LUANNE JONES

Sweethearts of the Twilight Lanes

AVON BOOKS

An Imprint of HarperCollinsPublishers

This is a work of fiction. Names, characters, places, and incidents are products of the author's imagination or are used fictitiously and are not to be construed as real. Any resemblance to actual events, locales, organizations, or persons, living or dead, is entirely coincidental.

AVON BOOKS
An Imprint of HarperCollins*Publishers*
10 East 53rd Street
New York, New York 10022-5299

First Avon Books paperback printing: March 2001

Avon Trademark Reg. U.S. Pat. Off. and in Other Countries, Marca Registrada, Hecho en U.S.A.
HarperCollins® is a trademark of HarperCollins Publishers Inc.

Printed in the U.S.A.

10 9 8 7 6 5 4 3 2 1

For Patrick

If you hadn't fallen in love with bowling
I might never have gotten the inspiration for this book.
You're a great kid, an enthusiastic bowler,
and the best son any mom could hope for.

Acknowledgments

So many people helped with their support and encouragement in making this book a reality. I would like to acknowledge and thank my wonderful agent, Karen Solem, who had faith in this project and my ability to pull it off, and Lucia Macro, for her impeccable taste in buying it and for her insight in taking the original story and kicking it up a notch. Also to the members of the SWG: Anne Marie, Cathi, Dee, Gail, Kay, Lea Rae, Laura, Mary Ellen, Nancy M, Shirley, Silver, Silvy Tess and Tom!

And to the PQUALS—Sharon, Diane, Lynn—thank you for listening. I'm glad to be a part of your "team."

Prologue

"Good gosh-a-mighty, Miss Theresa Jo Redding." The words slurred in a soft blurring of sexual growl, soft southern accent, and likely most of a fifth of fine aged whiskey. "That sure is one awful pretty party dress you got on."

Tess turned her gaze from her own image in the vanity mirror.

The most beguiling pair of blue eyes in Georgia looked straight through her.

She held her breath as if that could hold in her fears and hopes, to hide them away so that he could never use them against her. She could do this. She could do anything if she had to.

He stepped inside from the tiny shadowed hall that connected her room to her suitemate's. In crossing that threshold, he seemed to grow taller, his shoulders became broader, and his wicked, wicked eyes more intense than even she remembered.

And she did remember. How could she forget those hands on her, that mouth and all the sweet, impossible promises he had whispered in passion and then forgotten? She touched the small gold heart dangling on the chain around her throat.

If only he had appeared at her door a few days ago, when he had first gotten back in town. If only he had bothered to so much as pick up the phone once and call her in this past year. If only he had shown up tonight for her graduation with his heart on his sleeve instead of a flask in his pocket, then she might have been able to forgive him. But he hadn't, and "if only" was a game Tess had no interest in playing.

"Yes ma'am, a mighty pretty party dress." He dragged the back of his hand across his shameless smile.

"If you're so fond of it, Flynn Garvey, maybe I should loan it to you sometime."

"I think I'll have to pass."

"Oh? Why is that?" She ignored his moving slowly about her room, gently touching her things, seeming to absorb every detail. She let her fingers slide from the heart, and the single diamond set in it glittered like ice against her flushed skin. "Not into cross-dressing? Have I finally discovered some form of decadence in which you are not inclined to indulge?"

"Truth be told . . ." He stopped directly behind her.

Her back went rigid.

"It's the neckline." He skimmed his knuckles along the bare skin exposed by the back of the dress, then let two fingers rest at the pulse point just above her collarbone.

She held her breath, waiting for his hand to dip lower, wondering what she would do if he tried it.

"I never could pull off something this daring." He slid his fingers just inside the fabric at her shoulder, then bent down to whisper in her ear, "Unless, of course, you insist."

"You make a move to pull my dress off, Flynn, I'll latch on to the one thing you hold dear in life and see if I can't arrange a little removal of my own."

"You used to like it when I tried to get you out of your clothes, sweet Tess."

"I was young and foolish then."

"It was only last summer."

"A person spends too much time with you and they tend to grow up fast." She pushed his hand away, wishing she could rid herself so easily of the memories of her time with Flynn. "Well, you have that effect on people."

"I don't know about that." He straightened up and tugged at the waist of his form-fitting jeans. "Spending time around me doesn't seem to have matured Joe Brent none."

"You're a bad influence on that poor boy, that's all." She craned her neck to check the closed door across the way. Behind it, she knew Wylene Parker was breaking Joe Brent Spivey's heart. "I suppose you're the one who talked him into coming out here to try to convince Wylene to take him back?"

"No, that was his idea." Flynn picked up a photo of Tess's parents and little sister taken two years ago, just before her daddy died. He paused over it for a moment.

She opened her mouth, already on the defensive over some unspoken rumor or question about the family she had spent a lifetime protecting.

Flynn said nothing.

Well, who is he to talk, after all, she thought, sighing.

He set the picture aside, then rubbed his thumb over his stubbled cheek.

Seconds ticked by. But for Tess it only took seconds for her determination to waver. If she told him that she still loved him . . . could they still salvage what they had once shared?

Before she could open her mouth, Flynn aimed a cocky grin at her. "No, chasing after love lost was Joe Brent's brainstorm." He flattened his hand on his hard chest with a thud. "*I*, on the other hand, wanted to go over to the Lure and see how much of my family's fortune I could squander on watered-down drinks and siliconed-up strippers."

"Why do you need to go to some bar?" She

turned away so quickly that her barrette shifted and pinched at her scalp. That and only that explained the tears that warmed her eyes. "Aren't you drunk enough already?"

"Yeah, well, sure, I'm drunk enough, but it's been too damn long since I've spent an evening ogling nekkid women. Guess I'll have to go find me some . . . unless you'd like to oblige?"

"Get out of here."

"Then I'm off to the Lure. Think I'll see what I can pick up with my magic rod and reel." He headed for the door.

"Flynn?"

"Hmm?"

"Don't . . ." She bowed her head and covered her eyes so she could not see even his reflection in the mirror. "Don't drive in that condition. Promise me you won't."

He snorted out a hard laugh.

"Please?"

The room got so still she swore she heard him breathing, slow and steady.

"I won't, Tess. I promise." He spoke with a powerful quiet that reached deep into her wounded emotions.

Tess raised her head. She looked around, hoping for some sign that she had been wrong about him, that he still cared about her as much as she did him. But no one was there.

It was no act. Flynn Garvey did not love her. And

she had to accept that he had just slipped out of her life, most likely forever.

"Fini."

"Buh-bye."

"Good riddance."

A jangle, a clunk, a dull *thwump*—the sounds did not give away the specifics of the objects dropped into the small tin box by Tess's closest friends—the SuiteHearts.

Reni, the daughter of wealth, privilege, and doting parents who excused her wild streak with phrases like "she's just a little high strung."

Busty, blonde, and brainy to boot, Jerrianne Munroe, the only child of hippie-turned-preacher Jerry "Brother J" Munroe.

Wylene Parker, whose greatest wish in life had been to compete in the Miss America pageant but, having reached her full height at five-foot-two, never got any closer than Miss Dreamland Dairy Sweetcream Princess.

And Tess. Prudent, responsible, nurturing, boring old Tess, the grown-up of the group even when they were all still in elementary school.

Later tonight they would walk across the stage and into their future. It was a time of new beginnings for everyone—except Tess.

Tess clutched her own contribution to their private time capsule in her sweat-dampened fist. To honor the promise they'd all made, she did not so much as peek at the contents in the box. Her arm felt as heavy as her heart, unable even to push back the dishwater-blonde hair blown into her face by the late spring wind.

"C'mon, Tess. Let's get this over with." Jerrianne rooted around under the dipping neckline of her clinging sweater to adjust her bra strap. "We all have someplace to be tonight."

Tess didn't have anyplace to be, nowhere to go but back to the dormitory suite she'd shared with these three girls for the last four years. And it was empty except for tonight's clothes, a few boxes they'd take when they moved out tomorrow, and her most recent memory of Flynn Garvey.

"Get on with it, girl." Reni stabbed a finger toward the open box in the deep green grass. "My parents have hauled in half of Georgia for tomorrow's big unveiling of that damn statue they donated to the school. They're all in town and just champing at the bit to shower me with love and affection, not to mention checks and jewelry."

Tess stared at the small object in her hand and the tightly bound scroll of paper. She drew in a deep breath.

"If you are thinking of granting us one last Queen Tessa moment complete with a touching tribute to all we've meant to each other from sandbox to suitemates . . ." Reni's Georgia accent rolled out as thick and sticky-sweet as the generous coat of poppy-red lipgloss she wore. She put the back of her hand to her temple, a study in southern belle high drama.

The others exchanged glances.

Reni heaved out a totally annoyed "Ugh" and flicked her wrist easy as shooing a gnat away. "Then you can forget it, Tess, honey. We all have a lot to get done tonight, places to be, people to see, you know the drill."

Tess did not know. Reni and Jerriane and Wylene all had family they could count on to encourage them and to celebrate their successes. They had people willing to give of their love and time without first weighing what personal gain they might get from it. Tess now had only her little sister Anita Lynn and the few shimmering glimpses she sometimes saw in the shell of a woman that was her mother. In short, Tess had no one.

"Joe Brent's waiting to walk me over to the auditorium for the ceremony." Wylene checked the bangle watch circling her pale, freckled wrist.

"Why's he doing that?" Reni rolled her eyes. "Didn't that redneck butthead get the message that you two are broken up?"

"Watch your mouth," Tess warned. "Honestly, Reni, just once I wish you'd take other people's feelings into account before you speak. Wylene and Joe Brent have been together since we were all sixteen years old. When you say ugly things about him, how do you think it makes her feel?"

"I *feel* like that redneck butthead didn't get the message that we're broken up once and for all." Wylene shook her head. Her hair glinted in the light from the dormitory breezeway. "But if he wanted to come to Lassiter's graduation ceremony tonight, what could I do to stop him?"

"Two by four to the back of the head," Reni suggusted.

Tess glared at her.

"What?" Reni held up her hands. "I said to his *head*. Ain't like that's going to cause any permanent damage."

"Sometimes I wish we'd have all picked a college across the state, maybe across the country, instead of across town to go to, y'all." Jerrianne repeated the lament that had become her mantra over the past four years. " 'Course, my daddy wouldn't have heard of it and Tess had to stay in Mount Circe because of . . ."

Tess straightened her shoulders. Because of her family, because of her obligations, the conclusion echoed in her mind. Because her mother had lost her mind and her sister had lost whatever good sense she might have been born with. No one had to say it for everyone to know how to complete the thought.

Jerrianne looked away.

"Maybe you can't keep Joe Brent Spivey from coming to the graduation, Wylene, hon." Reni jumped in with far more conviction than called for. "But that doesn't mean you have to waste your time on him."

"I promised him I'd go out for a Coke after. I feel I owe that much to him, to make it absolutely clear it's really over—again. I'm taking that job in Dallas and leaving Mount Circe for good." Wylene plucked up the paper in her lap, her prediction for where they would be in twenty years' time, tied with a bright pink ribbon. She brandished it like Miss Liberty waving the torch of freedom, her eyes clear and her smile blazing. "After all, I have bigger plans for my life."

Sure, you have other plans, but what about the people you leave in your wake? Wylene's proclamation might have touched off the thought, but Tess had no illusions about who inspired it. Damn that Flynn. In the next instant her thoughts turned to poor Joe Brent. She knew how it felt to have someone you loved with all your being blow you off and move on without a backward glance.

"I'm just going to concentrate on the positive. That's what I'm going to do." Wylene laughed. "I'll explain to Joe Brent one last time that I'm done with him. Then for all I care he can crawl back into Flynn Garvey's convertible and they can drive over a cliff."

Tess winced, although she did see some appeal in her friend's solution.

"Is Flynn back in town?" Jerrianne directed the question to Tess.

Tess shrugged, feigning total disinterest in the matter.

But Jerrianne must have seen the flicker of pain in Tess's eyes, because she tipped her nose up and did what any good southern girl would do if she thought some boy had hurt her dear friend. She talked trash about the low-down skunk. "And here I thought this town was shed of that king of all good times and instigator of most bad behavior when he went off to college up north."

"Well, if it isn't the right Reverend Brother J speaking out of the mouth of his only child." Reni snorted out a laugh and held her hands up. "Hallelujah! It's a miracle!"

"No, a donkey speaking is a miracle, Reni—except when you're around, then it's just business as usual." Wylene wrinkled her nose.

Reni laughed harder.

"I know what you mean, Jerrianne. I don't understand what Flynn's doing back here either." Tess folded her arms, like that would shelter her hurting heart. "Historical differences aside, I always did think that was one nasty trick, unleashing the likes of Flynn Garvey on those unsuspecting folks—even if they are Yankees."

"Well, they must have caught on to him, 'cause they kicked him out." Reni sneered. Not many people can actually sneer and pull it off, but Reni could and she kept right on at it as she spoke about Flynn. "My parents are friends of his family, you know."

"Family?" Tess bristled at the term. "What does that horndog know about family?"

"Just because in all these years no one has been able to pinpoint who his daddy is—and not for lack of trying on just about everyone in town—does not mean he doesn't have any family." Wylene gave that tentative smile. The girl would take in a rabid badger and forgive it for biting her because that was its nature after all.

Tess had never developed that quality and she did not foresee starting now on Flynn Garvey's behalf. "Sure, he has his mama and look how he's done her. Mr. God's Gift to Easy Women has put his mother through pure hell."

"Gee, Tess, don't let your manners hold you back, tell us how you really feel about the boy."

"I'm not saying anything anyone else in town hasn't said, or thought, Reni. Flynn himself flaunts it by going around saying stuff like"—She puffed her chest out and raked her hand straight back through her hair in a fair to middling impersonation—" 'I was born a bastard and I'm committing the rest of my life to acting like one.' "

Jerrianne nodded. "That's right."

"Is that what he got thrown out of college for, Reni?" Wylene's eyes sparkled. "Acting like a . . . a . . . you know?"

"Oh, worse than that." Reni leaned in.

Jerrianne and Wylene followed suit.

Tess clenched her fist around her contribution to their personal time capsule and looked up into the late afternoon sky.

"It was a terrible scandal, involving a professor's wife, two one-way tickets to an exotic South American locale and a—"

"Are we going to bury this box or simply bore it into the ground with a bunch of idle gossip?" Tess glowered at her friends.

"You're the only one who hasn't put her memento in. We're waiting on you, Theresa Jo Redding," Reni reminded her.

"Fine." Tess extended her hand. "No peeking now."

"No one has looked," Jerrianne assured her.

"We made a promise," Wylene said.

"Besides, the shadow from the dorm is so black you can't make out what a single thing is in that damn box—no matter how hard you squint." Reni sighed.

Tess dropped her offering into the box, keeping her gaze locked with Reni's. Despite the fact that they had been her best friends since Tess had bonked her on the head with a Josie and the Pussycats lunch pail in a fight over a boy, or maybe because of it, Tess did not wholly trust the girl.

"That's it, then. Guess it's time to say good-bye." Wylene tossed her scroll into the tin box.

"Goodbye for now but not forever." A note of near panic colored Jerrianne's voice.

"Of course not." Wylene flashed the smile that had won her a handful of local beauty titles. "We'll make sure that no matter where life takes us, we'll stay friends."

"If nothing else we'll see each other in twenty years, when we dig this thing back up." Jerrianne tapped on the metal lid with her ultralong, fake fingernails.

"Twenty years," Tess murmured. She couldn't imagine it. She hardly knew what she'd be doing in the next twenty minutes, let alone so many years in the future. "In twenty years we'll . . . why, we'll all be in our forties!"

Wylene groaned.

Jerrianne blinked as if trying to bring that image into focus.

"*You* all might be in your forties, ladies, but not me."

They gave Reni what they commonly called "the Look."

She shrugged it off. "The women of my family happen to possess the secret of eternal youth."

"Some secret!" Metal met metal with a decisive clank as Tess closed the lid on the box. "You just aggravate every living soul you encounter half to death. By comparison to the haggard, worn, and wary faces you create around you, you merely *look* younger."

Reni turned away, her face a mask of angelic innocence. Then she placed her hand on her chest, one finger raised to Tess in a gesture she most certainly didn't pick up in their six-week course in charm and etiquette at the YWCA the summer they were ten.

"I hope you marry well, Margery Irene Pittman." Tess laughed even as she snatched away the offending finger on her friend's chest and gave Reni's hand a squeeze. "Because *only* someone who loves you and/or is contractually obligated to do so will put up with you for the long haul."

"That's why I have you." Reni squeezed Tess's hand in return, then flung it away. "That's why we all have you, Queen Tessa. Because we know you will always put up with us no matter what big asses we manage to make of ourselves."

"Don't count on that," Tess warned.

"But we do," Jerrianne said, her head bowed just a tiny bit. "We count on the fact that you'll stand by us no matter what . . . no matter what we've done, Tess."

"Or what we may do." Wylene winked and scrunched up her nose. "No matter how big a mess we may make of things, we know our Tess will see us through and do whatever she can to bail us out. Just like you do for that ingrate sister of yours and like you always have for anyone you love. Isn't that right, girls?"

The praise wrapped around Tess's chest like a

vise, tightening with every accolade. "Oh, I don't . . ."

"It's true." Reni snapped the lock shut on the tin box, then handed it to Tess. "Like it or not—and I suspect that deep down you do like it very much, girl—you are the anchor that holds the SuiteHearts of Lassiter College together."

"Anchor?" Funny, that's just how these uninvited expectations felt. She looked into the faces of the girls that only seconds ago she had ached to think of leaving, then at the box that Reni held out toward her. No one was waiting for her. Flynn Garvey had used her and tossed her aside. Tess had no plans for tonight or the far-flung future staring her down from the other side of graduation tomorrow. Suddenly most of that didn't seem so bad.

"Let's get this over with." She chucked the box into the deep hole they'd dug at the southwest corner of their dormitory's lawn. "The sooner we finish up here, the sooner we can each get on with our lives—our very separate lives."

Not giving a thought to her manicure, she sank her hands into the damp, rich soil and shoved it over the top of the box, ready at last to bury her past and to look toward the future.

Flynn was dirt. No, no, too easy on himself. He was the stuff dirt pointed to when it wanted to lift its self-esteem and said, "Yeah, I may be dirt but at least I'm not Flynn Garvey."

Only two people had given a damn what became of him in this life and he had treated them both to a double fistful of heartache. He had his reasons. Good ones. Those reasons would give Tess blessed little comfort now.

He'd cruised aimlessly over town all evening—around the campus, past the Lure, even past the dairy. He'd seen a few familiar faces and found out a few things that surprised even the likes of him along the way.

Now he sat in front of the Salvation Brethren Fellowship, just off Main Street. He had no illusions of finding religion in this storefront dispensary of gospel and good works, but he did think he might get some sound advice and a kind word.

When you're the kid that everyone in town had given up on before you drew your first breath a kind word went a long way.

"I know you don't need shelter for the night, but something has brought you here." Jerry Munroe, founder of the fellowship had been at the building. When he saw Flynn drive up he'd come out and leaned against the car. "Care to tell me what it is?"

Flynn shut off the car. The spare key felt strange in his hand when he had expected the full key ring that had gone missing tonight. Almost as out of place as him in a spot like this, talking to a man of

God. "You one of those kinds of preachers who absolves people of their sins?"

Despite the fact he was built like a stick bug, Brother J mustered up a big-bellied laugh.

"I didn't think so. Even if you were, I doubt you could help me."

"I can listen. Lotsa times all a man needs is a sympathetic ear to listen while he figures things out for himself. Did you do something you want to talk about?"

"I hurt someone I really care about. I did it for a good reason, but . . ."

"Your mother?"

Flynn forced out a cold chuckle. "I'm talking about someone else this time. Someone who trusted me and I had to show them what a mistake that was, how getting hooked up with me wasn't in anyone's long-term best interest."

"What do you mean *show* them? Why didn't you just talk it over? Explain yourself?"

"Man, if I could explain myself, do you think I'd be such a loser?" Flynn laughed for real this time.

"You're not a loser."

Flynn gripped the stick shift and looked away. Even he drew the line at calling a preacher a liar to his face.

"You're a young man who's been dealt a lousy hand in life, but you've also had your share of blessings. You're smart and you've got a solid moral lodestone in you."

"Me? Moral?"

"Yes. It is in you. Obviously it is or you wouldn't have come here seeking. You certainly wouldn't be this heartsick over how you left things with this girl—"

"I never said it was a girl."

"I may be a widower and no young buck, but I am still alive enough to understand it's always about a girl." Brother J gave Flynn's shoulder a squeeze. "And the fact that what you've done grieves you so, tells me there is hope for you yet."

"You think?"

"I know."

Flynn almost believed. Almost.

"Just go talk to her. Set things right."

"I can't give her false hope."

"Then give her something better: the chance to heal."

"I don't understand."

"It's the wound we don't flush clean, the piece of glass under the skin, the sliver we can't find that festers. It stays tender. It makes us weak. Left untended over enough time, it can eat us alive."

Flynn looked away.

"You going to do the right thing?"

"Thinking about it." He leaned forward, both elbows on the steering wheel. "You know, it might surprise you to hear this, taking into account my reputation around town and all, but I like you, Brother J. I admire you."

The other man nodded. "Well, I don't know as I'd go advertising the fact, but I like you, too, Flynn. I see the seeds in you. One day you'll be the kind of man others admire."

He sat up straight; his throat clenched up, but he managed to ask, "You really believe that, don't you?"

"I'm a preacher." He dropped his hand on Flynn's shoulder. "Would I lie to you, son?"

Son. The simple word warmed him and steeled his resolve. He'd head back over to Lassiter, to Tess. He might have to take a few more turns through town to get his nerve up, but he'd do it. "Okay, then. I'm going to go do the right thing."

"Good for you. You won't regret it."

Over the roar of the engine as he pulled away, he muttered, "I hope not. I sure do hope not."

1

Present Day

—SIMPLY SOUTHERN—

*A magazine devoted to the distinctive style
and grace of the southern lifestyle.*

TESS REDDING, Editor in Chief
Magnolia Oaks Heritage House,
Mount Circe, Georgia

Tess ran her fingertips over her embossed letter-head. This was who she was. Or at least, who—to even her own amazement—everyone saw her as. Editor of her own magazine on style and good taste, the author of four books on the same, and the inadvertent benefactress to an entire community.

She rolled her black fountain pen between her

thumb and forefinger, smiled, then slowly began to write.

Her antique rocking chair creaked as she sat back. Brilliant sunshine slanted in onto her open, airy porch, creating a glare on the linen paper. The blue swirls of her perfect handwriting dried quickly in the sun's warmth.

Tess lifted her face toward the light, pausing to gather her thoughts. She wanted to get the words right. She had to find a way to express her feelings that left no doubt as to her intent yet befitted a woman once dubbed the Martha Stewart of the South.

Dear Reni,

Please find enclosed . . .
one swift kick in the butt!

Tess dropped the sheet of stationery to the painted white floor. Careful not to wrinkle the crisp white paper, she pressed her foot down onto the page, then lifted it up for closer inspection.

The dusty imprint of her Dreamland Discount Mart canvas sneaker made a convincing visual aide of what she'd gladly do to her friend's backside, given the opportunity.

Tess loved Reni like a sister, but like a sister she sometimes wanted to wring that girl's scrawny, diamond-encircled neck.

Using a couple of back issues of *Simply Southern* magazine as a makeshift writing desk, she threw one leg over the arm of the chair with no regard for how her cut-offs rode up to expose the white skin of her inner thigh. She had bought this land and this house, with its huge porch designed to shade the house and channel the gentle mountain breezes, with seclusion in mind.

Seclusion and privacy. Sweet privacy. What must that be like? To live in a place where no one knew you or your family and had no interest in finding out about them? She had never known a time when people didn't feel obliged to speculate about her poor mother's plight.

And no one ever spoke of Millie Redding without the adjective *poor* cropping up a good half-dozen times followed by a lot of head-shaking, a few stealthy sidelong looks, and at least one "bless her heart."

Later on, Tess's sister's all too public rebellion against the family took the place of speculating over Mille's condition. And Tess would be a danged fool to think her own name hadn't salted a few wagging tongues from time to time. That was life in Mount Circe, and she could only do what she could do to guard herself against it—keep her mouth shut and her eyes open, and behave herself at all times.

She turned her attention back to the letter she'd begun and poured out her feelings just as she might say them right to her friend's face.

What the hell are you thinking, girl? You want to buy your Granny Pistol's old house? What on earth for?

Reni's grandmother had earned the nickname "Pistol" at her mother's knee and had milked every last drop of nuance from the pet phrase before she passed on to her reward and into local infamy at age one hundred and two. Her granddaughter had taken up the banner almost since birth. Tess had often envied the candor and vivacity of Margery Irene Pittman's self-indulgent family, so different from the careful, anxious household Tess had grown up in. But fond memories of a pampered upbringing hardly explained her friend's plan to buy a ramshackle old mess of a house and move home again.

From anyone else I'd chalk up this half-baked idea to sloppy sentimentality. Not from you. No, ma'am. Not from the girl who wore heels and pearls and nothing in between beneath her college graduation gown and, when everyone else threw their caps in the air, proceeded to flip up her back hem and show everyone where they could plant their good-bye kisses!

You cannot come back here, Reni, not even as a part-time resident. It just wouldn't work. You have some wildly overromanticized memories of this place which have set you up for a big letdown.

And that speech you gave me about longing for a simpler way of life? For you, sugar, slipping into a coma would be a simpler way of life. Coming back to Mount Circe is death. Death by boredom. Death by gossip. Death by ever watchful eyes, unforgiving hearts, locked-up minds, and cheeks clenched so tight that when certain Junior Leaguers walk past you can hear a subtle squeak, squeak, squeak that is definitely not coming from their new Faragamos.

I know whereof I speak because Flynn Garvey has already tried what you're contemplating. Moved "home" about a month ago. Mount Circe's very own prodigal son returneth—except no one here seems ready to kill the fatted calf and rejoice. They seem more than happy to let him wallow with the pigs, like that's where they think he belongs.

He stays alone in that big old house on the Hill. It's been empty for a couple years, since right after his mama passed, you know, and not kept up at all. Rumors drift by about him now and again, each one juicier than the last.

Flynn. Tess laid her head back and tried to churn up any emotion regarding Flynn Garvey. Anything. Anything at all. It was an exercise she had indulged in at least once a day since word of his return had reached her ears.

To say she felt nothing would only add another lie to the fire. She would not delude herself like that. She did feel something when she heard that man's name, when she thought of those fallen-angel, Elvis-blue eyes, when she recalled the last time she saw him.

Her cheeks grew hot. Dull pain like a fist contracting tighter and tighter rose high in her chest. Anger, embarrassment, yes—she felt those, and once in a while a streak of sheer panic at the thought of running into him unprepared. And if she were going to adhere to her strict resolution to never lie to herself, she felt something more. Felt it but refused to confront it.

She turned to her letter again, focusing solely on the task at hand, as she always did when she had a job to do.

The whispers and innuendoes fly around this town about anything new or different, and Reni, honey, you (and Flynn if we are going to be brutally frank) fall smack into that category. I can't stand back and watch it happen to you. Not that I'll be around long to watch it if my plans come through. That's another reason for you not to come back. If I make this deal happen, I'll have to leave here for good.

Tess lifted her face to the breeze. Leaving Mount Circe? Was that what she really wanted or was something else driving her decision? She'd started the business here because she'd had a sick mother to tend and a little sister who had grown from a child wanting someone to push her on a swing to a young lady who needed to be pushed from the nest. Those things took time and money, and both her mother and her sister looked to Tess to provide.

She had stayed here to do just that, but now Mount Circe had become her home. Could she really just up and walk away from it without looking back? She didn't know anymore, but her path was set and she did not know how to turn back. She had to move forward with her plans to expand her magazine or settle for the fact that she'd never be more than a regional phenomenon. Still, the repercussions of her decision weighed heavy on her mind.

I guess by now you have figured out why I'm sending this in a letter instead of using the regular e-mail route. Dawgs, Margery Irene, can you venture what it would do to my image as the patron saint of small town southern belles if that e-mail went awry? I'd be burned in effigy! Tastefully, of course, and in a lovely arbor of cultivated native greenery, on a fire created of hand-hewn hickory chips, soaked in spring water to produce the maximum effect. But burned nonetheless. It would be the end of my career, just as it's really starting to take off and drawing the attention of some deep-pocketed backers.

You and Jerrianne are the only ones I can trust with this information. You two are the only ones who know that I am just a few nimble negotiations away from up and moving my whole operation to Atlanta. Most of the magazine's real operations are already there out of necessity. Only a few workers remain here, and they freelance mostly. Still, moving the official headquarters, the place associated with the whole feel of the magazine, from this place to a city that size is a huge step.

Much as I would love to have you close at hand as that all happens, I cannot sit by and let you do this without voicing my objections. Ardently. In a very Simply Southern whomp-upside-the-head way.

I'm only thinking of what's best for you. I know you feel at odd ends since the divorce, but please, do not come back here all filled up with hope of recapturing something that never really existed. Do not come back thinking Queen Tessa can make a speech, pull a few strings, and make it all better. Queen Tessa is history. Just like all the things you think you remember about this place. History and fiction.

I blame myself for your misconceptions, of course. I've made a career out of embroidering the truth of this small-town way of life, of packaging and promoting Mount Circe as the nearest thing to heaven this side of the Mason-Dixon. But you know better than that, girl, surely you do.

The delightful diner I write about in my books and columns is only the crummy Chat 'N' Chew Café where the same old men sit all day telling the same old raunchy jokes and solving the world's problems.

Hacker's Five and Dime has a new coat of paint but the merchandise looks like Ollie Hacker orders it via a time machine with its dials stuck at 1965.

There's a new law office over the barber shop and they have turned the Rebel Tavern into a museum of southern culture. But no matter how many scented candles they burn in that place it still reeks of cigarette smoke, booze, and the lingering odor of sweet Vidalia beer-battered onion rings. Remember those? They practically had to call in the EPA to figure out how to dispose of the grease they fried those things in, it was that foul. Good-gosh-amighty, I miss those onion rings.

Tess missed more than the onion rings. She missed adventures with her dear friends late of a summer night in their hometown. She missed their laughter and their long talks. She missed romance and the guilty pleasure of sneaking away to meet . . .

a certain young man . . . under the brightest moon she'd ever seen that one, magical summer.

She blinked and a bath of tears soothed the sting in her eyes. She sniffled.

She missed being young and having countless choices spread out before her like a banquet. She missed the woman she had always dreamed she'd be by now. She missed the feeling that she could still be that woman, if only . . .

There isn't much else to miss around town as everything else is still here. People still size you up according to which of the three parts of town you come from. Plantation Pines redneck or a white-collar dairy worker living in Dreamland, they still don't measure up in the eyes of the bluebloods with big houses on the Hill. Town is still only three tree-shaded blocks of Main with the red brick First Baptist Church keeping watch over the east end and St. Elizabeth's ornate cathedral and cemetery dominating the west. Football is still the primary passion in the fall, the Fourth of July picnic and parade the social and civic highlight of the entire summer.

The Lure maintains its claim as northern Georgia's finest nude dancing club and bass fishing outlet. Still has that classy motto—"Live Bait! Live Girls!"—painted on the side of the aquamarine cement building, too. Twi-

*light Plaza Shopping Center sits empty now,
but the Twilight Lanes Bowling Alley is still
"open twenty-four hours a day to provide fun,
fitness and fine eatin' since 1951."*

*You see, nothing really changes here, Reni,
nothing except the seasons.*

The soothing *clink-clink-a-clang-clink* of the
windchimes Tess had salvaged from her own grandmother's house drew her attention away from the
letter. Not everything in her tiny little town in the
Georgia mountains was as stifling as she'd tried to
convince her old friend. She thought of her family,
who had been in these parts as long as there had
been dirt to plant in. She thought of the people who
worked for her, and of the beloved town fixtures that
brightened the dreary sameness of the familiar
place.

*Go by the library any Saturday morning and
you'll see Jobie James sitting on the front
bench hollering at every female that comes
out, "Hey, girl, whatcha readin'?" Jerrianne's
daddy still runs the Salvation Brethren Fellowship out of a storefront on Second Street. He
still drives a beat-up old van with scriptures
stenciled on the side and has that sad, scraggly ponytail trailing down his back. He doesn't
do the street preaching so much anymore
though sometimes come a balmy Saturday*

night, if you've got the windows thrown open, you can hear the old gospel hymns done up on steel guitar and drums shaking the rafters of the Fellowship Hall.

I see Jerrianne daily, though we rarely talk about anything personal. It's hard not to be aware that I am her boss no matter how long we've known one another. And then there is the whole unpleasant Anita Lynn factor. Leave it to my baby sister to go after one of the Suite-Hearts' boyfriends. I know that was many years ago, but it's not the kind of thing Jerrianne can ever just put aside. Not when she has to explain to her sweet little boy why his father never married his mother or why Ed never comes back to visit. Though, in truth, I think it's her father more than Jerrianne's feelings that keep the man away. She's long over that louse and a wonderful mother to Max. A wonderful mother and a right-hand "man" to me. She could do anything, Reni, if she'd just get up the courage to tell her daddy she's not a little girl anymore and ask him in all Christian love and forbearance to butt the hell out of her business. But who am I to tell anyone how to run their lives?

Joe Brent is between jobs. Again. Wylene keeps food on the table and the kids in clothes with her home-based business. I told you about that, didn't I? Wylene Spivey's House of Charm and Cheerleading? They converted the garage into some kind of studio. I'm ashamed to say it's been open a year and I have yet to get by to see it. I tell myself it's because we're both so busy but, sugar, it's a lie.

I cannot say for sure that he hits her. If I could you can bet your ass I wouldn't let that continue. I know he is a big bully and he intimidates her. Though I've never caught him at it myself, I think he makes her feel like garbage. Like garbage, Reni, our Wy!

It breaks my heart to know what fantastic dreams she had when we were young, then to see her today, to see how she lives. I call her sometimes but I never know what to say. We make small talk. She tells me her cheerleading team made regionals. Or that Jolene and Brentelle placed in one of those absolutely frightening junior beauty pageant things she insists on entering her girls in. Or Joe Brent has her on a diet and won't let her get away to meet me for lunch—that kind of thing.

Every single time before I hang up I want to say, "Leave him, Wylene. Leave that rat-bastard. I'll help you. Reni will help. Put the girls in the car and just leave." But I never say it. I know if I do she'll feel she has to choose between loyalty to her husband and our

friendship. Am I a jerk to not say what I think?
Or am I, as I tell myself, just keeping the lines
open, keeping myself available if she should
ever get her courage up to walk away? I don't
know.

Tess gripped her pen. She kicked her leg out and
back, making the rocker sway gently. She clenched
her teeth. She had only wanted to warn her friend
off of a foolish move, and here she'd gotten all nos-
talgic then gone off into sappy self-analysis.

She felt unfocused like that too often lately. She
blamed it on stress, on having too many irons in the
fire, on feeling unsettled about the pending business deal and unsure about leaving the place she'd
called home for all her life. But sometimes it made
her worry, made her think that maybe she was
becoming like her mother in ways she dared not
contemplate.

Well, that's it. I've begun to ramble. I'm telling
myself it's stress and if you believe otherwise
you can keep your big mouth shut. Mouth
shut? Dawgs, I've forgotten who I'm writing
to! The most I can hope for is that you limit
any obnoxious opinions you have to the
greater Houston area.

Got to run now. Don't buy that damned
house! Which was all I really wanted to say

when I started this note an hour and one jaunt down memory lane ago. Don't try to come back home because you can't. Your home is anywhere but here now. Learn from what I told you about Flynn Garvey.

Before she even realized what she'd done, Tess had underlined that last sentence—twice. She stared at the man's name, shut her eyes, then sighed and went on.

Off to the Salvation Brethren Fellowship this afternoon. Photo shoot for the Christmas issue already. Yes, Christmas in mid-July, but that's the nature of this business. After that, we're up to our behinds—which at our age is not quite as deep as it would have been a few years ago!—in work.

We have to work up a presentation for none other than Phillip Pearcy McLaughlin. Do you remember him at all? Spent most of his time traveling but came back to Georgia to retire in Atlanta a decade ago. It's at his insistence we will be moving there so he can have the magazine close at hand. He's one of those wealthy recluse kooks we grow here in the South like kudzu.

Oh, that reminds me, give your family my love! Call your mama in Miami and she'll tell

*you the same thing. Don't come back to Mount
Circe, 'cause nothing here is what it seems!*

*Much love always,
Tess*

Tess let out a long sigh and splayed her hand over
the pages. She swallowed hard to push down the
whorl of fear and anticipation rising in her throat
and folded the letter into three perfect sections. She
slid the paper into the envelope and sealed it before
she had a chance to reconsider. She had someplace
she had to be, people waiting for her and a plan for
the future. She would not let anything or anyone
keep her from it.

2

"Ho, Ho, Ho—Holy S—"

Reverend Monroe cleared his throat.

Flynn turned toward the mirror to take a good long look at what he'd been reduced to. "Saint Nick."

"Not yet." Old Brother J's shaggy blond ponytail had turned a yellowed white but his eyes were still vibrant.

With joy or madness—Flynn was never quite sure which. Thinking of the scheme the old guy had cooked up regarding him and this crazy magazine shoot only muddled the possibilities further.

Brother J thrust a fur-trimmed red hat into Flynn's hand. "But you're getting there."

"That's assuming 'there' is the place I want to

go." He shoved the hat down low to cover even the hint of his light brown hair.

Brother J went right on adjusting the hem of the baggy pants over Flynn's black boots, which were, in fact, hip waders that the preacher wore for river baptizings. The pants were stuffed with pillows and hidden beneath a red velvet costume. "You can't fool me, son, I know exactly where you want to be and have no doubt you'd do whatever it takes to get and *stay* there . . . or should I say here?"

Here. Mount Circe. Flynn narrowed his eyes and stared out the open door into the shaded street. From here he could see the back of the library and the parking lot of the Rebel Tavern in its new incarnation. A sign pointing the way to Magnolia Oaks Heritage House, home of *Simply Southern* magazine, stood watch over it all.

The only person who ever really loved him had chosen to live in Mount Circe, even though it meant a lifetime of pretending not to hear the hiss of gossip behind her back or to see the smirks on faces as she passed.

She had grown up here and here she had stayed when she needed the strength and comfort of friends and family. She did not find it for herself but never gave up hope that it might one day be extended to her son. It had not been. But then, out of fairness, Flynn would not have embraced it. In fact, the only thing he had ever applied himself to with his whole heart in his youth was a steadfast pursuit of the town's contempt and condemnation.

Now his mother lay buried in the cemetery at St. Elizabeth's. Found peace at last, he hoped, in this town that she had cherished so much that she endured loneliness and heartache to make a home for him here.

Home. What hackneyed, bogus, and ridiculously sentimental clichés had *not* been written about the word? He looked out the door at the gangly-limbed boys sitting on the backs of the park benches, their music blaring, sure they had all the answers. Across the street an American flag snapped above a weathered barber pole. Beneath it, two old men leaned on canes and spit tobacco into a can with rust on the rim. They laughed. Probably because they knew there were no answers, only a handful of enduring beliefs and hope.

There was always hope, wasn't there? Flynn had based most of his adult life, his work, and now this last-ditch effort to bring peace and closure out of his troubled past on the conviction that one should never give up hope. Peace, closure, hope—that's what had brought him back home.

Heat rose in Flynn's cheeks. His throat closed up. When he had sat on the young Turks' side of the street he'd have made a joke at getting emotional over this dim spot in the southern landscape. But looking out at the familiar sights of Mount Circe

now, those clichés did not seem so silly. When he
heard the word *home*, this is the place that filled his
mind and heart.

A film of sweat dampened Flynn's upper lip. The
smell of spirit gum holding the thick white beard
and mustache to his face made his nose twitch. "Has
anyone bothered to point out to the purveyor of
Peach State pretentiousness that it's nowhere near
Christmastime?"

"No reason to."

Flynn opened the heavy jacket and fanned it,
which cooled his skin but did nothing to ease the
twisting in his gut. "It's July."

"She knows." Brother J gave Flynn's pantleg a
good yank to get it in place.

"In Georgia."

"Uh-huh. They always start production on the
Christmas issue long about now. Way it has to be,
I'm told. We don't mind anyways. Kinda livens up
the dull side of summer to throw us a little Yuletide
shindig before we slide on into the dog days."

"I can't believe you'd go along with her nonsense."

"Nonsense?"

"You read the stuff she writes in her books about
this place. Its like she's tried to cover the whole
damn town in doilies. She makes it look like something it's not and never was."

"I like the things she says about this town."

"But it's not real. Candied mint sprigs sticking

out of fruited-up lemonade served in cut crystal glasses on the honeysuckle-covered veranda? When did you ever know anyone in Mount Circe to do that?"

"Well, there was this one fellow, wore hats and started every other sentence with 'Land-a-goshen,' lived with his mother. Now he just might have done something like that." Brother J laughed.

Flynn scratched beneath the fake beard. "You know what I mean. For most of us, iced tea on the front porch, that's fine enough."

"I suppose."

"Anything more is like icing on a cow pie, I tell you. Might make it look a he—a whole lot better, but I still wouldn't want it on my plate for dessert."

"Amen."

"So you do agree with me?"

"About that cow pie, sure but not to comparing it to what our Tess does."

"Our Tess," he muttered. For a moment he thought about pointing out that she was not their Tess, that they were hers. They owed everything to her and that obligated them all to her and her whims. Flynn, of all people, knew that was no way to live. He exhaled and kept his thoughts on that to himself. "It's just that there's so much around here has a lot more meaning than the frills and phony stuff she fills the pages of her magazine with."

The minister tugged a small pocketknife from his jeans and flipped it open with his jagged thumbnail.

Dropping to one knee, he went to work scraping some mud from the toe of Flynn's boot.

"I just don't like the phoniness of it all. If it's one thing I hate, it's the idea that skirting around the truth is some kind of noble alternative."

"To what?"

"Anything!" Flynn shifted his feet so that he no longer had to face the image in the mirror of himself as the icon of childhood mirth and joy. "It's that murky ground in the middle, neither black nor white, not truth nor lie. That gray area that lets us justify that keeping the dark at bay is just as good as shining the light. It's a dangerous place. Get too comfortable with it and you're sure to lose your way."

"Yes, you can, son. You surely can."

"Then I'm a little surprised you allow her to drag you into it."

"It's how the business works."

Flynn glanced around the dank building. Jumbled rows of battered metal chairs sat scattered over the warped wooden floors. Windows painted over with vivid tempura paint cast strange shadows all about them. Parked just beyond the door, something folks liked to call the Salvation Deliverance Van waited, held together by prayer and heaven alone knew how many coats of paint.

He laughed. "What do you know about business, Brother J?"

"Around here, everyone knows about Tess Redding's business, son—how it runs, what she expects, and who benefits from seeing it succeed."

What could Flynn say to that bit of wisdom and truth? He saw the changes the *Simply Southern* operation had brought to a town that had teetered too long on the verge of caving in on top of itself. Even Flynn had to concede grudging admiration for her accomplishments. There was no denying it— Tess Redding had worked a miracle here.

"Yeah, well, she always was the one they all counted on in her little gaggle of friends, even when we were kids." Flynn started to push his hand back through his hair, recalled that he had the Santa hat on and settled for swiping some sweat from his brow. "Your daughter ran around with her, right?"

"Did and does. Works for her now. Tess's business puts food on my child and grandchild's table as well as plenty others 'round town."

"So you remember what they used to call her?

"What? You mean Queen Tessa?" J chuckled.

"That's right. *Queen* Tessa." The name fit. There'd been something special about Tess even back then—and something untouchable, out of reach for a boy like him with no daddy and not a lick of common decency. "Looks like Her Highness finally made her own phony little kingdom out of the whole town."

"It ain't like that. Ain't like that at all." J fit the

blade of his knife back in its sheath, then raised his arm for a hand up off the floor. When they stood eye to eye again the older man tapped the end of the closed pocketknife against Flynn's chest in a way of warning, no threat implied. "If it wasn't for Tess, our food bank would be empty. We'd have no funds to provide and there'd be too many more hungry folks with their hands out, needing whatever we could scrape together."

Flynn set his jaw and didn't say a thing.

"Every time she mentions my work in her books or magazine, donations come winging in from all over. Sometimes so much we are able to do things over and above the food bank, clothes closet, and church services."

"That so?"

"Bought books for the Dixon boy when he went off to college and couldn't afford them. Gonna get a group together to fix up Miz James's house so the county can't condemn it when she's gone and put poor Jobie in an institution."

"Sounds like Ms. Redding is pretty well respected around here. Sounds like lots of people count on her."

"They do, and with good reason."

"Not like some of us, huh?" Flynn closed the jacket over his padded belly and slid the belt into its brass buckle. "Not born into respectability, never did anything to earn it, not in this town's eyes."

"They didn't understand how much you did for

your mama. Or know what you've done with your
life these last ten years, the good work you do on
behalf of other single mothers . . . and fathers, for
that matter, I suppose."

Flynn grunted. He'd had to recover child support
payments from four, maybe five mothers in the
decade since he committed himself to that work by
creating the Anna May Garvey Foundation for Children's Support Rights. That number paled in comparison to the countless fathers he'd tracked down
like the heartless, conniving, looking-out-for-their-
own-mangy-asses-while-their-kids-did-without rats
that they were. He clenched then unclenched his fist
and shrugged. "I do what I can."

"Word is, from service organizations all over the
South, you do what no one else can." Brother J patted him on the back. "Folks 'round here don't know
that, though. They just don't know you like I do. But
they'll come 'round."

"I have been more accepted around town than I
every suspected I'd be. Accepted, mind you, not
welcomed. But just the other day, Ollie Hacker did
tell me that if I planned on moving my business
here, I'd do well to hook up with the Lion's Club
over the Jaycees."

"See, now that shows how far you've come
toward finding your place here."

"Yeah?"

"Sure does. It's sound advice. He ain't leading
you down no path. The Jaycees got the snob appeal,

I'll grant you that, but you can't beat them Lions for a first-rate pancake supper." J nodded.

"That's a *good* thing, huh?"

"It is if you're hungry." The older man's hand stilled on Flynn's shoulder. "You're on the right track, then, son. I'm mighty proud of you."

Flynn shut his eyes and savored the feel of the kind touch and genuine approval. He'd gotten so little of that growing up and had shunned it as an adult, feeling nothing he did ever really earned it. Now he treasured this small show of Brother J's trust and support. It meant more to him than all the money on earth. More than the millions he had been given in a trust fund from a biological father who had never approved of him—or called him son.

"Yes, you're on the right track." Brother J cinched up the belt holding the pillows and hip waders to Flynn's middle. He stepped back to survey his handiwork. "But we got to get back to work. If she catches us standing around jawing Tess'll come bearing down on us like a freight train straight out of h—"

Flynn cleared his throat this time.

J let out a belly laugh. "Let's get you into your chair over there so they can get some pictures of you with the kids."

"Kids?" Flynn jerked his head up so hard that his beard slipped. He winced at the pull on his skin on the spot above his lip where he'd put the spirit gum.

He caught a mouthful of synthetic white hair. It took a couple of tries to spit it out. "When you roped me into this you never said a word about my having to be around *kids*."

"Didn't think I had to." The other man pushed the beard back into place. "You're Santa Claus. Santa just naturally goes with kids, right?"

"Not this one. Brother J, I am no good with kids."

"You can't convince me a fellow who's dedicated himself to making folks do right by their own children ain't any good with young 'uns."

"Hey, I'd walk through fire to help a child, Brother J, I truly would. But no way am I going to sit in a chair, plop one on my knee and endure the www."

"The Worldwide Web?"

"The wailing, wheedling, and wetting on my pants leg."

"Aw, that just goes with the territory."

"Then I'll leave that as uncharted territory, if you don't mind. Not that I wouldn't mind having a couple kids, someday . . . in the far-flung future."

"Now, now. Every man's got to look his destiny in the face at some point. Look's like your time is today."

"Destiny I can stare down without a fear or a flinch, Brother J. But a child? They scare the s—"

Brother J popped the elastic band holding the beard against Flynn's head.

He cupped his hand over his stinging ear. "I was going to say stuffing. Kids scare the stuffing out of me."

"Oh, what for, they ain't gonna bite you." J slapped him on the back, then swung around and started off, calling out, "Well, not most of them, anyways."

"Bite? Oh, no, that's it." As the preacher disappeared behind a heavily curtained door at the back of the room, Flynn yelled after him, "I don't want anything to do with a bunch of whining kids."

"Then I suggest you stop acting like a baby." The soft click of high heels and the delicate swish of fabric accompanied the rich, melodic Georgia accent of a woman ready to whoop ass first and take names later.

Flynn turned to catch a glimpse of her over his shoulder. Like someone peering at a solar eclipse, he instinctively knew that looking directly at Tess Redding for the first time in all these years would be a big mistake. And he was right.

Like something just stepped off of a tissue paper-and-tinsel-rope throne perched on a flatbed truck in the annual Christmas parade, she planted her feet just inches from his. The lights set up for the photo shoot gave her hair the illusion of bright liquid gold and chased any shadows age might have etched on her face. She didn't seem to have aged a day since he last saw her, in fact, on the night of her graduation from college fourteen years ago.

She laced her arms, one over the other and honed in on him. "Acting rather childish about this, aren't we, sir?"

"We? Ms. Redding, I wasn't aware *we* were doing anything, but if we were, I can't imagine it would be something childish." He let his gaze settle into hers and held it there for one, two, three seconds, beyond the point when most people began to squirm at the bold intimacy of his eye contact. "Myself, I prefer something of a much more . . . adult nature."

She blinked but said nothing. He'd gotten to her. Struck speechless, no doubt, by his blatantly seductive response to her sarcasm. The woman who held the town in her fist had fallen into the palm of his hand.

He'd had some concern over how he'd handle his latest first encounter with Mount Circe's gilded belle. Now he realized he needn't have worried. She had not really changed so much since that night so many years ago. He had handled her then and he would now. He chuckled deep in his throat and raised his hand to stroke his chin.

His fingers sank into the billowing fluff of his Santa beard. *Shit.* She had no idea who he was and for thinking he was clever and sexy . . .

"Maybe later you can indulge in some adult pastimes—like filing taxes, turning your head and coughing for the doctor, and sitting all the way through church without spoiling your big boy pants." She brushed a fluff of white fur from his deep red velvet sleeve. "Right now, we have some children to entertain."

He straightened his shoulders like he hadn't just acted like the world's most arrogant moron. "I hope by *we* you are referring to you and eight tiny reindeer, Ms. Redding."

She needed only to raise her eyebrows to give him his answer.

That woman had fire and a backbone like steel. He saw it in her eyes, her posture, and the way she didn't raise her voice to make her point.

"No?" Knowing she couldn't see his practically patented boyish grin under his beard, he wiggled his eyebrows and laughed as he said, "As in no apologies necessary, I presume?"

"As in no way can I allow you to back out of this photo shoot at the very last instant."

"Ah." He nodded, intent on the way she managed to fuse gentleness into her no-nonsense approach.

"No apologies necessary on my part for that"— she tipped her chin up—"I presume?"

He jerked his head to one side in a make-do nod. "You're a lady with a job to do."

"And you're the man I've hired to do that job, so if you please . . ."

"You have no idea who I am, do you?" Marvel, not malevolence colored the question.

"You're Jolly Old Saint Nick."

He ignored the determined jibe. " 'Cause if you did know who I was, I suspect you wouldn't be so all fired-up to make me fulfill my obligations here today."

"I am always 'all fired-up' about fulfilling obligations."

"I'll bet you are." His affirmation rang with more admiration than he'd planned. "But you have to understand, I'm not the right man for you."

She opened her mouth as if to answer, then shut it again. A troubled look passed over her face, which she seemed to chase away with a shake of her head and deep breath. "You'll do just fine, I'm sure of it."

"When Brother J reeled me into this project, he never mentioned talking to children."

"Why did you think he got you suited up like that?" Her face softened with playful amusement. "To showcase the variety of outfits available in the clothes closet for the needy?"

"I thought they'd pretty much just take pictures with you." He left out the part about how he assumed she'd take front and center, hogging the credit, making it seem like she invented the very season of goodwill toward men. "This is not my usual line of work, you know. I'm not a professional."

"I know." She smiled. "We try to use regular people from around here whenever possible. It brings much-needed money into the community and gives the magazine the feel of authenticity."

Authenticity. The single word snapped him back to his senses. Charming as this woman might be, he doubted if she had an authentic bone in her body— or idea in her magazine. "No disrespect to you, but I'm telling you, you don't want me for your Santa."

"I'm afraid I don't have any other choice."

"Get Brother J to do it." He started to remove his hat to seal his resignation.

She put her hand out to stop him. "That's simply not possible. The kids would be onto him quicker than a duck on a June bug."

It had been a long while since Flynn had heard that expression. Listening to it tumble so easily out of the polished perfection that Tess had become made him smile, despite his reservations. He lowered his hand from his head and stepped a little closer to her. Intimidation rather than seduction might best rattle her cage, make her show her true self and get him off the hook. "They'd be on him that fast, huh?"

She held her ground without going haughty and stiff the way many southern women with too high opinions of themselves would. Instead she met his gaze, wet her lips and gave a slow nod. "That fast. And that's why we need you. We need someone the children won't recognize by voice or mannerisms. In a town this size that's not an easy bill to fill, what with so many folks close kin and kissing cousins to one another."

He liked standing this close to her, he discovered. He liked the fact that she smelled of fresh soap and sugar cookies, not some fancy perfume. He liked the graceful gestures of her hands and the way her hair went slightly out of place when she tilted her head. And he especially liked watching her lips moved as she said "kissing cousins," all slow and drawn out.

"You make a good . . ." He cleared his throat to shake off the huskiness he found in his voice. "You make a good point, ma'am, but still—"

"Brother J said he'd found the perfect candidate in you and I trust his judgment."

"Hope you don't take offense in my saying this, but sometimes I think Brother J is a few loaves and fishes shy of feeding the multitudes, if you catch my drift."

Her lips twitched. A healthy glow not even the most skilled makeup artist could reproduce rose in her cheeks. Her eyes glittered with repressed laughter.

For a great big phony, she did a damn pitiful job of hiding her reaction.

"Still and all, I stand by Brother J's choice." She reached out and put her hand on his. "I believe you can do this."

He sensed in her touch nothing patronizing or manipulative. In this costume, she did not know him from Adam. She had every reason to believe he was nothing more than some poor nobody with nowhere else to go, come to take advantage of Brother J's kindness. In a sense, he supposed, that was as good a description of him as any. Still, her hand was as kind and gentle on his as the caress of a mother to a child—and it damn near killed him.

"Look, I won't lie to you, the photo shoot is important to me. But I won't do it today if I have to stick in a substitute that the children will recognize. I won't do a picture spread at the cost of disappointing a bunch of kids who have had way too much disappointment in their lives already."

"I . . . I just don't see how I can . . ." If she'd asked him to do it for her, or for the magazine or even for the town, he'd have had a hard answer ready for her. But she asked for the kids with a sincerity he did not think she had the capacity to fake.

"Please?"

She could have scooped him up in a bucket and poured him into the Santa throne, he was suddenly that big a pile of mush, ready to do her bidding. He groaned out an overplayed sigh of disgust and shook his head. "Frankly, Ms. Redding, I don't see how I can refuse."

3

Jess had heard about women wanting to play Santa and the naughty girl. Fiction, she'd thought. The contrivance of an unimaginative, lonely male writing letters to men's magazines that began "I never thought this would happen to me . . ."

She touched one fingertip to her lower lip and stole a sidelong glance at the mystery man in the big red outfit. She knew absolutely nothing about him, except that he had won Brother J's unequivocal trust. That and, despite insisting he wasn't the man for the job, the fact that he was absolutely the best Santa she'd ever seen.

"There you go, sweetheart. Your six-month Santa checkup is right on target. Keep up the good work."

A little girl with hair the color of the red Georgia

clay slid from his lap. The camera flashed at just the right instant to capture the reluctant Santa reaching out his hand, ready to rescue the child should she slip or stumble.

The girl's bright new shoes, a gift from the magazine, had hardly hit the floor when she turned to him and whispered, "You won't forget, will you?"

"No, darling." He put his hand beneath her chin. "I won't forget. I promise."

The blissful satisfaction beaming from the child's face said she believed him. So did Tess.

She had no reason to, of course. No man had ever given her reason to believe anything. She folded her arms over the stifling tightness of her green taffeta bodice. Some folks around these parts might want to tell you that Tess didn't seem to think very much of men. But they'd tell it wrong.

At thirty-six, curling up in bed night after night all on her lonesome, sometimes she wondered how she ever thought of anything *but* men. Or one man. Not one with a name or a face she'd ever laid eyes on but a man she knew only in her heart.

A man who gave as good as he got whether in a verbal exchange, a business deal, an emotional commitment, or a good old-fashioned no-holds-barred roll in the hay. A man who would love her for who she was, really, down deep, not for what they imagined her to be or for what she could do for them. A man who now and then said things like "Don't worry your head about this, now, I'm here to take care of everything" or even just "You look tired, hon, let me get dinner tonight" and then did. That kind of man did exist, didn't he?

She turned her face toward the halo of light in the dim room and found herself snared by the intensity of the stranger's gaze.

He did not look away or seem the least bit embarrassed that she caught him staring at her.

If he smiled, she could not see it beneath the ridiculous beard. But she didn't care, not as long as she had those eyes to sink into, deeper, then deeper. She had not seen eyes like that since—

A wave of cold apprehension washed over her. *Could it be?* He was back in town, after all. She tried to look more closely without looking like she was looking more closely. No, the eyes were too dark to be Flynn's, too many lines fanned out from the corners. She make a quick study of the hands she had so admired and immediately decided it could not be him. These were the hands of a man who knew how to pitch in and work hard, how to lift a child with the ultimate care, or grip a tool with equal skill. Those were not Flynn's eyes, not his hands. She would recognize them, wouldn't she? Even after all these years?

If she could only see something more of him, then she'd know for certain.

Fashion magazines often ran surveys to discover what women first noticed about a man. Answers like "the eyes," "his smile," or the classic nonanswer, "his personality" made Tess believe those women

must have been filling out the forms with their
mothers peering over their shoulders.

Give her a set of broad shoulders, muscled arms,
a hairy chest, and a tight tush any day.

The stranger flexed his long fingers over the
curve of the chair's arm.

And hands. Big, strong, capable-looking hands
scored big points with her, as did a few other things
that a lady *never* mentions.

She tipped her head to the right.

He cocked his to the left.

She thought back over the brief conversation
they'd had. She tried to place the voice that came
muffled through the thick beard but she could not.

Beard? Had she lost sight of the one most impor-
tant clue she had here? This man was playing Santa
Claus. This man came with the recommendation of
Brother J.

Therefore this stranger could not be Flynn Garvey. She had definitely let her imagination get the
better of her. She ran her fingertips inside the V of
her stiff, turned-up collar.

The stranger's gaze followed the movement
downward. It lingered only long enough to make
her skin tingle with vivid awareness of his attention
to her body.

Her breathing grew shallow.

He focused intently on her mouth when she
pressed her lips together. Then he raised his glittering eyes to hers again.

"Don't move a muscle, Santa!" Jerrianne's order cut through the moment like a hot knife through warm butter. "We want a few pictures of you reading the magazines before we wrap up today."

What the hell was wrong with her? Tess fidgeted with the papers and things on the nearby table as her assistant went gliding by with a mockup of a holiday issue in her hand. Had she actually been flirting? With Santa Claus? And on the job, no less. Had she lost her ever-loving . . .

Tess cut herself off. She had not lost anything but a few carelessly squandered minutes.

"This won't take but a second, then you can get out of that getup." Jerrianne handed the man a fresh white handkerchief. "I'll bet you're just about to burn up in that thing."

"Thank you." He accepted the cloth with gratitude and dabbed it at his brow, then around his neck. "It was getting a bit steamy in here."

Feeling certain everyone present sensed the sexual undertone of his remark, Tess wet her lips, ready to cut him down to size.

That's when the Santa with the sexy eyes winked at her.

Winked. It was so damned corny it should have made her groan. It almost did.

Taking the kerchief back, Jerrianne handed him the prop magazine and walked away.

He studied Tess's picture on the cover.

"Hold the magazine up, please," the photographer urged in a near monotone. "Make us believe that this is the source of great inspiration for you, that it gives you ideas."

"Oh, but it does." The man stroked the edge of his thumb slowly over the image of Tess as a cross between a southern belle and the mistress of the North Pole.

Tess shivered.

"It gives me a lot of ideas," Santa murmured.

A *little* steamy in here? Tess snatched up a clipboard from the table and began to fan herself furiously. It was indeed.

The camera flashed.

She blinked. What she doing? This was one of the most important photo layouts of the year. She could not afford to let herself get tangled up in a forbidden flirtation with a total stranger. Hardly the behavior of a woman hoping to become the next national symbol of style, taste, and elegance. Now more than any other time she had to stay focused.

Tess lifted her chin and shook back her hair, like that could settle her sensible, aloof, mature self back into place. When she lowered her gaze to the man again she wore the detached expression she'd perfected as a young girl that said "no hunting, no fishing, no trespassing."

The man on the gold and red throne held out his hand. "Wouldn't you like to climb up onto my lap and tell me what you want?"

Her attitude changed from "no trespassing" to "come on in" in a heartbeat. "Oh, you know that I would."

"What was that?" Jerrianne came up behind Tess and slid the clipboard from her hand.

"Nothing. Nothing." Tess pursed her lips so tightly that she practically whistled as she exhaled. Then she realized that the man had been talking to someone, and it wasn't her. "Who is he talking to?"

A movement just beyond the circle of light around the large chair came in answer. Tess narrowed her eyes to make out the small sandy-haired boy. Tess smiled and whispered Jerrianne's son's name. "Oh, Max."

Max kicked the toe of his sneaker against the edge of the platform and hung his head.

"Look, Jer," she elbowed her old friend. "Max snuck in to steal a minute with Santa."

"He didn't! Oh, Tess. I'm so sorry."

"About what? He's not hurting anyone."

"He did beg and beg for me to bring him in today but I made it clear he wasn't to get in the way."

"He's not in the way."

"Hi." Her mystery Santa motioned for the child to join him.

Max stuck his hands in his pockets.

"Come on. It's all right." A soothing strength infused the masculine voice coming from behind the faux beard.

"Max, you come away from there." Jerrianne motioned to her son.

"Leave him be, sugar. He just wanted to get close to Santa." Tess could relate to that.

"You don't understand. I told him not to do this and he's disobeyed me. I catch enough grief over every little mistake I make with Max as it is, if Daddy walked in and saw this—it would just be one more piece of proof about how bad it is raising a boy without a husband."

"Okay, don't worry, hon." She gave her friend's shoulders a quick squeeze. "I'll take care of it and if your daddy walks in, I'll take the blame."

Max put one foot on the platform and his knee poked through a hole in his jeans.

Tess marched forward.

At the sound of her footsteps, Max lurched forward and thrust his upper body over the arm of the chair like it was the last passing piece of driftwood in a rain-swelled river. "I know you ain't Santa Claus."

"What?" The man raised his hand to the fur trim of his hat like he wanted to rake his fingers through his hair, then stopped himself.

Tess moved in, not exactly sure how to handle it but certain only that she could do the job. "Max, is there something special you want to—"

The boy only stole another panicked look at her, then fixed his whole being on the man who had warned Tess he could not deal with children. "I fig-ure you're just someone my Aunt Tess hired but I heard my grandpa talk about you and that's why I come in here."

"Santa's had a busy day, sugar." Tess inched in closer. "Why don't you let Aunt Tess see if she can help instead?"

"Yes, you see . . . the thing is . . ." The spray-painted chair creaked as the bogus big guy shifted his weight and shuffled his feet.

"I got to talk to you, man to man."

"Man to man, you say?" Humor and compassion filled the man's response.

Tess knelt, trying to keep everything under her control.

Max ignored her entirely. With the most serious expression she'd ever seen on any child not looking back out of her own mirror, he said, "People don't think I know stuff. They talk soft and spell things around me and think I don't get it, but I do."

If possible, the stranger's eyes grew darker. "Do you . . . I suppose you're way too old to sit in my lap, right?"

"I'm not a little kid anymore. I'm eight."

"I understand." The man leaned forward, his hands folded between his knees. "Why don't you tell me what you want, son? If it's humanly possible, we'll get it done."

The boy nodded, then stretched up on tiptoe, cupped his hand to his mouth and began to whisper into the stranger's ear.

Her stomach knotted at being lopped out of the

loop by her godson and a man in a Santa suit. Especially when she was the only one here with any real power to help the boy get whatever he wanted.

"Yes, I see." The man's fingers engulfed one sticklike little arm, while his other hand spread out to cover the boy's back from shoulder blade to shoulder blade. "That *is* a problem."

What is a problem? Tess wanted to demand. "You know you don't have to whisper, sugar. We're all Santa's helpers around here and Aunt Tess would like to—"

"That's not necessary." Santa put her suggestion in check with a raised hand.

"But, I—"

"I've got this under control." *Back off.* He didn't say it, but then he hadn't had to, his tone got the message across.

A strained murmur carried a palpable prickling tension that worked its way through the crew. No one spoke to her that way. Ever.

"I don't believe you understand, Santa." It actually hurt her to smile this brightly and speak so sweetly, but she pressed on. "You're in *my* magic workshop today and here, *I* am the one who keeps things under—"

"Don't worry, Miss Redding. You don't have to do a thing." He gave Max a sturdy handshake to cinch the arrangement. "I will take care of this personally."

Every fiber in her being wanted to tell him to take

that attitude, wrap it in gold-tone foil paper, and put it where Rudolph's nose don't shine. That urge ran smack dab up against the only things that could shut her up: her godson's presence, the eyes of a man which held overwhelming promise, and the fact that he had spoken the words she had always longed to hear. *I will take care of this.*

She stepped back and held her hands open.

Max whispered one more thing in Santa's ear, shouted "Bye-bye" to Tess and his mom, then darted off like his heels had caught fire.

Tess shot her arm out. "Max, come back here!"

"Let him go." The man stood and loosened his oversized brass buckle. "I'm telling you, it's covered. Would you just trust me?"

"I have no reason to." She took a deep breath and got the distinct odor of rubber and river mud.

In a matter of seconds, Jerrianne appeared to whisk off the heavy coat as he peeled out of it. "Thanks for being so sweet with my boy."

"*Your* boy?" He whisked the hat off his head. "I didn't realize."

"I hope he didn't bother you too much."

"Not at all."

She started to say more and Tess knew exactly what she wanted to ask, but when he handed Jer the hat and turned his back she did not pursue it.

"Don't worry, sugar, I'll find out what Max said to the man," Tess whispered. "You know I won't let you down."

Jerrianne mouthed a "thanks" and hurried to put the props away and wrap things up.

With a wave, Tess shooed away the photographer and his assistant, then fixed her attention on the stranger.

Seemingly unaware of her, he rubbed his long, blunt fingers back through his short brown hair, which glistened with sweat. He pulled the tail of his white T-shirt up and wiped the hem across his eyes, then under the long phony beard. This was a man, acting completely masculine without any pretense. A take-charge man, who had done what he had to do without whining—much—who, despite his own concerns, found it in himself to be tender when the situation called for it.

What she could see of his body befitted the kind of man she had just seen in action—not the slick six-pack abs and bulging biceps of a kid building his body into something that ended up looking more like a plastic action figure than a real man. A *real* man. Comfortable in his skin, in a suit, or in jeans— or out of them—that's what he exuded.

And the best part was, he was a total stranger. She could make a dad-gum donkey's ass fool of herself in front of him and never have to worry once how it might reflect on her in the community. That, she decided then and there, was his appeal.

He arched his back, stretched and let out a low, deep moan.

Granted, it was not his only appeal. She crushed

a handful of her taffeta skirt in her fist. "As I said, I have no reason to trust you in this matter, Mister . . . ?"

"I don't care whether you trust me or not." He shrugged the suspenders of the hip waders off. "My getting the job done is hardly contingent on your opinion of me."

"There's no need to get hostile."

"Wasn't being hostile, I was being honest. Though I can see where a woman in your position might confuse the two."

"The only thing I'm confused about here is what has gotten up your . . . hip waders."

"Maybe it's a feather from this." He tugged free the last pillow and pushed it into her arms. "Now, if you'll excuse me, I have to go find a way to get this beard off."

"You can't just walk away from me."

"Watch me."

"I am not through with you!" That sounded harsh even to her ears and she'd heard herself say some pretty bitchy stuff.

Still, he did not give a backward glance. He just kept right on clomping out of the room with bits of white beard stuck to his damp neck and Brother J's hip waders shimmying with every step.

Flynn blew through the heavy curtains that separated the room they'd done the shoot in from the long hallway at the back of the building. The curtain hooks scraping the metal rod did a fair imitation of how this whole event had grated on his nerves. Well, maybe not the whole event. He had enjoyed talking to the children more than he had expected.

His thoughts touched on the last little guy he'd spoken to, and a weight sank in the pit of his stomach. His single-minded mission of finding and confronting his father would drain enough of his time and energy. How could he take on the plaintive request of a little boy with no one else to turn to?

The real question was, how could he not? To ignore Max's problem because it didn't dovetail with his own goals would negate everything Flynn had tried to do with his life this last decade.

He sighed. At least he was free of Tess Redding. He scratched his chest with both hands as he'd longed to the whole time she'd tried to badger him into letting her take over the boy's plight. If he could just grab the solution to take the beard off, then slip off the rest of this costume, he could get out of the Fellowship Hall before she caught up with him. She'd never know—

"Just for the record"—her voice sounded considerably hotter than the cool draft stirred as she flung the curtains open—"I didn't say I didn't trust you, just that I didn't have any reason to—yet."

He grunted something between a laugh and a growl, and started toward his best avenue of escape, the men's room at the end of the hall.

"Okay, fine," she called out after him. "I trust you. Is that what you wanted to hear? You big baby."

"Baby?" He froze in his tracks, and turned just his head. She'd said it to command his attention, of course, but he doubted she'd thought out how the simple word could be turned on her. "Hmm. After the way you so openly flirted with me, lady, shall I take that as a term of endearment?"

"Flirted?" She laughed but it sputtered out so weak and awkward that he almost felt sorry for her. She recovered with a toss of her hair and a cutting look, her eyes half-shut. "You call that flirting?"

No, he called it manipulation. That well-schooled way too many Georgia peaches had of playing a man along with unspoken temptation in order to win his cooperation. Only one woman had ever succeeded in pulling that act on him in his thirty-eight years.

And he was not going to give Tess Redding that chance again. He turned. "Actually, I'd call it whoring yourself to get your way."

She put her hand over her mouth, her eyes big as saucers.

"But if I did say that you'd probably slap this beard right off my face and, seeing as it's stuck on pretty good, that might smart a bit. So I'll just say see you around instead." He gave a salute with two fingers and started for the restroom again.

"We made an agreement to act like adults, didn't we?"

Though he heard her coming up quick behind

him, he did not hurry his pace. When he swung his
arm out to push open the door, she fit herself in front
of him so fast that he had to jerk his hand back to
keep from grabbing her breast.

"Or was I thinking of some other man wearing
rubber, velvet, and plenty of padding to make up for
his . . ." she trailed her gaze pointedly downward
then up again. ". . . shortcomings?"

"Hard to tell." He folded his arms. "I'm sure one
does meet so many of those kinds of men in your
line of work."

"You'd be surprised."

He conceded to her show of good sportsmanship
with a chuckle.

"You did a very good job with the children
today." She tugged at her collar. "You impressed me
and I don't impress easily."

"That I believe."

"And you can believe me when I say, I really
hope that you can help Max. I do so want to trust
you."

"Yeah, well, I want a pony and a place to ride it
but I guess we'll both be disappointed."

"Oh, I don't know. I live out in the country and I
can afford a pony. Maybe if you tell me what Max
asked for we could work out a deal."

Pride had kept him from letting her take over for
him up until now but she'd just made it matter of
principle. "Much as I'd like to come out to your
place for a ride . . ."

She clutched her collar shut all the way up to her throat but she did not take her eyes from his.

He smiled like he knew what she was hiding under the fancy coverings—because he did. "I believe I'll have to pass."

"It was a joke, for heaven's sake. Only trying to lighten the mood. Who do you think you are, anyway?"

"I am one man in this town who will not be beguiled, belittled, or bought off in the name of the greater good of Tess Redding and *Simply Southern* magazine." He sidestepped her and splayed his hand over the rough wood of the men's room door.

She nailed him with a glance from the corners of her eyes. "Big talk for a man wearing stinky hip waders and a Santa Claus beard."

"Cheap shot, but then, did I expect any better?" He had, and that's why the catty remark riled him all the more.

"At least you have some expectation. You know who you are talking to, who you feel so free to insult while you hide your face and refuse to give me your name."

"That's rich, coming from the slickest sham artist in town—Queen Tessa."

"How do you know that name? You're not . . . I had myself convinced you couldn't be, but you are, aren't you?" Her touch felt so tentative on his arm that he knew if he flinched she'd withdraw it.

Damn fool that he was, he did not move a muscle.

With her standing so close that he could see the genuine concern in her eyes, he didn't want to move and he didn't want to keep up the game of antagonizing her.

So much time had passed since their last encounter. Today he had found too many things to admire in the woman she had become for him to ignore them. Even now she had dogged him not for herself but for the sake of a child who had everything at stake when she had nothing to gain by doing it. Maybe he'd carried the notion of her betrayal so long it had blinded him to the fact that she had changed. People changed. He was living proof of that.

"I know your nickname because we go back a long way." Maybe it was time they made peace. He held his hand out to her. "It's Flynn, Tess."

"Flynn Garvey." Her face went pale.

"I'd take off the beard to prove it to you, but—"

"Flynn Garvey, you dirty son of a—" She snatched the fake beard off so fast he hardly had time to prepare for the ripping pain. "It *is* you!"

"Ow!" He stumbled back, one hand on his stinging lip where only fuzz remained of the full white beard. His eyes watered. He coughed. He clenched his teeth to keep from cutting loose with a string of curses that, if it didn't bring toads or lightning or some other curse raining down on his head, would surely bring Brother J running. "Have you gone crazy?"

Her eyes flashed with pain that even he could not miss when she raised her head and whispered, "Get out."

"Now is that any way for the ultimate symbol of southern hospitality and graciousness to talk?"

"Out."

"I should have known better than to think you'd grown anything but more ambitious and more bitter."

"You should have known not to come back to Mount Circe, or if you felt you had to come back, to stay as far away from me as possible."

"Believe me, those are my plans from this point on." He rubbed the pad of his thumb over the raw skin under his nose. "Guess it's not all water under the bridge between us, is it, Tess?"

"I wish it were." She stuffed the beard down the front of his gaping hip waders, turned, and headed back down the hallway. At the curtained doorway she stopped, fixed him with the look that kept even the likes of Reni Pittman in line, and summed up. " 'Cause if there was any water under this bridge, Flynn Garvey, rest assured I'd drown you in it."

4

"Tell me the truth, Jerrianne, am I in way over my head?" Tess shut her laptop and surveyed the wreckage that was once her desk.

"Probably." Her assistant heaved another armload of files onto the already life-threatening tower on the credenza. "But then, I don't see that as a problem."

"Why?" Tess rummaged through the sea of sticky notes, the waves of mail and the normal flotsam and jetsam of hair clips, paper clips, and emery boards awash on her desk. "Because if I went under for the last time no one could find my body in this mess for at least a week and that would give you your first vacation since Max was born?"

"Well, there is that." She tipped her head. The afternoon sunlight streaming in through the rows of tall windows made her ponytail a flash of blonde brightness. "But the main reason I don't see a problem with you getting in over your head is because I know you're the master of treading water until you can build a boat and set your course again."

"I appreciate your faith in me, sugar, even if I do wonder how well placed it is." Tess worked her fingers under a pile of fabric samples and yanked out her leather appointment book. She looked at it and blinked. That wasn't what she was looking for, was it?

"Everyone has faith in you, Tess. Speaking of that very thing, your sister called."

"When?"

"Must have been pretty early. She left a message on the machine."

The notations in her appointment book looked like a montage of foreign words and chicken scratchings circled, underlined, and exclamation-pointed to within an inch of their lives. Tess heaved a sigh because she dared not pitch a fit. "Don't tell me, let me guess. She needs money. I'm not being fair to her. Daddy must be rolling over in his grave seeing how mean I am treating my only baby sister . . ."

"That's about the size of it. What shall I—"

"Erase it."

"You sure?"

"Jer, you of all people know how much I have given that girl, how much she has taken."

"From all of us."

"I spent my childhood and young adult life, and I

mean *spent* it, like hard-earned, down-to-your-last-dollar cash, creating some kind of home life in a house where there was damn little to work with and nobody to help out."

"I know."

"At the time I thought I was doing right by Anita Lynn. Now, seeing what a mess she has made of her life, and the lives of . . . others . . . I know how wrong I was to spoil and coddle her." Tess shut her eyes tight, then opened them again and pulled her shoulders up. "Well, no more. Erase the message. And keep on erasing any messages from her that are like that one."

"Will do." Jerrianne reached down and plucked up the pen Tess had misplaced moments earlier and handed it to her. "Is this what you wanted?"

Tess tossed the appointment book on top of the heap. The pages fluttered as it fell open. "Yes, thank you."

"You're welcome. And by the way, maternity leave is *not* a vacation."

"I know, I'm just . . ." She stuck the pen behind her ear and began rifling through things again.

"You're rattled."

"Of course I'm rattled. Why wouldn't I be? Do you have any idea what all I have on my mind right now?"

"Oh, I have an idea." The cocky sashay in her walk conveyed as much as her playful tone. She feigned an intense interest in watering a tiny potted

African violet that had gone to that great garden in the sky over a week ago. "I have a pretty good idea what's occupied your mind this past week. It doesn't have anything to do with business, either."

"Everything in my life has to do with business anymore." Tess swiveled around in her chair, stopping only when her knee bumped two stacked boxes marked ACCOUNTING. She pulled her legs up and tucked her bare feet underneath her.

"You don't fool me." Jerrianne shook the watering can and a few drops of water flew off the tip of the nozzle.

"I'm not trying to *fool* anyone." Was it her imagination or had she said the word *fool* twice as loud as the rest of the sentence?

"Good, cause you're doing a lousy job." Her friend didn't seem to notice. "I saw the way you flirted with a certain Santa man before you knew who he was."

"Oh, please." She opened her laptop, caught a glimpse of her pinched, weary expression in the darkened screen and shut it immediately. "I don't have the time or the inclination to flirt with anyone. Do you know what all I have pressing in on me right now?"

"No, but I can just guess what you want pressing in on you." She ran her fingers over the long, curved watering can spout in a gesture too innocent looking not to be totally deliberate. "Or should I say, who? You know, Flynn—"

"Jerrianne Munroe, don't you make me run tell your daddy you've been trash talking."

"I just said—"

"You said that man's name, and around here, that's nothing but unadulterated gutter talk."

Jerrianne wrinkled up her nose and set the watering can down with a *clunk*. "I don't care what you think. Flynn Garvey is all right in my book."

"Then we need to get you a new book. This one's missing some vital pages."

"Listen, that man has made more headway in finding Max's father and getting some back child support out of him in the past week than I or my daddy, or even you, Tess, have accomplished since Ed and Anita took off together."

"I know." Tess put her head in her hands. Just thinking about Flynn churned up knots as big as boulders in her stomach. It always had but until last week, she could simply push it away. It was the past. She could not change it and she would not dwell on it. Until he showed up again, she never allowed herself to think about Flynn, the hurt she'd dealt him and the horrible truth he knew about her. Now she had no choice.

"It's no secret you have some issues with Flynn."

A dry, humorless laugh snagged in the back of Tess's throat.

"But if you ask me—"

"No thank you." She held one hand up. "If I asked you, Jer, you'd tell me that all I need to resolve those 'issues' would be a dog collar, some whipped cream, and two uninterrupted hours in the Come and Go Motor Court over behind the bowling alley. That about right?"

"Oh, no, Tess. Whatever is between you and Flynn goes much deeper than that." Jerrianne moved to the door and leaned against the frame. "You'd want that room for way more than two hours."

"What I want . . ." She forced the unwelcome image of Flynn's strong arms around her naked body out of her mind. ". . . is to get back to work."

"Fine."

Tess flipped through the pages of the appointment book perched on the highest pile on the desk until she found the red circled date in September with the time and place she'd be making her pitch to P. Pearcy McLaughlin. "We only have six weeks until we give our presentation. We're way ahead on production so we can devote as much time as we need to getting the paperwork and projections polished. Everything has to be in perfect order."

"It will be." Jerrianne started to leave, then poked her head back in. "Oh, there is one more thing you need to know about Flynn."

"I don't want to know anything else about Flynn. I don't want to hear his name uttered in my office again. Do you understand?"

"Yes, but I—"

"No. I can't afford the distraction even talking

about that man can become to me. I have too much to concentrate on already."

"The world won't stop spinning if you take some time to relax now and then, you know."

"How can I relax when so much is riding on me making the right decisions?"

"You always make the right decisions."

Tess clenched her jaw and shut her eyes.

"From the time you took that job as a reporter at the *Vanguard* and wrangled your column on southern style into a weekly special section that got picked up all around the state, you've made the right choices. You've done good."

"I've gotten lucky a lot, and yes, made the right *business* choices . . . so far."

"So far is pretty danged good, honey. Your books have been bestsellers snd this one"—she jerked her thumb over her shoulder at the framed cover of *Simply Christmas: Celebrating the Holidays with Southern Style*—"helped you launch the magazine and got you on those New York morning shows."

"That's hardly as big a deal as this next step may prove, Jer."

"Sugar, anything that gets you standing inches away from Matt Lauer is a *big* deal."

"But what if I'm doing the wrong thing by trying to expand the magazine at this time?"

"You're not. You've done the research, you know the time is right."

"What if I can't get backing from McLaughlin?"

"So what if you don't?"

"And what if I *do*? What will it do to this town if I move *Simply Southern* to Atlanta? We only have the small staff here, but they all need and love their jobs, and the secondary money we bring in from people visiting the Heritage House and coming to patronize the places we highlight in the books and magazine, it means a lot to a lot of people."

"They'll survive."

"Will they? The dairy has been steadily laying off workers every year."

"There are other businesses in town. And Mount Circe should still draw some tourism trade."

"Oh, right, the Museum of Southern Culture will pull the travelers in off the highway right and left. They'll swarm in in droves to see the handful of Civil War relics and the Jimmy Carter exhibit complete with two whole cases of unopened Billy Beer."

"Don't forget they do have Miz James's little pink autograph book on display now—with all the names of the stars of *Gone With the Wind* in it."

"Written by Miz James herself, no less."

"The tourists wouldn't know that."

"At least not until they got a gander at it and shared the thrill we all had when we first clapped eyes on the scrawled inscriptions of such luminaries as Vivian Lee, L-e-e, Clark Grable, and Olanie D. Havlinn. She didn't even come close on that one."

"She did get Butterfly McQueen right, you have to give her some credit for that."

Tess laughed. "Jerrianne, you know, of all the SuiteHearts, you are the sweetest. You try to find something good in everything, don't you?"

"And you try to find something to worry over."

"I was born worried."

"I believe it. You've carried the weight of the world on your shoulders ever since I've known you."

"But not for much longer. If we can get ol' Pearcy to invest in us, we can build an empire so big we'll hire people to do the worrying for us." She snapped her fingers triumphantly.

Jerrianne shut her eyes. "I can't wait."

"Me neither. But we have to wait. The old boy is near impossible to get in to see and he refused to work us in until this day." She tapped her finger on a page, then moved back around the desk. "Until then, we have to make sure everything runs smooth. We can't afford even the hint of trouble."

The bell on the main door of the building rang out to let them know they had company.

"And for future reference, when I say trouble I do mean Flynn Garvey."

"I . . . uh . . . I better go see who that is." Jerrianne stood stock still.

Footsteps echoed in the marble foyer on the floor below them.

"Are you going to see who that is or shall I?"

"No!" Her assistant thrust out her arm with all the subtle ease of a mother flinging her body into the path of a moving car to spare the life of her only child. "That is, no, you stay put. It's my job to greet visitors, not yours."

Tess nodded.

Jerrianne twisted her fingers together but her feet did not move.

"Then go."

"I am." She hesitated, then sighed and hurried out to meet their guest.

People wandered into her place of business at the rate of three or four a day. Locals brought out-of-towners by and vacationers passing through Mount Circe often stopped in to tour the old restored mansion and headquarters of the magazine. Then there were the die-hard devotees who came from all over the South to pay homage to what they saw as the last bastion of gracious living.

Occasionally entire bevies of belles would descend on the place in all their finery. More than one gaggle of Junior Leaguers made the pilgrimage yearly, expecting the royal treatment—which they got.

"Welcome to Magnolia Oaks Heritage House, would you like to sign the guest book?" Jerrianne laid the accent on extra thick today.

Must be a man in the group, Tess thought. Not that it mattered beyond Jerrianne's nervous habit of shifting into hardcore hypersouthern sweet-thang mode around men. Male or female, school kids or senior citizens group, everyone who walked through the doors of this house received a welcome worthy of a conquering hero.

"If I sign it, do I have to use my real name?"

Except him! Tess stormed to the doorway knocking against her desk and almost toppling the fabric samples, files, and her appointment book to the floor in her wake. She shoved the clutter back into its precarious position as she called out, "That had better not be who I think it is."

"Hi, honey, I'm home!" Flynn's voice carried up the stairs like the noxious odor of a skunk under the front porch floorboards.

In three steps she put herself at the top of the grand staircase, hellbent on throwing that pest out. "This is not your *home*, Mr. Garvey. In fact you are about as welcome here as flea-bit cat at a pedigree dog show."

"Said the lady with her claws showing."

"The only thing I'm showing is *you*—to the door." She pointed with a flourish worthy of the Queen of England, or at least a very highly placed Atlanta debutante. "Good-bye, Mr. Garvey."

"Tess, that's what I tried to tell you upstairs, that Flynn needed to drop by here today so I could sign some papers." Her assistant looked up the stairway waving several pages like the white flag of surrender. "And, well, here he is!"

"Here I am." He held his arms wide apart. His expensive suit jacket fell open.

The polished veneer of an unmistakably expensive cotton shirt, silk tie, and summer-weight suit could not obscure the true nature of the man standing in her foyer. The terms *comfortable*, *cocksure*, *lean*, and *hard* sprang to her mind, though not necessarily in that order.

Time, she decided then and there, was a woman. And Flynn had sweet-talked her into showing him the ultimate kindness. How else could anyone explain the way this man wore his years so well? Aging had refined in him a visible strength and ease that his physical body could not wholly contain so that it cast a sense of purpose and presence about him. That created an image altogether bigger than life.

Not a single strand of gray tarnished his closely clipped golden brown hair. No lines marred his face unless he smiled, and then they only accentuated his killer blue eyes and hard, brazen mouth.

"Yes, here you are, indeed."

"Tess, I'm sorry. I should have had him come by my house, not work."

"No need for apologies, Jerrianne." He said her assistant's name but his gaze burned straight through Tess. "This isn't the first time I've ever shown up unannounced and caught your boss with her . . ." He narrowed his eyes. ". . . guard down, is it, Tess?"

"Trying to provoke me won't get you anywhere."

"Amen to that." He tipped his head to one side to

speak to Jerrianne, his gaze never leaving Tess. "I spent the better part of one summer trying to *provoke* her brains out, but she wouldn't have any part of it. Guess I wasn't good enough for her. Though I never had any complaints about my provoking skills before or since, mind you."

Jerrianne hid her face behind the papers and laughed.

Tess clenched her teeth and gripped the cold wrought-iron banister at the top of the stairs. "That's it, Flynn. Get your smart-aleck doesn't-know-how-to-stay-out-of-places-where-it-has-no-business-going ass up here right this minute."

"Now you've done it," Jerrianne whispered none too softly.

"What happened to you showing me the door?" he called up.

"Now, Garvey!"

"She wants me." He put his hand to his heart and smirked and, darn him, made it look bone-melting, heart-stopping sexy.

"She wants your *ass*." Jerrianne's tone implied her boss wanted to nail his butt to the wall. The sly look she cast Tess's way said something else entirely.

"It's all hers." Flynn gave the other woman a wink as he started up the stairs two at a time. "But if she wants anything else from me, she's going to have to ask a lot nicer than that."

5

Flynn hoped to high heaven she did not even try to pull her "nice girl" routine on him. Shrill and shrewish, cool and sassy, those, he could take from her. He rubbed his hand along the back of his neck where the hair pricked up.

He'd had dreams all week long of her turning her considerable charms on him in ways that went far and above the call of even the most gracious southern hostess. He woke from those dreams sweaty and more frustrated than a grown man with plenty of options in the female companion department should ever have to be. Who could have guessed that even after all these years and the transgression that stood between them, Tess would still affect him that way?

He watched her walk into her office. With her every step, her fitted sundress accentuated the sway and curve of her round behind. Her hair gleamed like Tupelo honey and her tanned bare feet padded over the thick rug so silently that he could hear himself breathing. He could smell her hair and the way her perfume would cling to his skin after a night in each other's arms.

He could feel her. Feel the essence of who she was and feel the way their bodies would twine together, how she would take him inside of her, deeper and deeper.

"Pardon my office. It's not usually this messy, but . . ." She turned and motioned to him from inside the airy room. "Well, are you coming in or not?"

He hung back long enough to take a deep breath and fasten the button on his suit coat. Crazy as it seemed, she *did* still do it to him. "I'm right behind you."

"As I said, I hope you forgive the chaos around here—"

"Is that what you hope I forgive, Tess? Because if that's all you ask"—he held his hands out—"consider youself forgiven."

She dropped into her chair and raised her chin.

"If, however, you want me to absolve you of the sins of your past?" He leaned over the desk between them, one hand spread across a patch of green fabric and the other over the open appointment book. "That may take a little more convincing."

Her eyes flashed.

He smiled, just a small smile, to keep her off balance.

"I have no intention of asking for your forgiveness about anything." She folded her arms. "I don't expect it and I recognize that to your way of thinking, I don't deserve it."

There had to be a catch here. "What about to *your* way of thinking?"

"To my way of thinking you're the one who should be asking for my forgiveness."

"Ahh. Yeah, should have seen that one coming." He straightened, sighed, and made himself shift his focus to other things. "But then where you are concerned, I never had the knack for seeing anything until it hit me between the eyes."

"I know I hurt you then, Flynn. But I truly cannot fathom how you could still be agonizing over that all these years later."

"Agonizing? Pretty strong word from the person who said she'd rather see me drowned than let all this become water under the bridge."

She winced in a fetchingly sheepish way that was too unattractive to suggest contrived coyness. "What can I say? High drama was always a weakness of mine."

He smiled—for real this time.

"I reacted strongly, badly, I'll admit that. But I did it for a very good reason. I'm afraid of you, Flynn."

"Afraid?" He hadn't seen that coming. "Of me?"

"Of what you know about me. What you can do to . . . to all I've worked for."

"Why is it always all about you?" His words overlapped hers but he did not care. She'd delivered a sucker punch to the gut by spinning this personal issue into yet another concern about her ludicrous business. "What about me? What about my feelings in all this?"

"All I hurt was your pride, Flynn, a young man's pride."

"Don't discount how deep that can cut."

She nodded, then turned her head completely away from him. "I'll grant you that. Won't you at least acknowledge I've shouldered a lot of pain and regret since that awful night when . . . when everything changed?"

He didn't have an answer for her.

"I can't believe you can act like our whole relationship began and ended on the night of my college graduation, Flynn. What about that summer before you went back up north? I gave you something I held precious because I thought . . ."

He glared at her, daring her to go too far.

She shook her head. "It's not like I never made any sacrifices. That's all I'm saying."

For an instant it all came back to him, the heat of that summer and of their first time together. Even then, despite the aching fire of young passion, he knew she wasn't like any other girl he'd been with.

He had fought his baser urges, reigned in his own needs, and made love to her with a tenderness he had not known before or since. "It doesn't do a lot to bolster my pride to think you came to me that summer thinking of yourself as a sacrificial virgin."

"Make fun all you want. I hadn't bargained for any better from you. That's the exact reason your coming back has me on the defensive."

"I was kidding, trying to lighten the mood." He left out that he'd also needed something to chase away the renewed longing and emotional anarchy even the briefest memory of her inspired.

"Anyway, we both know that the issue that stands between us now is not"—she dropped her voice to a whisper—"that summer."

Was it shame or pain that put the hush in Tess's words? Knowing that would make a world of difference to Flynn.

"Only three people know what happened the night of my graduation, Flynn. Two of us won't talk, too much is at stake. But the third one, there's the enigma."

"*I'm* the enigma?"

She pressed her lips closed.

"*I* am the enigma?"

"You are the wild card."

"Koo-koo-cachoo."

"See? You don't take anything seriously. And that has me nervous as a cat in a room full of rockers."

"Long-tailed cat."

"What?" She put her chin in her hand.

He half-leaned, half-sat on the edge of her cluttered desk. "The expression's 'as nervous as a long-tailed cat in a room full of rockers.' "

"Oh." Her eyes met his and lingered there.

So much stood between them, time and anger, broken hearts and battered egos, but looking into her eyes now, Flynn knew one thing had not changed. He still felt compelled to extend her a level of tenderness and protection that circumstances told him she neither required nor deserved. "But you don't have to be, Tess."

"What?"

"You don't have to be nervous, or afraid. Not about me."

"Flynn, if people knew what happened that night, even though now it doesn't seem like such a very big deal, it could have far-reaching effects. There is no part of my life that information would not touch and there are innocent people who would be hurt, perhaps irrevocably. Can you understand my concern?"

"I've kept quiet all this time, haven't I?"

"Yes, and I thank you for it."

"No problem. I know how it feels to have your dirty laundry aired by everyone in this town."

"Air your dirty laundry?" She sat back and crossed her legs. "Flynn, the way I recall it, you know what it's like to wave your drawers in the face of everybody in town."

"That's not true, Tess."

"Oh no?"

"No." He placed his hand on the arms of her chair and leaned over her until only inches separated their faces. "I don't wear drawers."

"And I was beginning to think you'd changed." Her lips twitched.

"I have, where it counts."

"Oh, changing your underwear *counts*, at least with me. But then you know how I go in for all that fancy, frou-frou nonsense."

"I do." He reached his hand out, wanting to touch her cheek or brush back her hair. At the last possible second, he thought better of it and straightened, picking up a scrap of fancy fabric to rub between his thumb and forefinger. "I do indeed."

"Maybe the women you're used to spending time with aren't so fussy."

"You're losing your touch, Queen Tessa."

"I have no idea what you mean by that."

"Used to be if you wanted to know something you just got in my face and asked."

"I have no interest in your face, Flynn."

"But you're dying to know about my past, my *romantic* past. What I've been doing and who I've been doing it with since we last saw one another—aren't you?"

"I do admit I find myself curious as to why some woman hasn't snatched you up—"

He started to grin.

"And thrown you out a sixth-story window." She uncrossed her legs then crossed them the other way.

Any retort he might have had slipped away as he focused on her bare skin and the way her thighs moved under the fabric of her dress.

"Word around town, by way of your mother, was that you'd never get married. Don't think that didn't cause some interesting speculation."

He chuckled.

"She did keep the town apprised of your, uh, entanglements, by the way. The starlet, the heiress, the lady airplane pilot."

"She talked about those?"

"Anywhere anyone would listen—which was everywhere but the graveyard and the cow pastures."

"Sounds like Mama made some friends around here in later years."

"She did. I didn't know her well myself, but she did love to talk about you, and word got 'round." She wet her lips.

"I can just imagine what those words were."

"Me, I never could imagine you with a wife and children." She looked away only a moment. When she faced him again, a weak smile quivered on her lips. "Where would they fit in your brand-new red convertible?"

"Yeah, where would a family fit in my life?" He rubbed his hands together and cleared this throat. He looked around and saw the photo of Tess's family. Before he gave it much thought, he began to speak again. "Took me a long time to decide if I wanted to find a way to make those things fit. I finally realized I could never make room for a family, for any serious relationship, until I cleared away some the relationships of my past."

"Flynn . . ."

"I came back to Georgia to see my father, Tess. It's time to put the pain between him and me to rest."

"Your father?"

"Yeah, and that's all I have to say about that." He tugged at the knot in his tie, then tightened it again. "What about you?"

"Me?"

"Why aren't you married, Tess?"

"I'm married to my work."

"Not good enough. I need a better answer than that."

"Learn to live with disappointment."

"I have."

His quiet words affected her like nothing else he'd said. Her green eyes grew soft. Her shoulders eased forward out of the rigid good-soldier posture she put on for the world. "I've dated a lot in the last fourteen years. Almost got engaged twice and wasted nearly five years with a man who let his mama make all his decisions for him. She decided finally that I would not do."

Do what, he wanted to ask. What had she done,

and had she *not* done with these dates, those almost-fiancés, this mama's boy? He wanted to know if she had given to them what she had offered him that summer so long ago—everything.

"So now you know," she said, far too brightly.

He didn't know a damn thing that mattered, but clearly she was not giving any better answers. He nodded. "Thanks for telling me. I know it doesn't come easy to you to talk about anything personal, not to me, anyway."

"Like you said, you've kept my secret safe for a long while now. That's earned my trust for the time being. I can only hope that will continue."

"You can do more than hope, you can bank on it."

"Heaven help me, I believe you," she whispered. "For the record, I do believe you've come a long way from the boy who raced around town terrorizing decent folks half out of their wits."

"Did you just call the 'decent folks' of Mount Circe halfwits?"

"Not *all* of them." She settled back into the chair. "But there are enough of them who, at even the hint of scandal or indiscretion on my part, would go off half-cocked. And so help me if you make a joke about that, Flynn—"

"I wouldn't touch it with a ten-foot pole." He held both hands up.

"Oh, hon, you don't *have* a ten-foot pole." She gave him a brassy smile. "I should know."

"And you were worried about me and my mouth,

girl." Flynn chuckled. "Not that I mind. I kind of get a kick out of seeing Miss Peaches and Perfection show the real woman beneath the polished image."

"Careful, Flynn. We're starting to sound like two people who could come dangerously close to not wanting to kill one another."

"Scary, huh? And you thought this town wasn't big enough for the both of us."

"If by 'both of us' you mean you and your enormous ego, then, yes, I had my doubts."

"Tess, you are—" *Incredible.* He laughed. "You are going to be trouble, aren't you?"

"Funny, I thought the same thing about you."

"Thought? Past tense?"

She pressed her hands flat together, like a little girl about to say her prayers. "I'm not going to pretend that having you around when I'm about to . . . when things are very delicate with my business . . . doesn't make me ill at ease."

"Okay, fair enough."

She took a deep breath.

Flynn took one right along with her.

"But, as I told you before I knew it was you behind that Santa beard, I *want* to trust you. I really do."

"Good."

"And, truth to tell, you've already given me reason to do so in the way you've treated Jerrianne and worked on her behalf."

"It's what I do." He shrugged.

"You do it well."

"I can't afford not to, not when kids' lives depend on the outcome."

"You talk like a man who's found his true calling in life, Flynn."

"I have a strong motivation to do the work." He refused to take praise for work conceived and driven by unresolved feelings of anger, doubt, and disappointment over his father's role in his life. "Besides, I discovered I have a knack for it, making the contacts, tracking things down, not giving up until there is no stone left unturned."

She nodded like she knew exactly what he meant. She did not know. She could not. She'd grown up with both parents present and lots of friends who loved her for herself. He had had too much money, too much freedom, and damned little else. Compared to his life, hers had been a sweet ride down a lazy river. She could not possibly know how he felt or why he did what he did.

"Trick is," he said, as he shoved one hand in his pocket, "you've got to learn not to let your feelings trip you up."

"Says the man who got so carried away playing Santa Claus that he made a vow to a little boy and then proceeded to make good on that promise, trying to find Max's father, without asking for a red cent to cover even basic expenses."

Downstairs the doorbell jingled. A man's muffled tones mingled with Jerrianne's lilting replies.

Tess had him there. He had taken on trying to grant Max his wish out of nothing more than pure and sappy emotion. Tess had seen through him. He'd made it easy for her, too, and he didn't like that one bit. "Max didn't ask me to find his father, Tess, but nice try at finagling it out of me, just the same."

"Can't blame a girl for trying."

Not when there are so many other things you can blame her for, he thought. And almost in that same instant, he realized he didn't feel so much like blaming her for anything anymore. He just felt . . .

"Tess? Tess! Jobie James just dropped something off for the two of us down here. I think you'd better come down and have a look." Panic edged the controlled quiet of the woman's voice carrying up the stairway. "Alone."

He glanced at Tess.

A crease formed between her brows and she stood. "I guess I'd better go check this out. Are we done here? Has our talk accomplished anything at all?"

"I'd say it's given us a new understanding, wouldn't you?"

She nodded. "But that's hardly a working solution. I'm a plan well, work hard, reap results person, Flynn. I'd like to see us come to an agreement, an arrangement we can both live with."

"You want to draw a chalk line through the center of town and each of us take a side?"

"Tess? Did you hear me?" Jerrianne called again.

"I heard you, I'll be right down, hon." She bent to collect her shoes from beneath the desk. "I understand you have to work closely with Jerrianne right now. I even accept you've come back to Mount Circe and in a town this small, our paths may cross. All I'd like to propose is that for the next few weeks, we each make a concerted effort to avoid one another at all costs."

"The next few weeks?"

"Don't ask." She held her hand up to cut him off just as she started to slip her foot into her shoe. She wobbled.

Flynn lunged forward to steady her, knocking her appointment book from the desk. The slap of leather hitting the floor made her flinch. Or was it his hand on her bare shoulder?

"Thank you," she whispered and once again he found himself mesmerized by the movement of her full lips.

He swallowed, hard.

She laid her hand on his arm for support and slipped on the other shoe. The heels added enough height that all Flynn would have had to do to kiss her was lean in and do it.

"Tess, please! I really need to see you all by yourself down here." At Jerrianne's voice they leapt apart faster than a couple of fifteen-year-olds caught necking on the family sofa.

"I think that's a very good idea, Tess." He straightened his tie, then ran his fingers back through his hair as if he actually expected to find himself disheveled from the nonencounter. "Let's do that. Let's make every effort to steer clear of one another for a while."

"I think that's wise." She squeezed past him and hurried to the door. "Give me a sec to hustle Jerrianne into the office before you come down. I hope you don't mind showing yourself out?"

He laughed at the question. Here she'd just asked him to stay the hell out of her life, then hoped he didn't take offense at her not walking him to the door. "You never forget your manners, do you, Tess?"

"I wouldn't want anyone mistaking me for a"—

"Bastard?"

"Yankee."

"Six of one, half a dozen of another." He grinned, then bent at the knees by the fallen appointment book. "Go on down. I'll gather this up and put it back where it fell from, then head downstairs in a minute."

"Thanks." She started out the door, then poked her head back in. "Flynn?"

"Hmmm?" He stuffed some business cards back between the pages of the book.

"I just want to let you know that I trust you completely to honor our agreement about avoiding one another."

"Thanks. Believe it or not, hearing you say that means a lot to me."

She did not believe it. It showed in her eyes.

"Tess?" Jerrianne's tone took on a pleading nature. "I hate to be a bother, but—"

"Go."

She did.

And her leaving left Flynn feeling . . . conflicted. He had to admit he liked that they had come to some sort of truce, but he also regretted that he had not seized the opportunity to kiss her senseless. Now that they'd made this ridiculous bargain, he might never have an opportunity like that again.

He stood and listened, the book in his hands. He heard only the anxious tone of the women's voices below, no details of the conversation. Then a door shut and he knew the coast was clear. He gave the room a sweeping glance, said his mental good-bye to Tess one last time, placed the book on the desk, and gave it a quick glance to make sure it would not slide again.

A date, circled twice in boldest red ink, caught his eye. He knew he had no business snooping, but she had left him here with the thing in his hands. If she wanted to hide anything she would never have done that. So he looked. What he saw put ice in his veins.

P. Pearcy McLaughlin. That sorry sonofabitch. He'd granted an audience to Tess. He'd made time in his impossibly busy schedule for a woman who meant nothing to him while he did not have the time of day for Flynn. He would not make time to see or even speak to his own flesh and blood, his only son.

Flynn checked the date, then reached over and plucked up a business card from the stack on the desk. With a black and gold pen from Tess's desk, he scribbled down the information on the back of the card and tucked them both into his breast pocket.

He had given his word to Tess, and he hated the idea of having to break it. But there was something bigger at stake now. She had a way into his father's presence, something Flynn had been denied far too long. Much as he valued the trust of this remarkable woman, he knew what he had to do.

One way or another, he would have to convince Tess to let him go with her when she made that September appointment. Even if doing so meant he would have to completely obliterate the promise he had just made to stay away from her.

6

Dear SuiteHearts:

I know what you did in college. And now you are going to pay.

Tess stared at the bold black words on the stark white stationery until the letters began to blur. The paper rustled in her fingers as she turned it over, then over again, then did the same with the blank envelope it had come in. "What *is* this, Jerrianne?"

The other woman clutched an identical note and envelope in both hands. She shook her head and when she spoke her voice scarcely carried above the hum of the computer on her desk. "I don't know."

"Is it some kind of threat?"

"I don't know."

"Or a . . . a joke?"

"It's not a very funny joke, if it is. Pretty jerky, if you ask me." Jerrianne gave a helpless sigh, then snapped her fingers. "You don't suppose Reni would—"

"Call her."

Jerrianne had the phone tucked under her chin and her fingers flying over the familiar numbers before Tess finished the simple command.

If grasping at straws were an Olympic event, this effort would have put the two of them in contention for a gold medal.

"It's ringing."

Tess flicked the envelope flap up then down and tapped her toe. "Your note is exactly like mine, right?"

"Exactly like." She lowered the mouthpiece as she spoke. "The envelopes didn't even have our names on them, so it doesn't seem that it mattered who got which note."

Tess nodded. "What's taking her so long to answer?"

"She's either not in or not taking calls." Jerrianne held the receiver out so Tess could hear Reni's recorded message on the other end. "It's her machine."

"For heaven's sake, hang up."

"What? Why?"

Tess reached over and did the deed for her assistant. "Because if she did do this as some elaborate joke we are not going to give her the satisfaction of capturing our panic-stricken response on tape."

"Good point. And if she didn't have a hand in these notes?"

"Then she got one herself or it doesn't involve her." Tess assumed the second of the two. "Either way, it's the kind of thing best addressed in person, not playing phone tag with answering machines."

"So what do we do now?" Jerrianne wore a look of hopeful expectation. She needed answers and guidance and, as usual, she turned to Tess to make it all better.

Thing was, Tess not only did not know how to fix this mess, she had every reason to believe she was at the very root of it. "Didn't Jobie have anything to say about who asked him to bring the notes out here? *Anything* at all that would give us some indication who might have sent them?"

The office chair squeaked softly as Jerrianne shifted her weight. "No, nothing. He was mighty worked up, all proud of himself that someone entrusted him with the errand."

"But he didn't say who?"

"The most information I got from the poor fellow was that whoever sent him had paid him a dollar to run the envelopes out here and hand them to me or you in person."

"A dollar?" Tess folded her arms. "One lousy dollar for him to ride his bike all the way out here and find one of us? Maybe have to wait for who knows how long if we weren't around?"

"What did you expect, Tess?" Her friend laughed but not her normal, light, bubbly laughter. "Did you think the kind of person who'd send a note like this would be a big tipper?"

"But still, to take such unfair advantage of Jobie."

"They'd hardly be the first."

Jobie James was fifty years old if he was a day—maybe closer to sixty. It was hard to tell to look at his tanned but smooth face and greased back hair. Since his "peculiarities," as folks around town called his disabilities, kept him out of school, there was no frame of reference there. She only knew that for as long as she could remember people found little chores for Jobie to do to earn folding money. Most paid far more than the job was worth, but some didn't.

"You're right, Jerrianne, they wouldn't be the first to use Jobie unfairly. Whoever offered him that piss-poor bit of compensation had to know he'd do it for so little."

"So?"

"So, I suspect this is the work of somebody familiar with Mount Circe."

"More importantly, familiar with us." Jerrianne held the note up. "Or at least with one of us."

She would not let herself see that as an accusation. She would not do or say anything that might reveal her guilt in any way. "They spelled our nick-name right. *SuiteHearts*, for us being suitemates, not the other way, like we were a bunch of sweet young things."

"Nobody who knew the four of us very well would ever make that mistake." Jer swiveled her chair half a turn, then brushed her fingertips over the silver-framed picture of her little boy, Max. "But the note does say 'I know what you did in college,' Tess."

I know what you did in college, Tess. Her heart-beat thrummed in her ears like fat raindrops pound-ing on a tin roof. Jerrianne knew nothing, she reminded herself. Only three people knew what she'd done and only Tess knew *why* she had done it. And in the end it was hardly the stuff worthy of blackmail, but more a secret she kept to protect someone she loved—and herself—from hurt and humiliation. For someone to use that against her, they'd have to hold a powerful grudge. "Who would do this?"

The low, languid notes of a man whistling as he walked down the long marble stairs sent a shiver tripping up Tess's spine. The sensation did not stop until it reached the nape of her neck and made the hair there stand on end.

"Tess, you don't . . . you couldn't suspect . . ."

She stood stock still as if the slightest movement would draw the attention of the man crossing the sunlit foyer.

"Flynn?" Jerrianne whispered.

"Why not? He told me himself he has a knack for discovering things about people." Of course, in her case, he would not have needed to work at it at all. "Even when they don't want those things uncovered."

His shadow fell across the frosted glass in the closed office door. Both women held their breath until it passed.

"But he was here when Jobie came in and gave me the envelopes."

"And can you imagine a better alibi?" *Alibi?* The very word pretty much absolved Flynn in the whole matter, didn't it? Man and boy, when Flynn did anything he did it in plain sight, up front, no excuses and certainly no alibis.

The bell over the front door clattered and the heavy door whooshed shut.

"It doesn't make any sense, Tess, not with him having gone so far out of his way to help me and Max."

"I agree." She heaved out a big sigh and held out her hand to gather Jerrianne's note with her own. "Truth be told, the one person we can probably exclude as having any involvement at all with this little piece of dirty work is Flynn Garvey."

"So do we just sit back and wait to see if we get another note?"

The quiet strength that Tess had always relied upon reasserted itself at that simple question. She was not helpless and she would not be a victim, nor would she let her friends be made victims. She smiled and tossed back her hair and fixed "the look" full force on Jerrianne. "Since when has just sitting back and waiting for anything to happen been my style, sugar?"

"Since never, Queen Tessa."

"Then get your purse and come on."

"Where are we going?"

"That note was addressed to the SuiteHearts without any individual names. We couldn't get a hold of Reni but there is still another SuiteHeart out there. We are going to go and pay her a little visit."

"Turn left out of the drive, Jer." The safety belt cut across her neck as Tess strained to see around the house and between some low-hanging tree limbs. Flynn's red convertible still sat in a parking space in front of the Heritage House.

He took his time putting on a pair of sunglasses then pulled a card out of his breast pocket. He made a stunning portrait in contrasts. Tan skin, white shirt, black suit, cream-colored car seats, sun on his hair like some carefree boy but with the commanding presence, even at this distance, of a man with a true sense of purpose. He touched the card in his hand with one finger then looked toward the house. If she didn't know better she'd easily imagine him studying his instructions for an upcoming secret mission.

She laughed to herself. Some spy he'd make. He did not even notice that she and Jerrianne had skittered out the back way and climbed into her assistant's car. A small thing, really, ridiculously small, yet it made her feel wicked and wise to have outwitted him. Had he seen them it would surely have aroused his curiosity. Might even have encouraged him to follow them, just to see why they had run off after receiving the strange delivery. The one thing she did not want to do under these stressful circumstances was arouse and encourage a man like Flynn.

"Are you kidding?"

She startled. "What?"

"You said turn left? You can't mean to take the dirt road. That swings us all the way around almost out to your house then over behind the dairy before we cut back in to Wylene's subdivision."

"I'm not kidding." She glanced back at Flynn slipping the card back into his pocket. "Turn left. I want to go the back way."

"But it's so much faster to go through town."

"Through town or all the way around it, long way or short cut, either one adds up to a pretty quick trip in the grand scheme of things."

"So why go—"

"If we go on the back roads no one will see us."

"Who's there to see us but Flynn?"

Tess gave no answer.

Jerrianne turned the car left, her ponytail swinging as they bounced over the dirt road. She raised her chin for a glance in the rearview mirror then slowed the car. "There's a big black car pulling into the front drive. Should we go back?"

Tess squinted over her shoulder. "Do you recognize that driver?"

"Can't make him out, but here comes Flynn and looks like he's slowing to have a chat."

"Good. That will keep them both occupied while we hightail it out of here. Keep driving."

"Yes, ma'am." The words came out hard, petulant, and more like an employee than an old pal.

The summer sun glinted off the front of the car, the brightness broken up now and again by the dappled shade of trees arching their branches over the road. The routine swoops and slopes of the road she took to and from work everyday did not soothe Tess as they usually did.

They whizzed past the turn off to Tess's beloved home and rolled on until the battered Dreamland Dairy sign came into sight. The car slowed to take the long curve that led into Mount Circe and would take them to Wylene and Joe Brent's house in the old subdivision that had always divided Plantation Pines from Dreamland.

Tension hung between them in the quiet car. They need hardly have used the air conditioning for the chill their silence generated. Tess didn't care. She did not want to make small talk. She was psyched. She had to be or she would never have dared go over to the Spivey house unannounced. She'd have never had the nerve, not knowing what she might find, not knowing how it might make her feel.

But she had already put any fear behind her about that and about the notes they had received. Fear did not produce results. She needed results to concentrate on finding answers. That meant putting and keeping any and all petty annoyances out of her mind.

"What is it with you two, anyway?"

"I have no idea what you're talking about." She lied so automatically it jabbed at her conscience. Everyone knew that she and Wylene had a tenuous relationship at best, but no one, especially a fellow SuiteHeart, ever asked about it outright like this.

"I'm talking about you and Flynn."

"Flynn?" Goodness, when had her list of people she got edgy talking about grown so large she couldn't keep them straight? Since her mother's death, it had only been the two, well, three, and now Flynn and . . . Oh, hell, it might be easier for her to name the people she wasn't on edge about.

"What's going on between you and Flynn?"

"Nothing. And it's going to stay that way." That, at least, was the truth. "We reached an agreement to stay out of each other's way."

"Doesn't seem like a very long-term solution."

"I don't need a long-term solution, or anything else from him. I just need to keep things running smoothly until I secure McLaughlin's investment.

Until then I am not going to be deterred by vague threats *or* the likes of Flynn."

"And you honestly think you can do that?" They turned down the Spiveys' street.

"Can and will." Tess fought back the swell of anxiety rising in her chest.

The last house before the street dropped off into a grass-covered dead end came into view. The shutters, front, and double garage doors in stark white accented with pink trim stood out against the red brick of the tidy ranch-style house. A neat wooden sign swung from the faux gaslight lamppost in the yard to announce Wylene's business, while a hand-lettered poster adorned with hearts and flowers in the garage door window proclaimed, CLASS IS IN SESSION, DO NOT ENTER.

Jerrianne parked the car in Wylene's drive. Suddenly, the side garage door swung open and Wylene's class poured out. About half a dozen young girls, ranging in age from Little Miss Peachtree Princess contenders to potential candidates for the next Mount Circe High Homecoming Queen scattered over the lawn, chattering and giggling, primping and sashaying in glittering spandex and elaborate hair bows.

Tess smiled to remember the time when she had felt that strong and sure about life and her place in it. When all she needed to face down any problem was charm, confidence, and the perfect hairdo. She took a deep breath and could almost smell the bravado of youth combined with the hint of Aqua Net, and it gave her strength.

"Can and will take this bull by the horns, Jer, and wrestle it to the ground if need be. And the same goes for Flynn if he doesn't abide by our agreement." She got out, fluffed her hair. "Absolutely no doubt about it."

"Uh-huh." Jerrianne tipped her head and Tess turned just in time to see a gleaming red convertible glide by followed by a minivan. The van pulled into the drive beside Tess's car but not before she watched the convertible glide to a stop on the street in front of the house. Its arrival caused quite a stir among the girls on the lawn awaiting their rides.

"Can and will," Tess muttered under her breath, "just as soon as I strangle that man and—"

"Hi, Tess, sugar!" A dark-haired beauty, wearing oversized orange sunglasses and a skintight blue polka-dot outfit waved like she was seeing her husband off on a five-day business trip while her lover was already chilling margaritas on the back deck.

Tess slammed her door so hard it rocked the entire car, adding, "And Reni Pittman-Webb right along with him."

Flynn had lived in Boston and Chicago, and had even wasted a couple of years of his youth in California. He found they all had their unique appeal, but looking at this simple home-based business filled him with a warmth and wonder found no other place but in the South. *Wylene Spivey's House of Charm and Cheerleading.* He read the words burned into a cedar sign with scalloped edges and grinned. He glanced over the young girls who, right down to the tiniest one with her baby face and pigtails, carried themselves like each already had a crown on her head and a man wrapped around her pinkie finger. No doubt about it, he was home.

"Girls! Girls! You know the rules. No horseplay in the yard!" Wylene Parker—Wylene Spivey for the last fourteen years, God have mercy—came out onto her porch, clapping her hands.

Of all the friends, Wy looked oldest. Flynn made a quick study of her overteased hair, waiflike figure and drawn face. It didn't help that age or hair dye had given her once sassy red curls a dull, lifeless look or that she wore too much makeup, which settled into and accentuated the lines on her face. It didn't help that she'd lived far too many years with Joe Brent Spivey, a man Flynn could imagine strutting and posturing on the stage of a sleazy talk show just as readily as he lounged on the sofa all day watching them.

"Y'all line up in front of the garage door like you're supposed to and one by one go get in your mama's cars." She gave the youngest girl in the group a gentle nudge. The child walked in a weak zigzag pattern that merely paid court to Wy's demand, then broke into a gallop to one of two minivans parked by the dead end. The other girls broke ranks and hurried off to climb into the vans in the street and the one blocking the view of Tess's car in the drive. Wylene called after them, "Remember, the way you act when you come out of my class reflects on me and our work here."

Wham! Wham! The sliding doors of the vans, each a variation on a shade of blue, banged shut.

Wy did not give up but kept on talking to the last child as she headed off across the drive. "We want people to take one look at you all and say . . ." The van in the drive backed up. "Heavenly mercies! Look what the cat dragged in!"

Flynn decided he had definitely been away too long when he did not react quickly enough to cover his ears before the squeals of delight pierced the air.

"Jerrianne! Queen Tessa! I haven't seen you in a coon's age." Wy swooped down from the porch and launched herself into the two pairs of waiting arms.

"Don't you dare even think of leaving me out of that hug." Reni wiggled her way over, never more than one overly enthusiastic swing of her hips away from splitting the seams of her dress wide open.

"Get over here, then, girl," Tess demanded, her hand out.

And in the wink of an eye they were all together again, hugging, laughing, talking all at once, then hugging some more.

For some men, this sight only lacked a cat fight in a wading pool of Wesson to be the stuff of their wildest fantasies. Breasts met breasts, lipsticked mouths pressed to powder-blushed cheeks. Blondes, brunette, and redhead created a smorgasbord that included Tess's cool, leggy class, Jerrianne's sultry baby-doll innocence, Reni's obvious but fun-loving nature, and Wy's vulnerability hidden under a practiced persona.

Flynn had to admit he liked the picture they made, too, but not for some adolescent sexual kick. He liked these women. It was that simple.

He liked the way, the moment they laid eyes on one another, everything else fell away and there was nothing but them and their friendship. He liked that, in each other's company, they cast aside any notions of vying for masculine attention and instead lavished their admiration on each other. He liked that even though time and who knew what else had gone between them, they still loved and celebrated one another the way good friends ought to, but so seldom did. They had a special bond.

And at its heart was Tess.

"I ought to pinch the heads off both of you. You first, Reni, showing up unannounced after I told you not to come back at all. I don't know whether to hug your or choke you." Tess took her friend by the hand.

"Then just squeeze me till my eyes bug out." Reni wrapped her arms around her friend.

Damn it, that woman was like the sun. Wherever

she went, everything revolved around her, reached toward her, depended on her. And she never let them down. Whatever her mistakes of the past, Tess never let her dearest friends down and they counted on that.

Too bad they had come together today under such dubious circumstances. He pulled the note Reni had showed him from his pocket. His gut twisted. Who the hell would dare send this kind of vague but disturbing threat? Or if it wasn't a threat, whose sick idea of a joke was it?

He could find out. True, helping Max and Jerrianne had already taken more time away from the quest that had brought him home, from his plan to finally settle his relationship with his father. Lending a hand to Tess and her friends would distract him from that even more, but in the end . . .

Flynn shoved aside the shame that flashed over him and admitted that in helping Tess, he would also help himself. This cryptic cautionary note might prove his ticket into the meeting Tess already had scheduled with his SOB of a father.

But to accomplish that he first had to win Tess's trust. He had to gain access to the sacred circle that was the SuiteHearts.

"Is that?" Wylene shaded her eyes with one hand and went up on tiptoe, gaping in his general direction. "Why, it can't be! Flynn?"

"Hi, Wylene." He started to wave then thought it

might look too goofy for a man wanting to offer his services as righter of wrongs and protector of fair maidens. In midair he angled his hand out in a salute so odd it either showed him too cool for ordinary greetings, or said that he had come to an age where he'd lost all his good sense and most of his motor control. Fat chance he stood now of getting ushered into the inner sanctum, much less asked to play the white knight routine. "Good to see you a—"

"Get yourself over here right now so I can hug the stuffing out of you." She flung her arms open.

With a single glance that could singe an ice cube, Tess tried to warn him off.

But the blistering glares of a righteous woman had never deterred Flynn from going after his goal. In two long strides he came close enough for Wy to grab him around the middle and Reni to seize his arm.

"Isn't he just as cute as *ever*?" The words dripped out of Reni's mouth like syrup laced with well-aged bourbon—and a touch of arsenic just to quicken the pulse. "I believe you have grown more attractive with every passing year. Wouldn't you say so, Tess?"

"Oh, yes," she deadpanned, her gaze burning. "He just keeps growing and growing. Kind of like kudzu, only without the obvious charms."

"Charms?" Jerrianne laughed. "Folks hate kudzu, Tess. It climbs and creeps and inches its way over everything and into all kinds of places it doesn't belong."

"I know." She answered Jerrianne with her eyes on him.

Flynn laughed.

"You know, Flynn, honey, if you came by to see Joe Brent, he's not here." Wylene slipped into the job as hostess so deftly that a stranger would never have realized they'd just been steered away from the potentially awkward situation between him and Tess. "I don't know how long he'll be gone 'cause something got into him and he took off outta here like a house afire but I'd so love for you all to come in and—"

"He's not here to see that sack of—"

"Reni!" Tess's look found its mark.

Reni smiled at Tess then turned to Wy. "Flynn is here because I asked him to drive me over. I'm here because of the note."

"You got one too?" Jerrianne's touch on Reni's arm looked as fragile as her words sounded.

Tess, on the other hand, showed not even the hint of frailty as she grabbed Flynn's lapel. "You know about the note?"

Jer cocked her head at Reni. "How'd you get here so fast from Houston? We only just got our notes a few minutes ago."

"Notes?" Wylene looked from one to the other of them.

"I didn't get it in Houston, Jer, honey, I got it in town."

"What are you two talking about?"

"You mean you didn't get one?" Jerrianne asked. "One *what*?"

Flynn took the note from his pocket and handed it to her.

"I hadn't been at Granny Pistol's house more than fifteen minutes when Jobie James come loping up the walk with this. After I read it I headed straight for Tess's office."

"You went to your granny's empty house before you came to see me?"

"I bought it. It's my new home. It's where I needed to go first."

"You bought it? You *bought* it? Reni, I told you . . ."

"Oh my . . . oh my g . . . what *is* this?" Wylene held the paper up. It trembled in her hand.

"Well, it's not an invitation to a party." Flynn took it away and tucked it in his pocket as if by the simple gesture he could shelter them from the cruelty of the strange message. "So Jobie hasn't been by your house today?"

"I don't think so." Wylene shook her head. "But I was in classes all morning."

Flynn smoothed the flap down on this pocket. "I can—"

"*We* can handle this." Tess motioned to the group of girls. "I already have a few ideas on how to proceed, a place in mind where we can meet—privately—to sort through some things."

"Tess, don't be ridiculous," he said.

"I am many things, but I am never ridiculous."

He ignored her wounded pride and went on. "This is what I do, and by your own admission do well. I find people who go to great lengths to keep themselves and their secrets hidden."

She raised her chin but that did not keep him from seeing that it quivered, if only for an instant.

He put his hand on her back. "I ferret out information that even the police often can't. You didn't want to take this matter to the police, did you?"

"No!" Each of the women, not just Tess, agreed out loud on that matter.

Flynn tried not to smile at that.

Her fingers still gripping his lapel, Tess leaned in to whisper for his ear only, "But what about our agreement for you to stay clear of me?"

He shifted his eyes so that their gazes locked. He had set out to win her trust, but seeing that would not be possible today, realized he might just have to settle for the next best thing—extortion. "I didn't send those notes, Tess, but I sure as hell know what *you* did in college that might have inspired someone to write those words. Now, do you really want someone else besides me poking around in this nasty little situation?"

"Y'all quit telling secrets over there and let's us put this issue to a vote." Reni put one hand on her hip and raised the other in the air. "I say if we have to choose between the police and letting Flynn see if he can—what did you call it, sweetie, ferret out?— the perpetrator, we go with Flynn."

"Me too." Jerrianne added her voice and uplifted hand. "He's done wonderful things on Max's behalf already."

"I . . . uh . . . I probably should talk to Joe Brent about this before I cast a vote but then again since I didn't even get a note, maybe I shouldn't even—"

"That's a 'yes.' " Reni grabbed Wy's arm and raised it high. "That leaves you, Queen Tessa. You voting for the cops or for Flynn to start . . ." She wet her lips and smiled like she was about to say the kind of thing that got her lectures in Sunday school, then finished, all breathy and wicked, ". . . ferreting."

"Ferret?" Tess kept her voice low and her body close to his. "That's another word for a weasel, isn't it?"

Flynn grinned.

She gave a small shove as she released his lapel and sighed. "Fine. We'll let Flynn help but that's all he's doing, helping. This is our problem, not his, and we"—she pointed directly at herself—"are the ones in charge."

7

"I cannot believe you got us out of bed at two in the morning to haul us clean across town to *this* place." Despite her whining and foot-dragging, Reni still managed to work a little wiggle into her walk as they headed through the deserted parking lot.

"Oh, hush up. You were the only one of the three of you who wasn't even asleep." Tess yanked the glass door open and held it for the others. "I had to stretch the truth about an emergency meeting to get Jerrianne out of her father's house and Wylene . . ."

Wy came slinking in the door, jumpy as a cat, with her eyes wide. She clutched her purse over the snoozing snuggle bunnies on the T-shirt they all swore no one would know was her pajama top.

"If Joe Brent hadn't dropped off dead to the world watching TV on the couch, we might never have snuck Wy out the back bedroom window to join us." Tess reached her hand back toward her friend. "You sure the girls will be okay while you're out, sugar?"

"I'm sure. Jolene'll watch over Brentelle and Joe Brent won't bother them. Most likely he won't wake up till morning, but even if he does and finds out I've gone out, he won't take it out on them."

Tess wanted to press Wylene to tell her who he would take it out on, just to hear it from Wy's own lips. No. She did not *want* to ask or hear about it, but she did wonder if she should.

"I still don't see why we have to meet *here* and at this hour." Reni wriggled by them, fidgeting with the buttons on her shirt. She did not fasten them or in any way try to better conceal the top of the peach nightgown she had on beneath the white cotton shirt and black jeans.

Jerrianne shuffled past, the tail of her pink cotton gown flapping over her behind from under her sweatshirt.

If Tess had ever had any real cause to doubt her mental bearings, this was the perfect time. Only a person with a precarious grip on reality would find herself herding her friends—in their thinly disguised nightclothes—into The Twilight Lanes Bowling Alley in the middle of the night.

"This happens to be one of the only places open *at this hour* that is both safe and discreet." She said it to Reni, but she still had enough sanity left to know she was trying to convince herself. She wanted to justify this drastic solution to a fairly simple problem, a restless mind. Or was it a restless heart?

One thing for certain: the key word was *restless*. Tess had been prowling around the house since she got home from work that evening. Starting a project in the garden, only to abandon it moments later, flipping through channels on the TV but never watching anything. When she lay down to sleep, things went from subtle discontent to . . .

A flash of heat rose from her neck at the dream she had awakened from, a dream so vivid and compelling it sent her scrambling from the bed like it was on fire. But it was Tess who had been on fire. And the spark responsible was none other than the last man she could afford to warm up to.

"Flynn," she muttered between clenched teeth.

"What did you say?" Jerrianne asked as they paraded past a closed shop, no bigger than Tess's walk-in closet, which sold all manner of bowling supplies.

"I said, uh, go on in." She swept her hand out.

"We are in."

Cigarette smoke curled out of another side room with black plastic on the windows and pinball machines and video games lining the walls.

"Then let's grab us some seats." Tess smiled like the perfect hostess and pointed to the distant end of the almost empty bowling alley.

They all obliged. They always did. Tess had taken advantage of that fact when she rousted them out of bed and brought them here. She told herself she was being proactive, not letting the trail of the notes grow cold or allowing her friends to get too complacent. She glanced at them. Jerrianne yawned. Reni settled in a chair, then pivoted to throw her legs across the bank of beige and aqua seats. Wy checked her face in a small makeup mirror from her purse.

Tess had lied to them and to herself. She had come here to accomplish two things. She had to cement her control over whatever actions they took regarding those damned notes, and she wanted to keep at bay her dreams and desires about Flynn.

"You ladies gonna bowl or what?" A gangly young man in a green windbreaker pointed to the rack of bowling balls behind where Jerrianne, Reni, and Wylene sat.

Bowling? That was the last thing Tess intended to do here tonight. Careful to stand with her back to the lighted lanes and her face in darkness, she toyed with a belt loop on her jeans and poured on her best hushed and honey-pie tone, "We don't know the first thing about bowling, hon. We're just hoping to sit and talk a while."

"I'm sorry, ladies, I'll have to ask you take it to the lounge, then. These seats and this area is reserved for bowlers only."

The flickering fluorescent bulb over the shoe

rental counter and the glow from a row of vending machines gave off just enough light for Tess to read THE TWILIGHT LOUNGE on a set of double doors. Though it was at the far end of the building, she could still hear the driving beat of country dance music pounding out from it. She swore she even felt it pulsing through the electronic scorekeeper where she rested her hand. "Gosh, it's just so awful loud in there. I don't see how we could hear one another over all that commotion."

"Not to mention being bothered by gentlemen." When Wy put her hand to the back of her head Tess swore the woman's whole hairdo moved forward then settled back in place again.

"Gentlemen?" Reni snorted out a laugh. "What kind of gentlemen are you going to find at two in the morning, tanked up on beer in a bowling alley?"

"Not the kind of gentleman I ever run across—if you don't count Flynn." Jerrianne meant it as a joke but the reminder of the man's darker, dangerous side made Tess's heart race.

She took a deep breath and shut her eyes. Flynn wasn't in the lounge. She knew that. She'd been smart enough to drive by his house on her way to Jerrianne's to make sure he was safe at home. A precaution. She wasn't checking up on him. She certainly did not entertain any ideas about showing up on his doorstep. She'd never dream of rousing him from the depths of sleep, looking into those dark smoldering eyes, throwing herself into his arms, wrapping her legs around his strong, muscular body and—

"Fish or cut bait, that's all I got to say on the matter."

"What?" Tess opened her eyes to see the attendant picking his teeth with the nail of his pinkie finger.

"Either bowl or hit the lounge," he said.

"C'mon, sugar. You just can't toss us out." Tess focused on the young man. "There's only one other person using the lanes now. We aren't hurting anybody, can't we just—"

"These lanes are for bowlers. You take one up, you gotta bowl." He jerked his thumb over his shoulder to the counter, where the cashier stood watching a small black-and-white TV. "Sorry, them's the rules. Pay for lane time and shoes or move it to the lounge."

"You're losing it, Tess," Reni whispered as the kid sauntered off. "Reckon it's 'cause you're squandering your sexual energies elsewhere, so there's nothing left for the occasional flirtatious manipulation?"

One day she was going to kill Reni. She really was.

"If Tess had told him who she was, I'll bet he'd have changed his tune. Everyone in town—heck, everyone in all Georgia—knows who Tess is. Her name has cache," Wy said, nose in the air.

"Well, since the idea of coming all the way over the Twilight Lanes in the middle of the night was to preserve all our identities, that really wasn't an option." Tess knew she came off as snippy as a small dog defending a big bone, but she didn't care. She was losing ground here on every front and it had to stop. "For now it looks like we're stuck at least rolling a few balls at the pins and pretending we're having a game."

Wy sighed.

Reni groaned.

"Oh, what's the big deal, y'all?" Jerrianne stood up. "We'll just bowl. It's not brain surgery. I even brought my own ball."

"You have your own *bowling ball*?" Reni sounded as amazed as if their longtime pal had announced she had a third breast.

"Of course I do. What did you think this was?" Jer tapped the leather case under her seat.

"I don't know." Reni eyed the bag suspiciously. "Maybe I thought you had incredibly bad taste in purses."

"Very funny." Jer pulled the bag out and began to unzip it. "But you of all people should know, I reserve all my bad taste for personal relationships."

Reni cackled aloud. "Ain't that the tru—Hey! I think that was aimed at me."

"I can't imagine why." Wylene started rummaging in the dainty red pocketbook she'd clung to since they had spirited her away from her house.

"Well, I don't have bad taste, or a bowling ball." Reni's dark eyebrows arched to show everyone she regarded the two things as interchangeable. "So I guess I can't play."

"They have bowling balls here for people who don't have their own, Reni." Wy gestured with her hand still in he purse. "Pick yourself out one."

"Those? Are you kidding?"

"What's wrong?"

"Well, just anyone can use them. I mean, who knows who handled them last? They might have had a finger fungus or . . . or just eaten a chili dog."

"Y'all, this is getting pretty far afield from our purpose in meeting here tonight." Tess put her hands on her hips and surveyed the group. "We have got to discuss how to deal with whatever unseemliness is lurking in our pasts and those damned notes."

"Not to worry. I brought disinfectant spray." Jerrianne pulled a large economy-size blue and gold can from the side pocket of her bowling bag.

Tess blinked, jaw slack.

"For the shoes," her ever-efficient assistant whispered.

Tess covered her eyes. "Heavens, don't tell Reni about the shoes. She'll faint."

"Don't worry. She can wear my shoes." Jerrianne set the can aside.

"You have your own shoes?" Wy had stopped pawing in her bag and had taken to staring into it with the intentness of a desperate person looking into a crystal ball.

"I happen to like the game. Max and I come out

here with the kids from Daddy's church. That's why he and Daddy gave me this for Christmas last year." Both her hands sank into the leather bag. Then, slowly, as if she were unveiling a piece of flawless jewelry, she pulled out a pearl-pink bowling ball with a full-fledged, fit-to-be-embroidered-on-your-sorority-sweater monogram above the finger holes.

The thing even impressed the likes of Reni, who promptly announced, "I want to use Jerrianne's ball or I'm not going to play."

"What are you, five years old?" Wy snapped.

"Only emotionally." Tess glowered.

"I don't care." Reni folded her arms. "Be mean to me all you like. I have my standards. There are just some places I won't put my hands, and a stranger's balls is one of them."

"Since when?" Tess laughed.

Before Reni could reply Wylene chimed in. "Um, y'all? I have a little problem. I didn't know we'd need any money tonight and, well, it doesn't matter 'cause usually I have some extra money sewn into the lining of my purse—for emergencies, you understand?"

The other women exchanged glances. They understood far too well.

"But it looks like it . . ." She cut herself off and snapped her purse shut. "It must have fallen out."

"Don't worry, I'll pick up the tab tonight, hon. The important thing is we're here and we've got to make the best use of our time to chart our plan of action." Tess gave Wy's knee a squeeze, then looked up to include the others in that commitment, only to spot Jer at the shoe rental counter and Reni plugging quarters into the candy machine.

"What is wrong with those two?" she asked through clenched teeth. "Don't they understand how serious this whole business with the notes is?"

"They understand, Tess." Wy stood up and with her face so close now, Tess could see the lines of grim weariness that no amount of blusher or stead-fast denial could counteract. "They just trust you to take care of it."

Tess winced.

"If there is anything to take care of." Wylene put her hand on Tess's shoulder. "For all we know, it's just a prank."

"A bit too elaborate for a prank, don't you think? All those notes so precisely timed?"

"Not too precisely. Remember, I didn't get one at all."

Tess did remember and something about that fact plagued her, like an ache that has no tangible source. She loved Wylene. She always had, and would charge hell with a thimbleful of water if that's all she had to come to her dear friend's aid. But the almost detached calm Wylene showed over this whole mess did not sit well with her. She tried to reason it out in her mind. Maybe Wy—who had once wanted to take on the world but ended up car-rying the weight of it on her shoulders—just could not be shaken by a vague note. Especially if she did not see its relationship to her. Or maybe her reaction was nothing more than simple resignation. Not so surprising from a woman who could not even count her hard-earned hidden money as her own.

Tess wound her arm around Wy's slender waist and gave her a sideways hug. "What do you say we go rent us some of those high-style bowling shoes?"

"You sure you want to put up a deposit for mine? They're so pretty I might have to wear them home." Underneath the makeup and the mask of numbed fatigue, the old Wylene Parker shone through for just a moment.

"You'd be the hit of the pageant circuit, doll."

They walked toward the counter, where Reni and Jerrianne now stood in a huddle with the boy in the green jacket.

"It's going to be all right, you know," Wylene whispered. "You'll have all this sorted out and everything under control in no time."

"You really think so?"

"Of course I do. You *always* have everything under control."

"I wish that were true." Then why did she have such wildly out-of-control thoughts about a certain man who had suddenly imposed himself in her life, her work, and now her dreams?

"Of course it's true." They came up behind Jer and Reni. "Why, even now, you said you gathered us together here to make some plans, but we all know you've already got things sketched out in your head and that's pretty much the way things are going to be."

Tess smiled. She knew exactly what she wanted them to do, how they would approach the issues of their pasts and who would work with Flynn if they needed his help and expertise. She'd just run down the details with the girls while they bowled, then arrange for them to meet periodically to keep on top of things.

In the morning she'd start scouting around for a better—but just as discreet—place for them to get together. "You know, Wy, you're right. I will get this sorted out."

"Sure you will. You're our Queen Tessa, after all. Nothing is going to happen that you can't get a handle on."

"Guess what?" Jerrianne spun around to face them, her eyes lit up like a kid at Christmas.

Reni turned slowly toward them, her nose buried in a catalogue. "Did y'all know that you can buy bowling balls in every color imaginable, pearls, swirls, and even sparkles?"

"You always were a sucker for anything that sparkled." Wy gave Reni's hand a nudge and the huge diamond there flashed even in the low light.

"Oh, it's not just glittery stuff, either." Reni flipped another page. "You can get shoes and accessories, and even custom-order color-coordinated bowling shirts with whatever you want embroidered big as life across the back."

"Don't tell me." Tess put her hand to her forehead like a psychic reading the future. "Now that you've discovered bowling can lead to a whole new kind of shopping you're thinking of taking it up?"

"Something wrong with that?" Reni looked up from the glossy pages.

"Isn't it exciting?" Jerrianne took Tess by the arm.

She didn't want to, but she saw no hope of getting a straight answer unless she asked outright, "Isn't *what* exciting?"

"Apparently ownership of the alley changed a few weeks ago, which interfered with the summer leagues. So, starting next week, they're sponsoring a four-week mini fun league."

Tess tensed. "And this affects us how?"

"Isn't it obvious?" Reni sighed and closed the catalogue.

"Tess, hon, you picked the Twilight Lanes out as the ideal meeting place." Jer gave her a little shake.

In the background a ball rumbled down the lane.

"Who in their right minds would think to look for us—well, at least three of us"—Reni gave Jerrianne a sidelong glance—"in a bowling alley?"

"Okay, I get it. If you want to go on meeting here so that Reni has an excuse to buy a new shirt and shoes, fine by me. But we can't always come after midnight. Maybe we should reserve a lane."

"Tried that already." Jer shook her head. "Can't reserve a lane unless you join a league."

In the one occupied lane, the ball found its mark with a distinct *whocka*. Pins fell, spinning, scattering, crashing down, all except one. It wobbled and tottered then went still to await the inevitable, the last well-aimed blow to strike it down.

Tess knew exactly how that pin felt. Still, she had to ask, "So?"

"So? So, I signed us up, silly!"

"Can you believe it?" Reni laughed and gave Tess a light smack on the butt with the rolled up catalogue. "Last week you were telling me not to move home. This week I did. Then we got some pissy little notes that don't amount to a hill of beans in my opinion, and now . . ."

"Now the SuiteHearts are all together again." Jerrianne beamed. "And are forming our very own bowling team."

Across the lanes the ball thundered down the alley.

She was going to sort things out. She was going to take control. She had no intention of going bowling. Tess ticked off the ways she had been proved wrong in just the last few seconds. This did not bode well for the very concern that had driven her to this point in the first place—that she could find a way to keep her feelings for Flynn in check.

Whop. The lone remaining pin toppled.

Tess shut her eyes and swore under her breath.

8

"The number you have dialed is out of order or is no longer in service."

Flynn swore at the mechanical voice. It made him feel better to swear when things did not go his way. Since his return to Mount Circe, he'd become what his mama would call "no better than a common trash mouth."

"If you feel you have reached this message in error, please hang up and try again."

"Try again," Flynn muttered under his breath as he dropped the receiver into its cradle. He slashed a dark line through the last in a long list of possible telephone numbers for Max Munroe's father, then tossed the nub of a pencil aside.

A groan eased out from low in his chest and he

rubbed his thumb and forefinger over his stinging eyes. The dust collecting over every inch of this old house filled his nostrils with the scent of dried mold and old paper. He looked at the wall-to-ceiling shelves of hardback books in the room he'd grown up calling "the library" but which now served as his home office.

Not that he needed this office. He had one in Washington at the Anna Mae Garvey Foundation building. Corner office—big sucker, too. He didn't need that, either. He hadn't needed it for a couple years as the foundation had grown to encompass more staff and require less of him.

It wasn't a huge operation by a long shot, but it no longer needed Flynn to keep it running. Most of his work of late had come in the goodwill-generating figurehead department. That was not a place he felt comfortable. He had never needed the work for the money and now the work did not need him, but he'd still felt displaced. It had forced him to take a good long look at himself, to take stock of his life.

And that had driven him back to Mount Circe. He could not face the man he had become—hard, cynical, lonely—until he looked into the eyes of the man who had made him that way. Or so he had thought. Now . . .

Now he wondered if it wasn't a tidy cop-out to blame his father's rejection as the reason he didn't have a full and happy life. Still, he had wanted that man's attention, if not his approval, for so long that he could not quite take hold of the idea that confronting his father would not change a damn thing in Flynn's life. It would not bring him peace. It certainly would not bring him love—and he wanted love. He had not thought he did before, but since coming home, he understood that was the only thing he had ever really wanted—and the one thing he had no idea how to obtain.

A shaft of sunlight warmed his back through the sagging curtains. Fine particles shimmered and drifted downward, destined to form yet another layer of dust. Hard to imagine how anything so unsubstantial could permeate every room, every object, seemingly every molecule of air in the house.

Maybe love was kind of like that. Working its slow, subtle ways, almost unnoticed at first, one day a man might look up and realize he's half-buried in it, that it had become a part of every facet of his life. At least, that's what he supposed love would be like. He'd never been in love, not that kind of love. He wasn't even sure he'd recognize that kind of love, even if he ran smack dab into it head on.

Admiration, genuine affection, he'd had those a time or two with a woman. Friendship, sure. He'd certainly felt his share of respect for the fairer sex, though in some cases, grudgingly so.

If he could find all those wrapped into one package—and throw in a little blinding, intellect-numbing, animalistic, no-holds-barred lust—that might pass for true love in his book. Or keep him occupied until the real thing came along.

The thought of Tess sprang to his mind. Tess as a young, innocent girl ready and ripe, trusting only him with the sacred gift of her body. He thought of her on the night of her college graduation, so caring and yet capable of a great betrayal. Mellowed by time and seasoned by experience, he could now see she had been equally betrayed. Yet she had not become bitter or allowed her hurt to spill over onto those she loved.

He thought of her as he had seen her lately, all curves and sass, smarts and success. The skin on the back of his neck drew up into goosebumps at the image. A warning, the old wives' tale said, that lightning was about to strike.

Flynn snorted out a "huh" at his silly lapse into sentimentality and dragged his finger through the film on top of the picture frame on his desk. He supposed he should bring someone in to clean up the place, to make it appear somewhat livable. But what did he care about appearances? Not like any one ever came calling here. The house might be untidy, even bordering on disrepair, but that didn't affect him. The shower worked. The kitchen worked. He had fresh linens on his bed. What more did he need? *Besides a woman to share that bed, if only now and again,* he thought.

Tess. His gaze fell on the phone. A tightness

knotted up low in his gut. He heard the advice of the computerized woman on the phone, urging him, "Try again."

Try again? He shook his head. His whole life had been nothing more than a series of trying and trying again. He leaned back in the leather chair and propped his feet up on the desk.

For his first twenty-five years, he'd tried to be the biggest jackass alive, to burn through his allotted time on this earth at a record rate. When that hadn't happened he'd realized he'd have to try again and this time put his effort into making something of his life. He'd done that, helped a lot of people along the way, too. Still, he felt empty.

He dropped his feet to the floor and brushed his fingers over the silver-framed photo of him and his mother, taken when he was just a baby. Just like in some corny old ballad, his heart ached to look at it. Seeing his mother through the eyes of a man who understood the world and the choices people have in it, his heart ached for her all over again.

He curled his hand into a fist. He *had* to speak to his father. He had to speak his mind, to demand recognition for himself and his mother. He didn't give a rat's ass if the old man cursed him and had him escorted from the premises by armed guards. He had to look that man in the eye and make sure they both knew the truth, who was the real bastard between them. It might not bring him love, but at least it would abate the pain he carried inside. Then, maybe, that real love thing could finally happen for him, too.

So Flynn had to try again. Too much depended on it. Right now, he could only think of one way to get that chance. He drummed his fingers on the edge of the black telephone. Gritting his teeth against a really humdinger of a curse, he grabbed up the receiver. He jabbed the keypad to dial the number of Magnolia Oaks Heritage House, telling himself he only placed the call in order to update Jerrianne on granting Max's wish.

It's a dangerous line to cross when a man starts lying to himself, a voice in his head chided. *A man who'd do that is only setting himself up for a world of hurt. And over a woman, no less. Try again, pal.*

"Magnolia Oaks Heritage House, home of *Simply Southern* magazine, Jerrianne speaking. How may I help you?" The soft voice purred like a melody through the wires.

"Hi, Jer, this is Flynn. Is Tess around?"

"Why, hi, Flynn, sugar. Just what are you up to this bright fine morning?"

"Nothing special, but I—"

"You know, my daddy was asking after you just the other day, said you hadn't been around the Fellowship in a while."

"Yes, well, I've been awfully busy. If you could just—"

"Why don't you drop in and pay him a call soon? It sure would tickle him."

He swore that girl got more southern with every syllable. "Jerrianne, I don't really have a lot of time"—*or patience*—"for small talk this morning. Could you put me through to Tess?"

"I don't think she'll be nearly as tickled as my daddy would be to hear your charming voice."

"And yet, strangely enough, if I had to choose between two people I'd most like to tickle, Brother J would come in a distant second to your boss lady." He laughed. "But you *have* guilted me into paying your father a visit. Now can I talk to Tess?"

"Um, well . . . I . . . uh . . ."

"What's the matter?"

"I'm not supposed to tell you this, but . . ."

"You're going to eventually. Let's save both us a lot of beating around the bush. What's up?"

"Tess is on her way over to your house."

He sat bolt upright in his office chair and put his hand on the back of his neck, recalling the warning about lightning striking. "Why?"

"She was fixin' to call you up and go over her royal list of ground rules for working with you—"

"I'm assuming that's your name for them, not hers."

Jerrianne laughed. "I don't honestly think she realizes how high-handed her need to control every nagging detail comes off."

"I don't suppose she does."

"Of course, those of us who love her forgive her for it."

"Hmm."

"Maybe that's because we take into account the way she came up and how she had to be that way not just for her own survival, but for her whole family."

"Yeah?"

"You know, how her father depended on her to keep home and hearth and the happy charade of it all together after her mother got down with the depression so bad she hardly ever left her bed."

He hadn't known, but he made a note of it now. During the short summer he and Tess had spent together she had always shied away from talk of her family. Given his own circumstances, this had suited Flynn just fine. He did not press her. In that regard Tess had provided him with a refuge from the strain of his convoluted family life. Funny, after all these years, to learn he had done the same thing for her.

"I'm not sure I really knew that, Jerrianne, but it does explain a lot. Of course, it doesn't explain why she is headed for my house this morning."

"She'd skin me alive if she found out I gave you fair warning."

"Ah, planned an ambush, huh?"

"You know Queen Tessa. She has to stay in command of everything, even who knows what, when they know it, and how they receive the information."

"Believe or not, it's one of the traits I find most

endearing in her." Flynn chuckled. "And don't worry, I won't let on that you tipped me off to her coming over."

"Thanks. It's not a good day for me to be skinned alive—I just had my hair done!"

The sound of a car pulling up the last stretch of the long, curved drive in front of his house put Flynn's senses on full alert. "Got to go, darlin', I think the queen has arriveth."

"Act surprised," she cautioned.

"Don't worry. If it's one thing Tess still has over me, it's the element of surprise." He hung up, leapt to his feet, and strode into the foyer to wait for his guest.

"It's blackmail." When Flynn had yanked the enormous front door open mere seconds before she had the chance to knock, Tess had felt her command of the situation falter. To regain it, she seized the issue that had brought her flying over here today and leapt into the discussion without greeting the man standing framed in the doorway. "That's what it is, plain and simple. Blackmail."

"Nice to see you, too, Tess."

Not only did his languid tone, and slow, sexy gaze melt away every ounce of indignation in her, but his refusal to even acknowledge her extraordinary remark stole her thunder—big time. And worse, it pointed out that she had committed the near unforgivable, even in a moment of personal crisis. She had forgotten her manners.

"I, uh, good morning, Flynn." She straightened her shoulders and tugged at her pale blue cotton vest. "And how are you today?"

"I'm fine, Ms. Redding. And you?"

"I am being blackmailed, thank you ever so much for asking." The full skirt of her white dress flared as she started to march over the threshold of the man's home.

"I'd invite you in." Flynn stepped in her way so quickly that she thrust out her hand, purely on instinct, to keep from colliding with him. "But I was just on my way out."

Without missing a beat, she curled her outstretched hand into the rumpled fabric of his shirtsleeve. "Dressed like this? I don't think so."

He put his hand on top of hers. "Nice save."

He wouldn't say that if he knew how this most insignificant contact between them had her senses tingling. She raised her chin and narrowed her eyes. "Thank you, but salvation is the last thing on my mind today."

"Now, that's the kind of talk I like to hear." He dropped his hand and braced his forearm against the doorframe, still keeping her from entering. "If this is a new approach in door-to-door canvassing, it's got those magazine peddlers and Jehovah's Witnesses beat by a mile."

"I haven't come here to sell you anything. And while I might have some opinion as to where you will spend all of eternity, that's not what brought me here, either."

"What did bring you to me, then, Tess?"

"Can't I come in?"

"No. I told you, I'm going out."

"In that shirt? Not on a bet."

"It's clean." He angled his head down slightly toward his upraised arm and gave a sniff, then added, "Enough."

She tried the Look on him.

He laughed.

"Now see here, Flynn, I did not have to come all the way up to your big old mansion on the hill to be lied to right to my face."

"Yeah? Where do you usually go to get lied to?"

"You were not 'just about to go out' in a shirt that looks like you slept in it."

"Not everybody buys into the concept of never letting the flaws show, you know. Not everyone judges things wholly on superficial appearances."

"I'd act offended, as I'm sure that's what you were going for in saying that, but it's pretty clear your cutting characterization doesn't fit me, and you know it."

"I do?"

"You must. Because if I really were as superficial as that remark implied, it could not possibly have hurt my feelings." She folded her arms and lowered her chin to drive her words home. "And that's why you said it, isn't it? To hurt me?"

"I was making a point," he muttered.

"Next time use your head."

Mischief lit the depth of his eyes. "Now who's saying what to hurt whose feelings?"

"What?"

"You know how sensitive I am about my pointy head."

Tess set her jaw so that she would not, could not, break into a laugh or smile.

He combed his fingers back through his hair in familiar fashion.

"There is only one thing on earth I hate more than you being a total jerk, Flynn."

"What's that?"

"You being sweet and endearing."

"Don't get used to it. I'm still not letting you in."

"Why? You got a girl in there?" She regretted saying it before the soft *r* in *girl* had trilled off her tongue. Then, because mildly embarrassing herself by seeming to care about Flynn's sex life was not nearly enough for a woman of Tess's standing and ambition, she blurted out a bit too comically and way too loud, "Not that I care, of course."

"No, I don't have a girl in here. Truth is, state of this old place at present, I wouldn't invite anyone in that I cared to impress." He folded his arms over his chest, and smirked just enough to make her knees weak, then added, "You either, for that matter."

"I see. Well, at least you've let go of that ridiculous lie that you were going out dressed like . . ." She moved her gaze from his expensive loafers, worn without socks, his faded jeans, and just-out-of-bed wrinkled shirt, open enough at the neck to show his tan did not stop at the collar line. ". . . that."

Damn her voice for squeaking.

"I still don't see what's so wrong with what I have on." His smirk became a smile. He shrugged, or maybe he was just shifting his broad shoulders. Either way, the movement sent a ripple through her. He held his hands open and said, "I'm a regular guy, Tess. Sometimes regular guys go out of the house in clothes that they've slept in."

"I suppose, but—"

"Sometimes regular women do to."

He knew. That not-so-veiled comment was his sly way of telling her he knew all about the early-morning jammie jaunt a few nights ago to the Twilight Lanes. But how? She'd been so careful, so clever, so . . .

"You haven't been talking to Reni, have you?"

"Fine as an example as that is of a woman who would have no problem going out in her night-clothes, no, I have not been talking to Reni. Why?"

He didn't know. She could see it in his eyes. He had no idea about their excursion and clearly thought her reaction to be . . . well, about as normal as anything else she'd said since she showed up on his doorstep. "No reason. It's just another red herring. Tell me, why is it that every time I try to carry on a conversation with you it always seems to go careening wildly off course?"

"Maybe you just can't concentrate when you're around me."

She laughed and tossed her hair in what she figured as probably the worst depiction of coquettish contempt ever seen outside a middle school drama club presentation. "Hardly."

"Oh? Then I guess you wouldn't mind if I did this while we were talking." He edged in a little closer.

"Mind? Why would I mind?"

He dropped his gaze to her mouth. "Or this."

She gasped in anticipation, knowing full well it left her lips parted and ready for the kissing.

He reached toward her. Then, so gently it scarcely felt like more than a breeze, swept her hair back off her shoulder. "Now, tell me again, why did you come here? Concentrate."

If he hadn't given the last directive, he'd have had her in the palm of his hand, quite literally. She stepped away from him. "I don't need you to tell me what to do, Flynn."

"I wouldn't dream of trying, Tess."

"Good."

"I have more productive things to do with my time than that, like beating my head against a brick wall."

"My, you do have an obsession about this pointy-head issue, don't you?" She folded her arms and gave him just enough of a smile to cut the sting of her remarks. "Have you sought help?"

He folded his arms too. The soft wrinkled fabric contrasted with the hard muscles of his chest and arms. "I thought you were the one seeking help, sweet Tess—my help."

"I never sought your help, Flynn, you manipulated me into having to accept it."

"At last we're back to where you came in, accusing me of blackmail."

"I wasn't *accusing* you of anything." They *were* back where she had come in, and with nothing to show for the effort. When Tess set out to accomplish things, they got done. For whatever reason, when she and Flynn teamed up, they got nowhere.

"So flouncing up to my door crying 'blackmail'—that wasn't just another fine example of your flare for the dramatic?"

"I was trying to tell you about a new development in the situation."

"Oh?"

"But now I see what a ridiculous waste of time that was." She turned on her heel and, careful not to feed his arrogance with more amateur theatrics, walked briskly to the long, wide steps of his home's large porch.

"Nice." His hands came together in hard, measured clapping. "Very nice. Hail Queen Tessa and all that horse manure. Now get your butt back here and tell me what's happened."

"I don't have to." She did not look back. From the creaking wooden steps, she set out across the unkempt lawn, not bothering with the brick walkway as she called out, "I was not the one who initiated your coming in on this, Flynn. I do not have to be the one who goes out of my way to make it work."

"Damn, I hate it when you're right." He said it under his breath but loud enough that she knew he wanted her to hear it.

In the shade of a big oak she stopped and put one hand on the hood of her car. The breezed kicked up the hem of her skirt and she raised her head, and glanced back at him over her shoulder. "You wheedled your way back into my life, Flynn. I don't exactly know why you did it, but you did. I'm not happy about it, either, but I had come to terms with the notion."

"I know." The stairs groaned under his weight. His approaching footsteps made a whisper-soft *swish, swish, swish* in the grass.

"Then, here I come to you with this latest twist, some important news, and what do you do?" She turned to face him. "I'll tell you what you do. You make a joke of it. You turn it into a chance to make a pass at me. You so completely miss the real meaning of the gesture that you think the whole thing is about you!"

He stopped at the edge of the massive oak's shadow, just a few feet from her. The brilliant sunshine glanced off his white shirt, making his shoulders seem broad as all outdoors.

Her eyes adjusted to the cool dimness of the shade, she could see every nuance of his face. She searched the faint lines that had not been there in his youth and found in him some remnant of the boy she had once loved with all her being.

"The real meaning of the gesture?" he asked, moving closer.

She put her fingertips to her throat, half expecting to find a small golden heart there on a golden chain. Her hand fell away. "I hoped that maybe, just maybe, I could trust you. If you weren't such a pigheaded donkey's behind, you'd have realized that."

"A pigheaded donkey's behind? I'd pay money to see that."

"Why? It's free to look in your mirror each morning, providing you can find a mirror with your house in the state you say it's in." Walking away from him, she let her fingers trail along the edge of her car until she reached the driver's side door.

Flynn could all but feel those cool fingertips tracing over his arms and back. He cleared his throat, looked away long enough to clear the image from his mind, then focused on her again. "The place is a mess, dust and neglect mostly. A little like the donkey's behind that lives in it."

She raised her head and offered him the perfect blend of sweet sadness and a serene smile. "I can't imagine you've suffered from much neglect in your life."

He swallowed hard. "Not by choice."

She nodded.

"I guess I'd better go—"

"Why don't you come in and—"

They had both spoken at once.

Tess laughed the quick light bubble of a laugh she always made when she felt self-conscious or embarrassed.

Flynn shoved his hands in his pockets. She had given him the chance to prove himself worthy of her trust and he had blown it. What made him think she'd ever try that again?

She sighed and put her hand on the door handle. "Flynn, I don't think this is—"

"Don't, Tess."

"Don't what?"

"Don't say it isn't such a good idea. Don't say it isn't going to work." He needed it to work, but not for the initial reason he'd insisted on getting involved.

For the first time since he'd come back to Mount Circe, Flynn put his issues and anger with his father aside entirely and focused on someone else—Tess. After everything, she still had found it in her to trust him, just a little. Just the idea of that shot straight through to his heart and made him realize that he felt the same way about her. Knowing that, he could not simply stand here and let her drive away. "Don't go, Tess."

"But, Flynn—"

"Come on in the house." He extended his open hand to her. "We'll figure this out together."

"If I had a brain in my head, I'd say no, peel out of here in a cloud of dust, and just do my best to handle this mess myself."

"I make a wicked glass of iced tea." He wriggled his fingers like someone straining to stretch a hairs-breadth closer to their goal.

"*Wicked* being the operative word where you are concerned, in my opinion." She stared at his open hand. "But they do say the devil you know is better than the devil you don't."

"So I've heard."

Gently, so gently he had to take a second look to be sure that she actually did it, she laid her hand in his.

As soon as he felt sure she would not snatch her hand back, he curled his fingers into hers, smiled, and started to lead her to the house. "Did you just call me a devil, Theresa Jo Redding?"

"If the horns fit."

He grinned and put his free hand to his chest.

"It's killing me not to make a wisecrack about horniness right now, you know."

"Noted. And I do appreciate the effort on your part."

"See, we're going to work together just fine."

"Of course we are." She let go of his hand and moved ahead of him up the porch steps.

He held back to take in the view and dang if she didn't throw in an extra bit of sass into her sashay to show she felt his gaze on her. A tightness he had not even been aware of in his chest eased then, leaving him to enjoy the tightness Tess's presence inspired lower in his body. She was one damn fine woman.

She opened the screen door and held it open against her back. She had to know how that silhouette accentuated the fullness of her breasts, the lines of her body, and even the roundness of her behind.

She was one damn fine woman, indeed.

She dipped her head down a fraction. Her hair fell forward over one eye. She smiled like a cat who had just lapped up a saucer of cream then purred, "We're going to get along just fine, Flynn. As long as you never forget—"

"What, Tess?"

"Who is in charge here."

He held his hand up as if taking an oath. "I swear on my honor—"

She cleared her throat.

"How 'bout on a stack of *Simply Southern* magazines?"

She cocked one eyebrow.

He chuckled, his hand still upraised. "All right, let's get serious then. I swear on the hood of my car."

"Your precious red convertible." Tess pointed to the garage where he kept his pristine auto.

"I swear on my red convertible—may the tires be stripped off, the chassis set on cinderblocks in the yard and the engine be yanked out and hung from chains in this very tree—if I ever, for one minute, forget who is in charge around here."

"Fair 'nough." She volunteered a gracious bow of her head, then turned to go inside the house.

Just as she disappeared over the threshold of his mother's house, Flynn started up the steps, muttering under his breath, "*I* am in charge 'round here, Queen Tessa, and ain't no hips or lips or woman alive going to change that."

9

Dear SuiteHearts:

Now that I have your attention, what is it worth to keep me from telling all I know? Think about it. Will contact you again soon.

Flynn set the note on the kitchen counter and picked up his tumbler of iced tea. "So, you going to wait and see what other information roles in?"

Tess fixed her eyes on the man leaning against the end of the cabinets. She clunked her glass down on the kitchen table and pressed her lips together.

"Look who I'm talking to." He laughed and slugged back his drink the way she'd seen some men toss back hard liqueur.

When he put the glass aside and dragged the

back of his hand along his lower lip to wipe away any moisture, Tess found the gesture coarse. Crude. And compelling. Masculine in the most unpretentious way.

"We're not going to wait, are we?" he asked, folding his arms. "We're going to jump in blindly with both feet and . . . and what, Tess?"

"Don't worry your pretty little head about that." It was just the kind of thing he might have tossed off teasingly to her, so it gave her an extra dose of satisfaction to say it to him. "I have a plan."

"Care to share it with me so I'll know where and how we're going to begin?"

"You'll begin where and how I tell you to begin. That's part of my plan." A bead of water snaked its way down her cold glass. "It's why I'm hiring you."

"You are not hiring me."

"Yes, I am."

"No, you're not."

An ice cube in her tea popped and cracked.

He set his jaw, then exhaled hard. "You try to pay me and I swear I'll donate every dime to Brother J."

"Far be it from me to tell you what to do with your hard-earned money."

He exploded with a short, robust laugh. "There's a first. Something you're *not* going to tell me to do."

"Dawgs, Flynn, you make it sound like I'm a total bitch."

"Do I?" He gave his glass a shake and the ice clinked and settled.

She noticed he did not deny her charge.

"Okay, so we're going to play it like you're the boss lady and I'm the hired gun."

"Heavens, you don't think you'll need a gun, do you?" She laid her hand over her breast.

"Just a manner of speaking, Tess." He smiled. "If I thought these notes were dangerous to anything more than your reputation, I wouldn't hesitate—"

"To use a gun?"

"You got some kind of weapons fetish?"

"I'm just not sure what to expect, that's all." She crossed her legs, then uncrossed them. She didn't know what to expect, not from the mysterious note sender, not from the secrets her friends would entrust her to explore, and certainly not from Flynn. "I don't like not knowing what to expect. Makes me jumpy."

"Well, next time you start feeling jumpy, just think of me." He lowered his voice and watched her with his eyes hooded.

She sat up as prim as an old maid Sunday-school teacher. "I hardly see how thinking of jumping you will make me feel any better."

"Think of me on the job, Tess." He cocked his head and clucked his tongue. "Where's your mind, girl?"

"I haven't lost my mind, if that's what you're implying."

"You know it's not."

She did know. Flynn could be wicked but he would not be cruel in that particular way. She touched her hair, her buttons. She laid her hand so flat on the hand-rubbed oak table she could feel the grain of the wood beneath her palm. "If you thought these notes posed a danger to anything more than the SuiteHearts' reputations, you wouldn't hesitate to what?"

"To go to the police."

"No." She raised up out of the seat enough to reach over and nab the note from the counter. Folding it in half, she ran her fingernail along the crease. "That's out of the question."

"Look, I understand the Mount Circe police don't rank up there with Sherlock Holmes in solving cases."

"Sherlock Holmes? I love and respect everyone on the force, Flynn—all half-dozen of them, right down to the janitor—but let's not mince words. Forget Sherlock Holmes, that lot could be out-policed by Barney Fife blindfolded and with his bullet in his other shirt pocket."

"Pretty down-homey frame of reference for a highbrow magazine editor." Flynn laughed.

"So I'm an *Andy Griffith Show* aficionado. Add it to the growing list of my deepest, darkest secrets. If you feel compelled to spill the beans about me to the local law enforcement, give them that tidbit, but say nothing about these notes to anyone. That's final."

"Why? I understand your wanting to protect your good name and all, but Tess, if the threats escalate, you have to notify the authorities."

"I won't do it. Won't stand by and allow you to do it, either."

"You're *that* afraid of the secret coming out?"

Part of her wanted to let him think that. He already thought her a bitch, what would a little more disdain from him hurt now? She drew in a slow breath and held it. The house smelled of being closed up too long. He had not wanted to let her in but he had asked her. He had asked her to stay. She told him she wanted to trust him, and so she would, as far as she could. "I can't let this go to the police because I'm afraid."

"Of?"

"What if one of the other SuiteHearts is behind it?"

"Tess you don't . . . you can't believe that."

"I don't want to believe it, but there's just something not right about the way Wylene is acting in all this."

"Wylene? How's she acting?"

"Well, like she's acting like . . . like she *is* acting." She thought of Wy at the Twilight Lanes, of that one flash she'd seen of the friend beneath the façade. "It's eerie, Flynn, the way she is. Too calm. Too detached."

"Maybe she thinks it doesn't really concern her, what with her not getting that first note."

"Exactly. She didn't get the first note." She tapped the paper on the table before her. "Isn't that odd that we all would get one, but not her?"

"You really suspect her?"

"No." Tess swirled the tea in her glass, watching it glide over the melting ice cubes. "That is, I don't want to. But she's not the girl we knew in college anymore. I can't read her. I don't know what she could be capable of. She seems so worn down, so distant."

"Consider her life. Consider who she is married to."

"Which only fuels my concern. If she found out about . . ." Tess couldn't look at him. "Well, wouldn't she have a good reason to want to seek a little revenge?"

"She doesn't seem like the type, Tess."

"No, I agree. But then there is the Joe Brent factor."

"Like he could come up with a plan as elaborate as this?"

"He doesn't need plans, Flynn. He has brute force."

"You saying he hits Wylene?" Flynn's fingers curled into a tight fist. Anger colored his lean cheeks.

"I've never seen a bruise on her. But that doesn't mean he isn't abusive to her."

He ground his fist into his open palm. "Amen to that."

"He has power over her and he uses it. And if everything we know suddenly became public knowledge . . ."

He relaxed a bit. "It might motivate her to leave him."

"Or it might make her stay, cut off from her friends with no hope of ever breaking free or making things better for herself and her kids."

"I guess you know what that's like," he said softly.

She would have challenged that remark if she only had the nerve to follow where the showdown might lead them. Instead, she folded her hands on the table and waited for him to speak.

"Okay, so no going to the police for now." He saluted her with two fingers. "Where do we start? Were you able to get any kind of sensible answer from Jobie? Could he tell you anything about the person who asked him to deliver the first notes?"

She shook her head. "No. I don't think he knew the person. Just kept calling him 'that fathead,' like that would tell me exactly who he meant."

"That fathead?" Flynn snickered into his tea. "I suppose a few likely candidates sprang to mind?"

She smiled. "You said it, not me."

He nodded. "Maybe I should go 'round and have a word with Jobie this afternoon, see if I can't get a better idea who it was."

"No."

"What?"

"I don't want Jobie stirred up over this. Next thing you know, he'll be hollering about it on the library steps."

"I can imagine that."

"Yeah, instead of his signature 'Hey, girl, whatcha reading?' he'll start shouting, 'Some fathead had me to tote envelopes out to Miss Tess's and it's got Mr. Garvey all het up.' "

"You know if you ever decide to abandon the magazine and book for a new gig, you have a promising future as a town eccentric."

"Spare me any high praise, it's likely to turn my head."

"So if we don't start with Jobie, where do we start?"

"I have that all covered, don't you wor—"

"Worry my pretty little head," he finished for her. "Yeah, got that. Didn't think it was funny the first time."

"Believe me, Flynn, I'm dead serious."

"All of this is serious, Tess. Though I'm not absolutely certain why. Let's face it, these notes don't even give a hint about what the sender knows or who they know it about. Yet you're taking it on faith that this is the real thing."

"I have to. We both know I do have something . . . something I deeply regret in my past."

"Yeah." He rubbed his hand over his face, obscuring his expression from her.

She laced her arms over her chest, folding herself into an impenetrable knot. "You do understand that I regret my actions that night, don't you, Flynn?"

He jerked his head up. His eyes found hers. "You wouldn't be here in my mother's home if I didn't believe that."

It wasn't a bid for reconciliation, but no anger or accusation colored his words or filled those searching blue eyes. "Well, apparently, the other girls have some things in their own pasts that they'd rather not come out, things that might rate a small-time stab at extortion."

"Whoever sent those notes might know something about any one of you, or even about all of the SuiteHearts, then?"

"That's what we figure. So I've hatched a plan that protects each of us."

"I'm listening." He braced one arm on the countertop.

"We take it one SuiteHeart secret at a time." She held her index finger up. "One by one we rule it out, or deal with it so that it's no longer a potential target for blackmail."

"And this protects each of you how?"

"Because only one person will know all the secrets. No public confessions. No more people having to find out about the things we'd rather keep secret than absolutely has to."

"Let me guess who gets to hear the private sins of all her friends." He ducked his head and smirked.

"Don't be sarcastic." Sarcastic did not describe the man's demeanor by a long shot. Strong captured it. Strong and sexy. And sure. Sure of himself and his ability to handle anything. And sexy.

Tess reached for her drink but found the glass almost empty save a few slivers of ice and the dregs of sugar and tea clinging to the bottom of the glass.

Flynn lifted up the pitcher, offering her more.

"It's not like I want to be in this position, but what are we supposed to do?" Needing to stretch her legs, or maybe just feeling restless in general, she pushed her chair back and stood. "Purge our pasts to Reni?"

"Heaven help you!"

Real as the cool fabric of her dress against her skin, she felt his eyes on her body. Heaven help her indeed, but she liked the feeling. She moved to the counter like a cat just up from a cozy nap, quiet and relaxed but tense just under the surface. She set her glass down in front of him, almost brushing her knuckles over his belt buckle as she did.

"More ice?" he asked.

"No, thank you, I like it a little warm."

"Warm and sweet?" He held the sugar bowl up.

She couldn't help noticing how some granules that had fallen from the silver rim now clung to his long, blunt fingers. His palms must be sweating, she thought. Hers certainly were.

He filled her glass.

She forced back her wayward thoughts and

gulped down a long drink of lukewarm tea. Then, cocking one hip against the cabinet, she said, "So that's my plan. Not perfect, but workable, don't you think?"

"Still seems like an awful lot of trouble to me just to suppress a bunch of stuff that happened fourteen years ago. Especially when I suspect most of those episodes don't amount to squat in the grand scheme of things and could probably be written off with nothing more complicated than claiming 'I was young when it happened.' "

Is that how he saw her indiscretion? A mistake of youth? She wanted to ask but she did not want to hear the answer. Because if he did or if he didn't, it would not change a darn thing, but it might make her hope that things could change and that would be a dangerous thing. "I think you're oversimplifying matters. Everyone has a thing or two they'd rather no one knew about. Young or not, we all have those very real regrets."

"Not me."

"Hmm. I've heard it said that it's not the things we did that we regret most, it's the things we *didn't* do."

"Oh?"

"Maybe that's why you don't have any regrets, there wasn't anything you didn't do." She traced her finger along the counter. "Not everyone is like you in that regard."

He smiled at her over the rim of his glass, that

lazy, sonofabitch smile that made her insides go liquid and he said, "Imagine that."

"You'd pretty much have to imagine it, wouldn't you?" She turned sideways so as to lessen the full effect of those eyes on her. "You did all your cavorting and transgressing right out in the open for everyone to criticize and enjoy."

"Not all, Tess." He leveled his gaze on her, his serious expression tempered with warmth and kindness. "Not *all*."

A delicate shiver crept over her at the memory of the secret summer they shared. Standing so close to him, she wondered if he sensed her reaction. She shrugged with one shoulder, hoping to give the impression that this discussion hardly rated any more effort than that. "Be that as it may."

"All these years, I still don't understand you, Tess. You know that?"

"Whether you understand me or not, I'm telling you the way things are going to have to be for us to work together."

"That so?"

"It is. You'll help me only by doing what I ask of you, when I ask it."

"So you've made this big deal out of coming here to hire me, yet you have no intention of telling me what you are hiring me to do?"

She said nothing.

"Great. That's just great." He turned his back on

her, ran his hand through his hair, then began to walk away, his words coming out as deliberate as each footstep. "I really don't want to sound dismissive of your desire to personally manage every last living bit of minutiae within a forty-mile radius of your imaginary kingdom, Queen Tessa."

She clenched her teeth.

He faced her again. "But that's taking it a bit too far, don't you think?"

"I'm sorry if it seems that way, but I must be extra careful. All this blackmail business is so ugly, it really has me on edge."

He tipped his head and crossed his arms. "Kind of puts a hitch in your get-along when you come up against something you can't sew lace on or glue dried-up flowers all over or otherwise embellish beyond recognition, huh?"

"So I'm a bitch and my work perpetuates fraud." She tried to sound bored despite the disappointment she felt welling up in her. "I've got it, Flynn. Is there anything else you want me to know?"

He glared at her, started to walk away again, then pivoted and took two pounding strides in her direction. "Just this."

Before she could gasp, he had her in his arms. His mouth took hers, seeking, demanding. No gentle, tentative kisses for this man. As with life and work, mischief or mayhem, Flynn gave this one passionate moment his all.

His muscled arms tightened to bring her closer,

so close she could feel his cotton shirt bunch up where it had come untucked. His belt buckle pressing against her.

Resist him! Shove him away! Don't let him do this to you! You cannot afford to lose your bearings now when everything you want is so close you can almost grab it. Neither intellect nor logic stood a chance when Flynn's tongue dipped between her warm, wet lips. Everything she wanted was there for her to take and she did. She wound her arms around him and gave herself over to the moment, knowing she would probably regret the instant the kiss ended.

No regrets? Flynn had a whopper of one brewing from the instant he took Tess into his arms. Taking risks, grabbing for whatever suited him at the time and worrying about the consequences later, those were traits he thought he'd long since left behind. But Tess did something to him.

She made him feel reckless, and invincible, and all churned up inside. She made him do things, feel things, want things that he had no business even imagining.

He sank his fingers into her golden hair. He pressed his body to hers and urged her to open her mouth to him with a gentle insistence he saved for only one woman.

She stiffened.

He anchored his feet just enough apart so that

when he took her deeper into his embrace, her thighs fit intimately with his body.

What started as a sigh eased into a slow moan as she yielded and parted her lips to him.

Another time, another woman, he would have cleared the counter with one grand sweep of his arm, lifted her up and gone for it right then and there in his mother's kitchen. But even this small intimacy with Tess tore at Flynn's conscience. It was wrong. The emotions and motivations driving it were blurred and unclear even to him. And every second he prolonged this kiss only fed his confusion and guilt.

He tore himself away, dragging Tess's moist breath into his lungs even as he did. "I'm sorry, Tess. I took that too far."

She staggered backward.

"I only kissed you to try to drive home a point."

"A point?" She touched one finger to her swollen lower lip, then raised her regal head and narrowed her eyes. "That's a clever euphemism for what you tried to drive home."

"I only wanted to teach you a lesson, Tess." He retreated a half step himself, but no more. "Instead I think I got a little education myself."

"You always did have to learn things the *hard* way."

"Yeah, yeah, I get it." He tucked his shirttail in, not giving a damn that it would leave his reaction to her more evident than ever. "You still do it for me, Tess. Is that what you want to hear?"

"Maybe I don't want to hear it, but maybe it's best that we do just get it out in the open."

"If 'get it out in the open' is another of your pitiful sexual innuendoes, I have to warn you—"

"Down, boy." She put her hand on his chest. "I only want to clear the air here, let you confront your obvious unresolved physical attraction issues about me."

"I have unresolved physical attraction issues? *I* have issues?"

"Good. Good. Get it out." She took her hand away. With her amusement over it all barely concealed, she beckoned him. "The first step to getting help is admitting you need it."

"I will if you will."

She lifted her chin.

"I thought so." He laughed. "Big talk from someone so afraid to ask for help from me that she devised this elaborate scheme, hiring me then not telling me what she is hiring me to do."

"I'm hiring you to start working on this first thing tomorrow morning."

"Tomorrow?" He'd made no inroads in getting in to see his father since he'd returned to Mount Circe. He'd made no substantial progress toward granting Max's wish in the last ten days. In fact, kissing Tess and cementing the deal to work with her had been the most productive thing he'd accomplished since he'd fallen out of bed this morning. He spread his arms wide to offer himself to her and the opportunity to salvage the day. "I'm available today. Why not get after it right now?"

"Get after it?" She picked up her nearly full glass and made a poor attempt at seeming to gaze into the tea and three or four remnants of ice cubes. "Do you have to make everything sound so vulgar?"

"Not into sugarcoating my words, Tess, not even when I'm in the presence of royalty—"

"Spare me the Queen Tessa jokes."

"—or just trying to do business with a royal pain in the ass."

"You didn't think I was such a pain in the ass a minute ago, when you practically tried to take a throat culture with your tongue."

"Throat culture?" He would not let her get away with trying to dismiss that admittedly unwise, but very real, act of passion between them. He moved in on her. "Tess, I apologize if I got too aggressive."

She backed up until she bumped the counter. "That's . . . that's all right."

"No, I was too forward." He trapped her neatly between his outstretched arms, his hands braced on the counter on either side of her hips. "But maybe you'll forgive me if you know I was just concerned about your health."

"My health?" She held her drink close to her

body, her arm creating a barrier between his chest and her breasts.

"Sure." He stroked the wave of hair that fell over her temple. He lowered his eyelids and fixed his gaze on those full, waiting lips. "I thought you might be running some kind of fever."

"Fever?"

The vibration of her breathy whisper fell on his mouth. He ran his knuckle down her cheek and smiled in anticipation of provoking one last payoff. "Yeah, because seems like every time you get close to me, sweet Tess, I get you really *hot*."

"Not just hot, Flynn," she murmured.

"No?" This was not the response he'd expected.

"No." She pursed her lips and hooked her fingers under his belt, then pulled him roughly toward her. "Hot and . . . wet."

The whole glass of tea washed down the inside of his pants in one lukewarm whoosh.

"Aw, Tess!" He jumped back and watched help-lessly as the stain darkened his jeans. "Why'd you do that? You had to know I was only joking around with you."

"So was I."

He shook his leg and a thin piece of ice slid down into his shoe. "You call this a joke?"

"If I'd have been serious, Flynn, I'd have poured the whole pitcher down there, ice and all, and cooled you off but good." She pushed her empty glass into his hand, then, giving his arm a shove with her shoulder, she flounced past. "I have to get back to work. Jerrianne and I have a meeting to do some number-crunching with our accountant from Atlanta."

"All right, go." He set the glass down, then swiped the back of his hand down his damp jeans. It didn't help. "We'll get together later this evening?"

She stopped her big old belle-style exit cold. An uneasiness came over her that did not fit a woman who had just doused a man's desire with weak tea and strong words. "I don't think we'll be done by then. You and I can start our work tomorrow."

Good as she was at hiding reality, putting a diamond collar on a junkyard dog, the lady made one lousy liar. He liked that about her. "I can come 'round after your meeting. How late can it run?"

"Oh, pretty late." She backed out of the kitchen in a move any first-year psychology student would chalk up to a subconscious need to cover her ass. Her action might have achieved that result, but her words did not. "Yes, I expect to run very late indeed. You know how it is when you get the four of us together."

"Four of you? I thought you said it was you, Jerrianne and the accountant? That makes three."

"Well, now you know why I have to hire someone to keep an eye on the books for me." She put her hand to her temple. "I'm terrible at math."

"You're terrible at lying."

"Yes, I am, but I am damn near lethal with a glass of tea, so don't push me, Flynn." She stepped back again, lifted her head high and shook her hair off her shoulders. "I can see myself out and I'll see *you* tomorrow morning."

He yanked his shirttail out, found a dry spot and wiped his hands on it.

"Did you hear what I said?"

"Yes, ma'am. I heard it." He watched her, then listened to the hurried click-a-clack of her shoes through the hallway and foyer. When the front door slammed hard enough to shake a cloud of dust down from the plate shelf over the kitchen sideboard, he laughed out loud.

Unzipping his jeans, he began to strip out of his wet clothes. "I heard every word, Miss Theresa Jo Redding. And I don't aim to pay heed to a one of them."

10

Perception is everything. The words of the consultant they'd brought in to give an unbiased review of the magazine's status still rang in Tess's ears as she hit the front door of the Twilight Lanes Bowling Alley. Why the simple credo nagged at her hours after the man had snapped shut his faux alligator briefcase and gotten in his preowned-but-pampered luxury car and driven away she did not know. But it did. Big time.

She suspected it rankled her to have someone say to her face the very thing she had denied to Flynn more than once these last weeks. Her work, her magazine, her life was not simply one big lesson in phoniness. She wanted to believe that. She had to. Otherwise, how could she go on? Why would she want to?

Every other aspect of the delicately woven fabric

of her life had begun to fray, if not yet unravel entirely. Her sister despised her. Her love life was nonexistent. She felt tired and testy and unsure of her mental state far too often for her comfort. And now someone was blackmailing her. The opportunity that taking the magazine to the next level had offered her had been her anchor, her best hope. Her best hope needed help.

Perception—not productivity, not possibilities, not perseverance—was everything. That's what the man had told her. That's what he recommended they keep in mind as they prepared their presentation for P. Pearcy McLaughlin. It did not matter how well they were doing, or even how well they knew they could do. It mattered how they looked on paper.

And on paper, *Simply Southern* and its outgrowth stank like yesterday's old fish. At least that's what the independent advisor thought. He had solutions, of course, but those solutions would cost her in both time and money. If she *had* money, she wouldn't *need* money, she'd argued, but he hardly seemed to get her point. And time?

Oh, sure, she had all the time in the world. After her regular working hours. And spending practically her every waking moment worrying over the little matter of extortion. And bowling practice.

She'd squeeze in polishing her company's perception on paper between fighting with Flynn and knocking out a few frames here at the Twilight Lanes. No problem.

Of course, if she went along with the recommendations, Tess had to face the fact that Flynn was right. She was a phony. Just thinking about it set her teeth on edge.

More than once over the past few years, as the books, photo spreads, articles, and the very persona of Tess Redding moved further and further away from any semblance of reality, she had questioned her choices. She had started her publishing career with the noble notion of preserving a way of life she held dear, a simple way of life. Now her life and the lifestyle she portrayed in her quarterly regional publication seemed anything but simple. Still, she had never strayed so far that she could not feel the heartbeat of the real South, the real Mount Circe, and plain old Theresa Jo Redding beating beneath the surface. If she went along with the consultant and gave in to McLaughlin's stipulation that she move to Atlanta in exchange for his support, she could no longer say that.

Flynn would be justified in his contempt of her. She tried to swallow but the mingling odors of nacho cheese, machine oil, and a thousand other undefined smells made it hard. So did having a cold lump of stubborn pride wedged high in her throat. Flynn was right about her. She did have it in her to do anything to get what she wanted, no matter who got hurt.

Because of him, she understood that about herself and she had to find a way to live with it—live with it or change it. The way Flynn behaved toward her, he obviously did not think the latter was even a possibility.

Tess dug her fingernails into the leather purse strap. She raised her head and employed a coping technique made famous by the ultimate Georgia belle: She refused to think about it—about Flynn, in her case—today. Tomorrow would be soon enough to deal with him and her decisions about the magazine.

Tonight, she had other priorities. She had to work on her bowling.

She marched past the pro shop and the room with all the video games whirring and pinging in it. Her eyes adjusted to the lighting and she scanned the length of the building. The place hummed with activity so she had to stop to search for the others.

A loud *ding-ding-ding* from the arcade, followed by Max shouting in triumph, told her that Jerrianne had arrived already. Tess just needed to pick her friends out of the clash of color and chaos scattered along the well-lit lanes. She squinted. She put her hands on her hips. She went on tiptoe to see over a hulking man with a small child hoisted on his shoulders. When she could not see around him, she decided to try another route.

"Lose something?"

Bent over, with her butt proudly stuck up and out, her head low and one hand thrust out to keep her from falling on her face, Tess only saw the pair of men's loafers stop just to her right. It was all she needed to know who had spoken to her. Fate and Flynn Garvey, it seemed, had struck a deal, conspiring against her to always catch her at her worst.

"Huh?" *Brilliant comeback, Tess. That really put him in his place.*

"I asked if you'd lost something." He took her outstretched arm as she straightened up. "Like your way?"

"My way?"

"What other excuse could the queen of southern style have for being caught in the Twilight Lanes?"

"I . . . uh . . ." She smoothed her damp palm down her jeans, exhaled through puffed-out cheeks, then jerked her head up to match his gaze. "Caught?"

"Yeah."

The implication did not sit well with her. Accustomed as she had become to having Flynn pop up when she least wanted or expected it, finding him here, now, did raise some disquieting possibilities. "Did you say *caught* in the Twilight Lanes?"

"Yeah, as in a place where a woman like you wouldn't be *caught* dead." He made a show of glancing around them.

She did the same. "Not as in you've been following me around and caught me here?"

"I did not follow you, Tess."

He seemed sincere, though she'd been fooled by

that act before. Still, she remembered Jerrianne's remark about a guy like Flynn hanging out in the Twilight Lounge. Maybe she should believe him, chalk up his appearance here tonight to mere coincidence. Whatever brought him, she had to throw him off the trail of her friends and their near-perfect scheme for holding secret meetings.

"Fine. I believe you. You didn't follow me. So what did bring you here? Hoping to pick up a few spares in the lounge? Or got all turned around in this big city and ended up in the wrong kind of gutter?"

"Bowling humor." He nodded, his eyes glittering in the low light. "I get it. Very funny."

She folded her arms. "You didn't answer my question."

He mimicked her stand. "You didn't answer mine."

No other man, no other person, intimidated Tess like this. Intimidated her and stimulated her at the same time. She wasn't afraid of the man, far from it. He challenged her. He did not let her get away with anything. Nobody else did that. Something about it thrilled her to her toes and yet made her want to slap him—or kiss him—senseless.

"Why are you here, Tess?"

Yes, he challenged her, but he was not in charge of her. She had this one tiny corner of her world still completely under her control and she'd be damned if she let Flynn walk in and take it from her. "Maybe

I'm here to check it out as a good place to feature in a story for the magazine."

He chuckled. That was all he had to do to call her a bald-faced liar.

If she had been a man she'd have decked him. "Where I go and what I do is none of your business. And in the future when we are not working together, if our paths cross by some unhappy coincidence—"

"My being here is no coincidence."

"You said you didn't follow me."

"Tess, sweet Tess." He shook his head. "When are you going to learn?"

Even feigned pity from him galled her to the very pit of her stomach. "Learn what?"

"That life goes on in its own way and people do pretty much what they damn well please, despite *your* directions and designs?"

"I think the fumes in this place have gone to your head. You're not making any—"

Without another word, he took her by the shoulders and turned her just so, then lowered his head beside hers and pointed. "I didn't have to follow you here, Tess. In fact as mysteries go, figuring out why you couldn't meet with me tonight provided a piss-poor excuse for one. Especially when I stopped by Jerrianne's and saw her climbing into her car dressed like that."

With Flynn's guidance, Tess spotted her friends. It had not been nearly as tricky as she had anticipated. "My heavenly days! No!"

"Much as I admire a woman who leans on her personal faith in times of crisis, I don't think it will offer you much help dealing with these ladies, Tess."

She shut her eyes but she could still see Wy and Jerrianne wearing the black and pink satin bowling shirts with *The Sweethearts* emblazoned on the back in huge white, sparkling letters.

"Hey, Tess!" Wy leapt up and began waving as Tess and Flynn approached. "Jerrianne, Tess is here!"

"I'd ask you not to call attention to us, Wylene, honey, but I hardly see the point of it, considering these." Tess pinched Wylene's sleeve between her thumb and forefinger. She'd rather pinch her friends for pulling this dumbfounding bonehead move. She kept a stunned smile on her face as she spoke, all the same. "And with our nickname on the back and everything."

"Isn't that the cleverest thing?" Jerrianne bent down and scooped up a limp shirt that had been draped over one of the three bowling bags placed in a row by the seats. She thrust it toward Tess. "Using the common spelling of sweethearts for our team name like that? Even you have to admit, Tess, that's just danged precious."

"Danged precious." She unfurled the shirt with her name on the pocket then lifted it for Flynn to see. "Yes. That was the term I believe I was searching for to describe all this. Danged precious."

"Double-dog danged." He gave Jerrianne a wink.

Tess wanted to give him an elbow to the gut but refrained. She might be Queen Tessa but even she could not fight a battle on two fronts. She needed Flynn as an ally in this.

"Aren't they fabulous?" Wylene did a quick turn worthy of her days on the beauty pageant runways and beamed a smile at them over her shoulder. "Reni did it. Ordered us all matching shirts, shoes, bags, and balls."

"One day I'm going to kill Reni," Tess murmured to Flynn without a trace of animosity in her tone. "I really am."

Flynn cocked his head and tucked his hands in his pockets. "She sure does like to throw her money around. I didn't realize she'd come into her inheritance yet."

"She hasn't." Jerrianne picked up a pink and black bowling bag and set it at Tess's feet. "Her parents have retired to Florida. This one's yours, Tess. She got you a ball but you can't use it until you have the holes drilled."

"Looks like nothing but top of the line." Flynn rubbed his chin, and jabbed the toe of his shoe against the expensive-looking bag. "So where does Reni get the money to do this kind of thing?"

Tess saw his line of reasoning in this. If the Suite-Hearts were being blackmailed for money, it would be important to know which ones had enough to make the effort worthwhile.

"Reni married well." Wy's worn face took on a distant, dreamy expression. "Even if she couldn't find it in herself to overlook misdeeds."

"Miss Deed, Miss December, Miss Daughter of Your Ex-Business Partner," Tess whispered to Flynn, to clue him in on just a few of the women who had come between Reni and her husband of ten years. "You name it, he did them all."

"Ouch."

"It did hurt Reni's pride, but don't kid yourself, it was one of those marriages that was over emotionally before the heat of the honeymoon had time to dissipate."

"The 'ouch' was for what Reni must have done to the poor guy."

"Let me assure you, he was anything but a 'poor guy' before they finished up in court. Reni married well, all right." Tess wadded her bowling shirt in her fist, knowing the others would not hear her. "But she divorced even better."

Flynn leaned his head close to hers. "Would it be impolite to say I'm not surprised?"

His breath stirred her hair and tickled her ear. She turned her head until she could look him square in the eyes, which, as an afterthought, might have been a mistake. She exhaled. "Impolite, yes, but not inappropriate."

He smiled.

Tess swore she could actually feel that smile on her skin, sinking into her being, pulsing through her with every beat of her heart. She wet her lips.

"You've made some very interesting choices in friends during your life, you know that, Miss Theresa Jo?" His deep, soft voice thrummed along her taut nerves.

She tipped her head to one side, blotting out the din and the disorder all around them. "Translation: I keep company with loose cannons, loose women, and loony bowling leaguers?"

"No, of course not."

"Hmm." She didn't entirely buy his innocent act.

"You don't just keep company with them." He took her hand and grinned. "You're their queen."

She refused to let him rattle her. "I wouldn't have it any other way."

"I know." He raised her hand to his lips and placed a kiss as light as an angel's sigh on it. "It's one of the things I find most compelling about you, Tess."

She wouldn't let him rattle her, but somehow he always found a way to do just that.

With her hand still in his, he held her gaze.

"I . . . uh . . . um . . ." She noticed he hadn't said he'd found her scintillating conversational skills compelling. No mystery there, of course. "Oh?"

"You just don't see that kind of loyalty much anymore."

She tried to take her hand away, but at the slightest resistance on his part, she relented. "I don't think it's all that rare a trait, really."

"I do." Grim lines framed his usually smiling

eyes and mouth. "But then maybe it's because of my line of work. When you see people willing to lie, cheat, hide, do anything to get out of something so vital as helping raise and care for their own children, well, you get jaded."

"*Get* jaded?" She made an exaggerated face, hoping to tease him into a lighter mood. "You forget you're talking to someone who's known you almost all your life. You were *born* jaded."

"And not a whole lot of things in my life have worked to dissuade me from that perspective."

Feeling the weight of her own role in adding to his outlook, she could only nod to show her empathy.

He raised his head, his blue eyes searching and a strangely sad smile on his lips. "But every now and then, when I look at you and your friendships, Tess, it makes me wonder if I judge things too harshly."

"Kind of funny to hear you speak to me about my sense of loyalty, Flynn, about judging too harshly."

"Yeah, I suppose it is, but that's how I feel. Every word of it comes straight from my heart." He turned her hand over in his and stroked her palm. "You're a good friend, Tess."

She pressed her lips together, ready to deny his claim when the look in his eyes made her stop. Her mind flashed back to their first encounter since he returned, when she thought he was just a kind-hearted stranger dressed in a Santa Claus suit.

She had sensed something in him then, before

she had to deal with all the emotional baggage of their shared past. She saw in his eyes now an innate quality that told her that he was a man to be trusted. A man who would step in to help her carry her burden if she would let him. She was not ready to let him—yet she also could not discount the effort it must have taken for him to admit what he just had about her.

"Thank you," she whispered. "That means so much, coming from you."

His head moved but he didn't quite nod. His lips twitched but he didn't quite smile. He did not take his eyes from hers.

He stood so near she could feel the warmth of his body through her T-shirt, see the way the dim light of the room made his eyes dilate. He took a deep breath and his chest brushed her arm.

The beat of the music from the lounge and the continuous vibrations rumbling down the long, slick lanes created a restless energy in her. She opened her mouth to say something, but when Flynn's gaze dropped to her lips, her heart skipped and words failed her.

The man was going to kiss her. Here. In public. In the crowded, noisy, smelly bedlam of the Twilight Lanes. And she was going to let him do it.

Let him? If he didn't make his move, she might just throw her arms around his neck and cry out—

"Hoist up your balls and show me a little hand action. Got a good stiff lane so no hooking tonight!"

Reni stopped behind the semicircle of seats just a foot or so away from Flynn and Tess.

"What? Are you nuts?" Tess gave her friend a light shove to the shoulder. "First you do this . . . this shirt thing . . . then you come in spouting filthy language? If you don't shape up, Reni, I'm going to—"

"What? Call my mother?" Reni shoved Tess right back.

"No, she'd only encourage you. But if you don't start showing a little discretion, I might just contact Brother J and tell him you've seen the error of your ways and want him to show you the way to get into heaven."

"Oh, hell, not that." Reni scrunched her eyes shut and winced like she'd bitten down on just about anything from the snack bar. When she opened her eyes again, she gave Flynn a little wave, then snatched up the hip-high handle to the suitcase-looking thing she'd wheeled in with her. "Besides, there's nothing dirty in what I said. It's all bowling lingo. I read it in a book. So you can just go screw yourself, Miss High-and-Mighty Gutter-Talk Guardian."

Tess gasped and grabbed Reni roughly by the arm, spinning her half around to confront her to her face. "You read a book?"

"All right. I watched a video, same difference." She snapped her fingers. "Now go and sit down with Wy and Jerrianne, the both of you. I didn't come here tonight to quibble about a bunch of meaningless crap."

"That's right. We came here for bowling practice," Jerrianne said as Flynn took a seat. She turned to him and put her hand on his arm. "Except Flynn, of course. I'm not sure why he came, but we sure are glad to have him here."

"I came by your house hoping to have a few words with Max—you know, keep him updated man to man."

"You're so good with him. He really needs to spend time around a decent man, to do guy things."

Flynn seemed uncomfortable with the praise. He rubbed his hands together, kept his eyes on the bowlers in the nearby lanes. "I don't know about that decent man thing, but I do get a kick out of hanging with the little guy. I was thinking about taking him fishing soon."

"My daddy makes one terrific grandpa, don't get me wrong, but it's important for Max to have other male role models."

Fishing? A role model? Was this Flynn Garvey they were talking about? Why had she never seen this side of him? And why did the possibilities of these newly discovered qualities in the man create a flutter in her stomach?

Flynn sat back in the chair. "I had thought, when I saw you get in your car wearing that bowling shirt, to come on out here and spend some time with Max."

"Is *that* why you came out here?" Only a deaf man with both hands over his eyes could have missed the challenge in Tess's question.

"It's one reason." His gaze followed her as she moved around to a spot opposite him in the U-shaped bank of seats.

She crossed her arms, almost daring him to say more.

He did not take the bait.

Tess plunked herself down. The vinyl-covered cushion sighed under her weight.

"I peeked in on Max in the arcade when I first got here." Flynn faced Jerrianne and Wy. "He's having such a good time, I figured I'd leave him be and come see what my favorite ladies are up to instead."

"Your favorite ladies are probably up to four ninety-nine a minute and they are just waiting by the phone for your next call." She wasn't being a bitch because she was embarrassed at wanting to kiss this man in public, she told herself. She only wanted him to come clean about his motives. "Why don't you tell us why you are really here?"

"I don't care if he's here to play big brother to Jerrianne's son or to set himself up for a game of hide the headpin with you, Tess." Reni pushed past them both.

Both she and Flynn started to object to that crude and erroneous analogy.

"I, for one, am very glad Flynn is here." Reni waved their thwarted protests aside and wheeled her bag around to put herself center stage, directly in front of the scorekeeper's table for their lane. "I have an announcement to make."

Wylene and Jerrianne perked up.

Tess and Flynn both folded their arms.

"No use in pretending here. I was something of a childrearing challenge to my dear parents." Reni held her hand up to dissuade any comment on that understatement. "I pushed the boundaries, sure, until I figured out there were no boundaries. Not for me."

"Where is she going with this?" Flynn asked.

"I have no idea," Tess whispered back.

"My parents indulged me. They indulged me because that was far easier than disciplining me. Whatever required the least investment of their time, effort, and emotions was just fine by them."

Tess exchanged a glance with Wylene and Jerrianne. Unburdening herself about her upbringing was hardly Reni's style. Something was up—and it was big.

"What was most expedient, they found, was buying people off. They got so used to it that they often did it without evening finding out if it was warranted." Reni swept her hand over the bag beside her. "That's what they did at Lassiter, without ever having bothered to notice that despite some wild ways, and with the help of some very dear friends, I had managed to come in eighth in our graduating class."

"I never knew that," Jerrianne murmured.

Tess had known, but she still did not see the connection.

"Before my folks even found that out, they had

commissioned a statue—A gift to the college that, the minute it was unveiled, would say to the world, 'It was by our generosity, not her own hard work, that our daughter made it through school here.' "

"Oh, boy, I remember this." Flynn propped his forearms on his thighs like someone watching the winning last-second play in the Super Bowl. "This is going to be good."

Tess had just the opposite opinion.

"With that in mind, I have come here tonight"— Reni raised one finger in the air—"to reveal my secret."

Tess shot to her feet. She could not allow this to go on. "This is not how we agreed to handle—"

"We didn't *agree* to a thing, Tess. You told us how it was going to be. And while I absolutely think your plan is best for everybody else here, for my particular situation, well, there's a better way. A simpler way."

"Be that as it may, this is neither the time nor place." Tess took a step forward.

Wy scooted to the very edge of her seat. "She's right, Reni. You can't just . . . blurt out the truth right there in front of God and . . . and all these bowlers."

"I don't know of a place where she can divulge her secret without God knowing about it." Flynn leaned forward, his folded hand between his open knees. "But as for the bowlers, they're occupied with their own business. As long as y'all keep your voices down, I don't see any reason why Reni can't do this here and now."

Tess opened her mouth to explain exactly why they could not do this here or now, but it was already too late.

"Thank you, Flynn. You have a good head on your shoulders, hon. And speaking of which . . ." With far more flourish than necessary, Reni ripped open the zipper on her oversized bowling bag, whipped down the flap, and yanked the contents out. "Ta-da!"

Jerrianne gasped.

Tess buried her face in her hands.

Flynn swore.

And Wy leapt to her feet, pointed in horror and cried out, "Holy stars, Reni, you're the one who decapitated DeWarren Lassiter!"

11

"You are trying to drive me beyond the brink. That's it." Tess stood in his foyer, her hands on her hips. "Beyond the brink, around the bend . . ."

"Yeah, yeah, and over the river and through the woods," he muttered, descending the stairs.

She shifted her feet. Her breasts bounced. A subtle jiggle, perhaps, to the untrained eye, but Flynn's eyes were nothing if not trained on Tess's body.

She stuck her chin up just enough to give her that annoying regal-bearing bullshit she loved to pull on people who'd put up with it. She probably thought the stance projected a "don't toy with me" attitude, but it only provoked Flynn further. Looking down at her now like this, toying with Tess became first and foremost on his agenda.

"I know I have a powerful effect on you, sweetheart. But I had hoped you could hold yourself back from going beyond the brink until we take care of this nasty business for Reni."

"It's not going to work."

He thrust the clothes he'd brought downstairs toward her. "Believe me, it'll work."

"I mean your trying to wear me down with your idiotic exercises in futility." She snatched the things from his hands without so much as a glance at them. "I'm telling you right now, it won't work."

"I'd hardly call trying to cut your friendly note-sending extortionist off at the pass an exercise in futility." He pointed in the direction of the downstairs powder room. "In fact, I thought it was the very reason we're working together."

"Our working together has nothing to do with reason, Flynn."

Like she had to tell *him* that. Reason? Hell, he'd overshot reason the day he put on a damn Santa suit in July and let them take pictures for a magazine that advocated everything he despised.

What place did reason have in his butting in on blackmail schemes and bowling practices? Or with coming back to his house after that practice to change into dark clothes and carry out a nefarious plan? Nothing about his deepening involvement with Tess smacked of reason, logic, or even old-fashioned horse sense.

Sure, it had started out as a means to an end, a

way of getting through to his father. But, on some level, he knew he'd never get through to that heartless bastard, no matter how many meetings he wormed his way into.

Yet, he was still here, still trying to help Tess, even though being around her made him crazy with a staggering mix of anger and awe, respect and regret and . . . other things that he would never get over wanting from her.

His head hurt. His heart felt caught in an ever-tightening cinch. And everything between his waist and knees ached from the clashing rhythms of desire and denial that thinking about her and being around her ignited in him.

She ran her hand over the clothes he'd handed her.

The hair on the back of his neck pricked up. And she had the gall to suggest he'd done it all to drive *her* over the edge.

"You can change in there." He pressed his hand to her back.

She hesitated, then sighed and headed the way he'd urged her.

"The door doesn't lock but you can trust me not to try to sneak a peek." He gripped the finial at the end of the sleek banister. "I'll just catch the show later on the hidden video."

"Ha ha." She stopped in the doorway and for the first time actually looked at what he'd given her to change into. "What *is* this?"

"If you wanted something better than my favorite

old sweatpants and Blues Brothers T-shirt, you should have let me take you to your house." It still chafed at him that she had refused to allow him to even drive her out to her home. "You know what they say, beggars can't be choosers."

"Yes, but I'm not a beggar." She smiled, not a trace of snobbery in her voice, and gave the clothes a gentle shake. "I know that because if I were a beggar, I'd go out and plead with total strangers for something better than these to wear."

He considered telling her he slept in those sweatpants almost every night but decided against it. "It's all I had that was black and would fit you."

"*Fit* being a relative term."

"I just washed them so you won't get any cooties or anything."

"You know, I just did an extensive article in the style section of my magazine on the importance of cootie-free clothing."

"Quit stalling and go change. We got work to do."

"I'll be right out." She slipped into the bathroom.

As the door clicked shut between them, Flynn fought to keep any thoughts of Tess in his home in various stages of undress out of his mind. He tried to calculate the logistics of his intentionally and unnecessarily complex plan to cope with Reni's absurd plight. He dug deep to work up a good gloat over his elaborate strategy to show Tess how ridiculous it was that she personally try to right each girl's youthful blunder.

He puffed up his chest and tucked his plain black T-shirt into his only pair of black jeans. This bogus adventure would teach her. This stupid late-night farce would show her once and for all who was really in charge.

"Okay." The door creaked and she stepped into the dimly lit hall with his favorite T-shirt skimming her breasts and the sweatpants that were like a second skin to him hanging low on her hips. "I'm ready."

"Yeah," he whispered harshly. "Me too."

He stepped back into the forgiving shadows to let her pass. So much for him toying with her. He'd wanted to show once and for all who was really in charge and that he'd done. Gritting his teeth, he folded his hand over the head honcho giving the orders from inside his pants and followed Tess at a decidedly stiff gait.

The narrow parking lot adjacent to the Lassiter College administration offices was vacant. Still, Flynn cut the headlights of Tess's sedan—his red sports car did not make the grade as a spy-mobile, he'd said—and coasted into the last space, in the darkest corner of the lot. They had not passed a single car on the drive over, though twice Flynn had claimed he thought he saw a light in the distance and ordered her to hit the floor. She hated to think about what a gullible moron she must have seemed when not once, but both times she'd dutifully crammed her body down between the seat and the dashboard. Both times!

Well, she would not be so easily tricked or controlled from now on. She'd hired Flynn to play the henchman, after all, not ringleader, and she wasn't going to let him reverse their roles again.

"Keep your head down. We'll both get out on your side of the car, then I'll get the things out of the back and we'll make our move."

She folded her arms. "Not so fast."

He had already slid across the seat. His body crowded to hers. His thigh met her thigh. His arm lay over her shoulder. His lips were near enough now to nibble on her earlobe.

"I don't take orders from you . . ." She paused to clear her throat. ". . . Flynn."

"Then how do you suggest we . . ." He pressed closer still, cleared his own throat, and finished as she had, his voice dropped to a serious tone. ". . . handle it."

Her lips parted. Her gaze fell helplessly into the pure sex and hint of mischief shining in his eyes. She touched her cool fingertips to the scorching skin just above her neckline. "I say we both get out on my side, you get the things from the backseat, and we get this taken care of."

"Then let's do it."

"Okay." For a split second she wasn't quite sure what she'd agreed to, but when Flynn pushed his body onto hers, she shut her eyes and did not argue.

"Oh! Oh! Whoa!" Her whole body started to tumble backward out the suddenly opened car door.

Flynn caught her before her head flopped onto the pavement and her feet flipped ever so elegantly over her ass.

"Shh. Tess!" He pulled her upright and gave her a shake. "If you're going to participate in a covert action, you have got to learn to be quieter than that."

"I'll try to watch myself," she muttered as she scooted out of the car. She knew he'd done it on purpose but how could she accuse him of that without admitting she was ready and willing for him to take her in his arms and do a little covert action of his own?

Her feet hit the ground. She made a quick survey of the area. All was quiet and dark, except for the two light fixtures on the front of the building and the hazy-edged halos cast from the two lampposts in the front lot. Lassiter lay before her much as it had fourteen years ago, a small campus wrapped in silence and serenity. Being here with Flynn, when all the rest of the town and college lay sleeping, dredged up memories she knew she should suppress at all costs.

Flynn only took a moment to retrieve what they needed from the backseat of her car, then came to where she sat on the curb. He crouched low and made a big deal of looking right, then left, then right again.

"You're making far too big a production out of this and we both know it," she said, content to let the sentiment both speak to Flynn about his actions and to herself about her feelings and memories. "I think it's getting out of hand."

"Ah, Tess." He curved his fingers around the back of her neck and urged her forward, then placed his mouth next to her ear. "Since when has what either one of us knows kept us from letting things get out of hand?"

He had her there. Literally. He had her. One move, one word, one kiss from him and she would have been his, at least for a few passionate mindless minutes. His touch, his voice, his very presence still had that power over her.

"C'mon. Let's make the world safe for spoiled rotten emotionally stunted brats like Reni." He gave her a wink, then took off.

She watched him move ahead of her, stooped at first, protecting the object they'd hauled from the Twilight Lanes first to his house, then here. As he reached the edge of the parking lot, he straightened and broke into a sprint. Without meaning to, she found her gaze skimming over his body, from the flash of short hair to the width of his shoulders, then down to his black jeans, which fit him the way jeans were meant to fit. Practically molded over a near perfect behind, they left enough room in the legs to invite her to picture the powerful legs under the stiff denim.

She fought to put the image from her mind but without success. Flynn's body—glorious, firm, agile, and naked—formed in her mind. She could all but feel the hair of his legs rasping against her calves and inner thighs, feel his weight pressing on her, into her.

The summer air hung thick with the scent of lush grass and the roses that crowded the flowerbeds throughout the campus. She tried to keep her mind on that, on anything in the present, but the familiar smells played havoc with her senses, enlivening her memories. She drew in a deep breath and held it. If she shut her eyes, she was there again, back to that summer and the nights when Flynn would come to her dorm and spirit her away. She could feel his hands on her breasts, his tongue pleasuring her, the way his gentle insistence turned wild and consuming when he could hold back no longer, when neither of them could hold back.

"Are you coming or not?" Flynn stopped behind one of the bushes that lined the side of the large brown brick building.

"I'm right behind you," she muttered.

"Then get a wiggle on." He motioned again for her to join him.

She hitched up the sagging waistband of his baggy black sweatpants. She squared her shoulders in the shirt she knew had once clung to his body, then marched up to where he waited.

"Remind me next time I have to go on the prowl

in the dead of night to bring along someone who actually grasps the concept of prowling." He put his hand on her head to coax her to keep low.

Tess clicked her tongue and cooperated, slapping his hand away as she bent her knees. "All right, I'm prowling. I don't know what good it will do, but I'm prowling my butt off here."

She stepped into the bushes, and when a wayward branch poked her in the ribs, she swore under her breath.

"Shh."

"You got it half right." She struggled to keep the bush from scraping her through her thin shirt.

"Tess, you've got to be quiet and take this seriously."

"Quiet I can do. Serious?" She held her hands up and looked around the deserted area. "I refuse to commit to that."

"Do you want to get the blackmailer off your back or not?"

"Of course."

"Then kindly can that attitude and get with the program."

"This plan is not going to have any effect on whoever sent those notes and you know it."

"How can you be so sure?"

"Oh, come on, Flynn." She didn't want to have to say it, but he would make her. She knew he would. She fixed her attention on extracting her shirt from the bush gouging her in the side. "You and I both know that Reni's ridiculous prank cannot be at the root of the blackmail attempt."

"No, we don't know that." He brushed her hands away and deftly as someone handling a frightened bird, freed her from the offending branch. "Of all of you, Reni *is* the most likely target for a simple case of blackmail. She has a crime, a coverup, and plenty of cash on hand."

A cool breeze stirred through the full trees lining the walkways that led to the classrooms, library, and the old dorm where the SuiteHearts has once held court.

"Look, it made sense when she said we should tackle her stupid mistake first and see if setting this right doesn't make the whole mess just go away."

The wind whipped her hair over her nose and into her mouth when she opened her mouth to launch an argument.

"Face it." Flynn swept her hair back and tucked it behind her ear. "Reni was right."

"Don't say that." She feigned a shudder to cover up her real reaction to his tender ministrations. "I don't think I'd know how to carry on in a world where what that girl says makes sense, where Reni Pittman-Webb is right."

"In a world where Reni is right that's about all anyone would do—carry on."

"Then by all means, let's—carry on our covert mission, that is," she added. She held back the branch he had removed from her side, speaking in a loud, teasing whisper, "Of course, if you were as serious as you pretend to be about this farce, you would have insisted we smear stuff on our faces like they do in the movies."

"Smeared them with what?" He strummed the side of his thumb down her cheek. "You going to rub shoe polish on that perfect skin of yours?"

"No, but maybe we could have used really dark makeup."

"Dark makeup." He gave a snort. "Great. At least you'd look your best for your mug shot if we get caught."

"And *you'd* be extra pretty for the all guys in Cellblock D."

He leveled his gaze at her. Even in the dim light from the distant parking lot, she could see the shimmer of laughter there. "Woman, don't you know better than to smart-mouth a man carrying a bowling bag with a severed head in it?"

"Lopped off of a statue fourteen years ago and buried under Granny Pistol's lilac bushes ever since," she reminded him. "This is such a nonproblem, Flynn. I don't see why—"

"Hey, you're the woman protecting the infamous vandal who dearly departed the likeness of DeWarren Lassiter's head from his body before his statue was ever even unveiled." He opened his hand to cup the side of her face in his warm palm. With his mouth so close to hers that each word blew warm and tantalizing over her own lips, he went on. "*I* don't see why you insist on taking this on for her."

"Like you said back at the bowling alley, I'm a good friend." She lifted her chin but not so much that his hand no longer caressed her face.

She liked feeling his touch on her. Liked standing so close to him that with each breath they risked total body contact. But more than that, she liked knowing she could depend on him even when she did not share his vision for correcting the problem and even when he did not share the principle behind her actions.

"You *are* a good friend, Tess."

So are you, she wanted to say. Instead she fluffed her hair and put on her best martyred look. "I must be. Why else on earth would I be sneaking around the Lassiter campus after midnight, still wearing my bowling shoes and in the company of a hollow-skulled hapless icon?"

"Not a very nice way to describe someone who's risking life and limb to help you."

"I was talking about the statue head." She pointed to the bag. "But the deeper we get into this solution of yours, the more I begin to wonder . . ."

"Hey, you want to march into the administration office and hand them the head of their founder on a plate, go right ahead. But do you honestly think Mount Circe's most recognizable citizen could do that and not have word of it leak out?"

She chewed at her lower lip, glanced down at the bowling bag, then held her hands out in surrender. "Lead on. Let's get this done."

"Okay. Campus security consists of the night watchman who got fired from the dairy for sleeping on the job. He drives around the buildings and shines his headlights on the doors every couple hours."

"How do you know that?"

He shrugged. "The way I found out about everything in Mount Circe, Tess. I just asked someone at the bowling alley. Two or three people were happy to volunteer that information and a whole lot more."

"And this is the place you've moved back to—a place where everybody knows everybody else's business." She shook her head. "I don't get it, Flynn. I just don't get it."

"What's to get? It's the closest thing I've ever had to a home. I don't expect a girl like you, someone who grew up in a real home, to understand why I'd settle for the next best thing, but—"

"No, actually, *that* I do understand, Flynn." She'd settled for the next best thing to a home, to a real life, to true love for far longer than she wanted to think about. She put her hand on his arm. "Perhaps more than you could ever guess."

He nodded.

"So, did you also happen to ask if there are alarms on the doors? If any are left unlocked?"

"Couldn't risk bringing that kind of suspicion on us." He unzipped the bag. "Besides, we don't need to go inside. We can just leave DeWarren and the explanation in front of the door. It's only a few hours till dawn. They'll find him quick enough."

"I should have made Reni take care of this herself."

"Why would she have to when she knows you'll come to the rescue?"

She knew that was a rhetorical question she did not feel like answering anyway.

"Let's get this done now." He edged along the side of the building, then stretched his arm out to hold her back. He checked around the corner. "When I say go, we make a run for it. I find a place to set the head that's safe but still visible and you find a place to leave the letter. Got it?"

"I've got it, but I can't help thinking in the back of my mind that there is an easier way to handle this."

"No."

"No?"

"No, we're not doing the battle of wills standing in the bushes with a hot head on our hands." He jerked the bronze sculpture from the bag. "We're here. We're ready. We're doing this my way or we're not doing it at all."

"The sneaking part is your way. The letter and the offer of an anonymous donation coming through an uninvolved third party if they drop any investigation is mine." She set her jaw.

"I'll make sure to acknowledge your contribution

when I write this chapter in my memoirs." He scanned the area, then gave her a curt nod. "Go."

They ran around the corner, leapt over a two-foot hedge, then charged up the stone steps to the front door of the large building in a matter of seconds.

Flynn settled the broken artwork against the corner where it would not attract attention from anyone driving by. "Bet that's gonna scare the piss out of the secretary when she shows up here to unlock the place."

"She's the same secretary who was here when I attended this place. She was a hundred and ninety years old back then." Tess worked the envelope under the crumbling rubber weather stripping at the bottom of the door. "Keeping the piss in her is the real test of your ability."

"I'll pass, thanks. You got the letter in?"

"It's in, let's get out of here." She took off running.

While she did not hear Flynn on her heels, she did not look back. Energized by the intrigue and sense of accomplishment, she pushed on, her eyes on her car in the lot just across the grassy lawn. She'd done it. One secret down, three to go. Nothing could stop her now.

"Don't take another step." Flynn's hushed directive hardly carried above the thundering of his footsteps behind her. "Get down! Quick, hit the dirt!"

She stopped where she stood, anchored her feet and crossed her arms like a deadbolt sliding into place. "Oh, no, I fell for that twice before, and I am not going to—"

Wham!

Flynn's full weight slammed against her.

The air rushed from her lungs in a surprised "oomph" as she plunged downward, the hard ground coming up fast toward her face.

With a last-minute bend of his knee and roll of his shoulder, Flynn alone took the magnified force of their fall. A fleshy thud. A muffled groan. And they lay still in the damp grass, her body sprawled over his like a rag doll.

"Are you crazy?" she demanded, pulling away.

He pulled her down to him, her head to his chest. His hand capped the back of her head. "Shh. I heard a car."

"Yeah, right. Don't think I don't know what you're up to here." Through the thin T-shirt and old sweatpants she could feel every hard muscle in his body under her. The scents of fabric softener on their freshly washed clothes mingled with the smell of grass and earth beneath them. She shut her eyes but could not blot out the thump-a-thump of his heart under her ear. "There's no car. You're just making me go through all this to get your evil jollies."

"Tess, honey, if I wanted jollies out of you I'd certainly find a better way than this." He put his finger under her chin.

"Yeah?"

"Oh, yeah."

Just then a car rolled past the building and the parking lot.

She groaned at having her suspicions proved wrong.

"See?" he asked.

She pulled away and this time he did not try to hold her back. A smarter woman would have justified the twinge of sadness she felt over that as a letdown after the big excitement. Tess sighed and sat cross-legged in the grass. "I still think that this elaborate scheme is some kind of payback for my trying to control the way I let you help us with all this."

"And you'd be right."

"Aha."

"I did want to show you how silly your preoccupation with these notes could get to be." He stood, brushed off his jeans, then held out his hand to help her to her feet. "But I also had your best interest at heart. Since Reni would not come forward and take responsibility for her conduct, I'd be damned if I'd have let you risk your good name on her behalf by trying to do this out in the open."

"If you'd *let* me?" She planted her fists on her hips.

"Tess." He took her hands in his, uncurling her clenched fingers as he did.

"What?"

"For once in your life, just let it go."

She set her jaw.

"Someone who cares about you is helping you. It happens. Get over it."

They stood there in the dim light on the old familiar campus, hand in hand and as close as they had been to seeing eye to eye in many years. Tess wet her lips. The man scared the pee-waddin' out of her.

No one else on earth that she could think of, including old P. Pearcy McLaughlin, who held her future in his money-grubbing hands, did that. And yet, as she gazed into those eyes that had once looked on her in almost holy adoration, then later cut through her heart like a blade ripping through a tender underbelly, she knew one thing. She could trust this man. She might not like his attitude or agree with his actions but she knew he was not in this to hurt her.

"We'll start looking into Jerrianne's secret tomorrow morning," she said softly.

"Can't tomorrow morning. Promised Max I'd take him fishing. We'll be at it pretty early. Have to drive out to that stocked pond place a couple towns over, so—"

"Don't knock before seven."

"Huh?"

"When you bring Max out to my house to fish."

"You're . . . you're inviting me out to your house?"

"Take the dairy circle road, like you were coming

to the Heritage House, but when you come to the corner with the blond brick house that has a sign out front reading NOTARY PUBLIC, PARK IN BACK, ALL SIZES don't turn off. Keep going straight."

"Got it."

He didn't ask about the meaning of the odd sign. Tess couldn't have told him if he had. But the fact that he didn't ask, didn't make fun, didn't even miss a beat over it made her think that maybe he wasn't so ill-suited to life in Mount Circe again.

"You can go out to the pond—Max knows the way, he can show you—early as you want, but don't come knocking on my door before seven. Got that?"

"Got it."

"They say what doesn't kill us makes us stronger. Do you believe that?"

"Sure. Why?"

"Because when this ordeal is done, I am going to be freakin' superwoman."

12

He was getting old—too old for this kind of nonsense, anyway. Flynn's muscles stubbornly refused to cooperate as he tried to lower himself to the edge of the dock on Tess's pond. He chunked the tackle box he'd borrowed from Brother J down on the gray wooden boards and the whole structure shimmied. Or did it shudder? The beams and supports groaned. He knew exactly how they felt.

Three scant hours of sleep simply would not cut it anymore. He used to get by on far less than that in his wayward youth, sometimes going without for days on end. Without sleep, he thought chuckling to himself. There was damned little else he went without in those days. Back then a late-night escapade with a gorgeous blonde and an early wake-up call would not have fazed him in the least.

This morning when the alarm blasted its obnoxious buzz in his ear at 5:30 A.M. he'd knocked the thing off the nightstand. In return the demonic clock had bounced off the bedpost and whacked him in the head but good.

He squinted into the first brilliant rays of the rising sun, rubbed his temple, and moaned. Half of hell's minions and all of heaven's holy horde working in concerted effort could not have dragged him from his bed that early, but one thing did.

"You gonna sit down on the end of the dock with me, Mr. Garvey?" Max Munroe dangled his legs off the planks jutting out over the small, still pond.

"Give me a minute, kid." He smiled down at the boy when the last thing he felt like doing was smiling. Mornings were not his thing. Kids were not his thing. Fishing was not his thing. But what could he do? He'd promised.

"Okay. I'll just sit here and practice dropping my line in the water." Max leaned forward until his face reflected back at them in the quiet water.

Flynn shot his hand out, ready to grab him by the collar to keep him from toppling headlong into the dank-smelling pond. But somehow between rod and reel and the way he stuck his tongue out just so and kicked his sneaker-clad feet back under the dock, Max achieved perfect balance.

The smile came for real this time, unbidden and

from a place so deep within him Flynn had hardly known it existed. He had promised Max they'd spend some time together but, not having had tons of experience with kids, he had no idea what they could do. He'd never had a father to play out that cornball Andy Griffith routine with him, going down to the fishing hole, skimming stones and all, but it seemed like the perfect solution.

When he'd suggested fishing to Max, the kid had hemmed and hawed a bit. He probably did not really want to do it, but finally the hunger made the boy agree. Flynn knew that hunger. Father hunger. The longing for love and approval so deep and real that it drove out everything else and left an empty, gaping hole.

So Flynn had pressed his case for fishing. Now, standing here with the wind whistling through the tall grass, the first light of day creeping over the mountains, and this great kid sitting here centering his whole being on dropping a fishing line into a skanky pond, he was glad he did.

No personal involvement. That had always been his style. He rarely even met the kids he worked so hard to recover back child support for. He didn't have to. He wasn't doing it for them, not really, not when you stripped it all down to the hardcore reality. He was doing it for himself and the kid in him who never went fishing with his own father.

Flynn wasn't proud of that fact. He wished he could make it more about the children and less about his pathetic childhood. But that's how it was. Something in him was screwed up that way and he was getting old. What were the odds he'd ever really be able to sort out his feelings and get his priorities straight this late in the game?

"I never fished nowhere but from my grandpa's rowboat, and then we didn't catch nothing." The boy looked up, his nose crinkled in a look of sober concern. "You think we'll catch something today?"

Flynn stretched, hoping to loosen his body up enough to get down on the dock without grunting like someone's granddaddy. "We'll sure try, kid. You ready to get started?"

"I guess." Max reeled his line back in but slowly this time, like he wanted to buy some time.

Flynn sat down. His jeans rasped on the splintered boards as he hung his legs over the side. He piddled and poked around inside the tackle box, to give Max the opportunity to spill whatever was on his mind. When he didn't say anything, Flynn pulled out a tub of worms, flipped off the lid and offered the contents to Max. "You need any help baiting your hook?"

He shook his head and fiddled with his fishing pole.

Clearly, something was needling the boy. An adult who knew how to deal with kids, felt confident of giving the right answers no matter what problem arose, would try to encourage the child to talk about it, let it out. Flynn knew that. He gave the tub a gentle shake. "Because if you need any help, you know, with the bait—"

Max raised his head. His eyes were dark. "Do you think the worm feels it when you put the hook through him?"

So that was it. Flynn exhaled his relief in one hard puff. "Naw. Worms don't feel stuff like people do."

Max absorbed the answer in silence, looking away. Finally, when he'd kicked his feet back and forth enough times to stir the beginnings of motion sickness in Flynn's already irritable stomach, he asked, "What about the fish?"

"What about them?"

"Do you think it hurts them when they get that hook through their mouths?" Max crooked his finger and placed it inside his mouth, pulling his cheek out like a fish on a line.

"No, I don't think it hurts them. They have small brains." He tapped his finger lightly against the kid's forehead. "They aren't that sensitive like us. They don't get hurt."

His pudgy hands dropped to his lap. "That's good, huh?"

"I guess." Flynn stared down into the wriggling worms in the white plastic tub. "If you're a fish."

"I wish I was a fish."

The air grew so still around them that Flynn could hear his own heart beating. In that one instant he knew exactly what the child had meant, how he felt, and that if he was anything but an uncaring jerk, he had to ask, "Why?"

"Then I wouldn't get hurt neither."

Yeah. He saw that one coming. Or had he *felt* it coming? Most adults would have tried to cajole the kid into a lighter mood or make some remark to downplay the boy's perspective, but Flynn couldn't do that. "You're worried about your mom and your situation living over the Fellowship and about what you asked me to do, aren't you?"

"A little."

"That's one of the reasons I wanted to spend some time with you, Max. I wanted to keep you updated on my progress."

The boy jerked his head up, his eyes wide with hope.

The sight sucker-punched Flynn low in the gut. "I wish I had better news for you, but so far . . ."

"Maybe if you could find my dad, maybe he could help." He spoke so softly, as if he dared not really voice it aloud, that a sudden breeze would have blown the very words away.

Flynn had stayed away from the tender topic of Max's father on purpose but now he knew he had to face it. "Is that what you really wanted when you made your wish? For me to try to find your dad?"

"Maybe . . . a little."

"That's not exactly what you asked for."

"I know, but I've been thinking . . ." He let his

voice trail off without explaining further. But then, as far as Flynn was concerned, he didn't have to.

"It's rough being a boy without a father. Believe me, I know."

"How?"

"Because I don't have a father either."

"Everyone gots a father. Nobody can get born without a father and a mother. It takes both of them."

"That's true." It takes both of them. To make a child and to make a life for a child—the choices of both parents played a role. "Does your mom ever talk to you about your dad?"

"Only if I ask, and then she tells me what she can. After that she just says she doesn't know what more to tell me."

Flynn nodded. Seeing how Jerrianne had allowed Max to take the lead not confronting the issue, approaching it openly and honestly with the boy, made Flynn think. He'd always focused on his father's shutting him out but never given much thought of his mother's role. Flynn thought nothing of using Tess to get through to his father, but the one woman who had any real power to make that happen had never even tried. Funny that it took a young boy to make him see that, to make him look at things from a different angle.

"Max, if you want to find your father, you should talk to your mother about that, not a stranger."

"You're not a stranger, you're my friend. You're going to help me make my wish come true."

"Max . . . I . . ."

"Aren't you?" The boy's whole being seemed exposed in that one, desperate look.

Against the kid's own wishes, he'd brought the boy fishing and here he was, the one getting snagged—hook, line, and sinker. He would help this boy make his wish come true if at all possible. "I promised I'd try and I will."

"No kidding?"

"I wouldn't kid you. I want to be totally honest with you." He put his arm around Max. "And I want you to be honest with me. 'Cause friends do that."

"Okay. Sure. I like being your friend."

"Then tell me honestly, friend, you don't really want to go fishing, do you?"

"I sorta wished you'd have a metal detector and we'd go looking for war relics and lost money and stuff."

"A metal detector? Is that right? Not fishing?"

Max nodded. "The couple times I went with Grandpa I spent all the time praying we wouldn't catch nothing."

"You did, did you?"

"Do you think that's a sin?"

"Well, I'm not a theologian—"

"Neither are we," Max piped up brightly. "We're Salvation Brethren."

Flynn laughed. "I don't think it's a sin for you not to want to hurt any of God's creatures, Max. I do think it would be awfully wrong for me to force you to do that just because of some dream I had when I was a kid."

"What does that mean?"

"It means . . ." Flynn checked his watch. It was not yet seven o'clock. He grinned and snapped the lid back on the bait tub. "It means instead of fishing, let's go up to Miss Tess's house and see if we can't get her to rustle us up a big bowl of cold cereal. What d'ya say?"

"I say, sure thing!" He leapt to his feet so fast the dock wobbled.

Flynn reached out to steady the boy and for an instant, he felt something he had not known in a very long time. He felt hope.

"Thanks, Mr. Garvey." Max beamed a broad smile up at him then turned and ran off the dock as fast as his legs would take him.

"Thank you, Max," Flynn whispered as he gathered up their things and headed up to Tess's house.

The light was on inside Tess's foyer. With daybreak still not quite upon them and the wide wraparound porch in darkness, Flynn could see inside her home plain as looking onto a lighted stage.

Through the long windows on either side of the doorframe and the large oval of leaded glass in the door itself he could make out a single form. Light glanced off her golden hair as she bobbed up and down, then side to side, he supposed trying to find the best vantage point to keep an eye on Max and him. Flynn slung the fishing pole up onto his shoulder, trying not to let on that he could see her.

She crossed her arms. Her thick chenille robe bunched up and open to expose the Blues Brothers T-shirt she still had on from last night's adventure. Tess had slept in his shirt. In his favorite shirt. The one he slept in. He took a deep breath, but that did not alleviate the prickling sensation of his skin drawing into big old goosebumps at the idea of his favorite sleep shirt skimming over her naked flesh.

She made him crazy. Crazy with desire. Crazy with longing. Crazy with her stubborn pretense that they had nothing but a common goal between them.

He knew they could not pursue a real relationship. He knew that boat had sailed many, many years ago. But damn it, why did they have to deny what they felt when they touched? Even if they never followed through on the passion they shared, why did they have to deny it entirely? It wasn't healthy and it wasn't going to make it go away. Today might be the perfect time to try to make Tess see that.

As Max scampered ahead of him on the walk, Flynn heard the chimes of an old clock reverberating somewhere near the door. Framed in the window, Tess turned her head to look as it *dong, dong, donged* out the quarter hour. Don't knock before seven. Those were her explicit directions and yet here he was, Max in tow, marching up big as life right to her door.

"Good gosh-a-mighty!" Her voice carried to them with the last clang of the clock.

He smiled to know Tess felt much the same way about his being here as he did. Standing on her porch with her just a few feet away behind that door made last night's decisions to meet here seem about as smart as inviting the devil to the Sunday School wienie roast—someone was bound to get burned.

"You sit on the porch swing, out of the line of fire, Max."

He knew she heard that, even though she now stood at the bottom of the stairs.

"I'll knock on the door then step aside," he said in a booming voice, trying to inject a little humor into an already awkward situation. "That way if she starts flinging frying pans first and asking questions later it won't put a dent in my purty profile."

A muffled curse confirmed she'd heard that, too.

Flynn knocked in far too jaunty a rhythm for this hour of the morning.

Inside he could see her turn and look up the long stairway then set her shoulders square and her head high. She was a daughter of the South, born resourceful and always resolute in the face of any stubborn obstacle . . . especially a man. She would not retreat.

Before Flynn's knuckles hit the door again, he

saw Tess bend at the waist. She flipped her head down then whipped her hair up and back twice. Violently. Going to work the old guilt angle by coming to the door all rumpled and grumpy, no doubt. But when she cinched up her belt, smoothed down the top layer of her hair and wet her lips, he knew she'd done it all in pure vanity. It puffed up his pride to no small degree that she wanted to look good for him.

"I told you not to knock before seven," she said as she swung the door inward. "But seeing as you've disregarded that and are here, I wouldn't want you to think me an ungracious hostess. Please, do come in."

"Coast is clear, Max, come on."

The boy darted between the two of them and made a beeline for the kitchen. "Did you eat up all the Choc-o-puffs, Aunt Tess?"

"I managed to hold back and save some for you, honey-pie. You know where to find the box in the pantry," she called after him. "Go on ahead and take the bowl into the den and see if you can't find yourself some cartoons on the TV."

"Thanks, Aunt Tess!"

"I wish I had that boy's energy." Flynn paused at the threshold.

"I don't think the world could stomach you with that much exuberance. He's already raring to go and it being barely the crack of dawn." She put her hands behind her back and leaned against the open door. If she flirted any harder she'd sprain something.

Or *he* would.

She arched her back in a way that all but begged him to say something he knew he shouldn't.

He cocked his head and narrowed his eyes at her, all concerned-like. "Did we wake you up, Tess?"

"No." She shook her hair back, dropped her chin, and looked at him through her lowered lashes. "I was already up. Why do you ask?"

"No reason." He shrugged and ambled inside, his hands shoved into his pockets. "You just have one of the most gawd-awful cases of bed head I've seen in a long while."

She stepped away from the door. It fell shut hard enough to make the mementos cluttered on the shelves in the foyer tremble. "Is there a reason why—other than wanting to get your insults in before the morning rush—you're here so early?"

"I wasn't insulting you, Tess." He reached out and touched her hair, stroking it back from her face. "I think it's sexy."

She looked startled for a second, maybe longer, then turned away. "Don't, Flynn."

"You started it," he said, barely above the measured ticking of the grandfather clock nearby. "Sounding all hoarse and breathy and looking fresh out of bed wearing my T-shirt."

She looked down, then tugged her robe closed and clasped it just below her chin. "I just wanted to . . . If I led you on, I'm sorry."

"Why?" He moved in front of her. "Why can't we admit that we still find each other desirable?

It's not like it's some big secret. It's damned obvious every time we spend more than two minutes together."

"Just because it's obvious doesn't mean we have to acknowledge it."

"I should have known you'd say that. That you'd rather hide the gritty truth beneath a false front."

She tossed him an impish grin over her shoulder and puffed her chest out a bit more than necessary. "Honey, I assure you, there is nothing false about my front."

"Don't I know it." He came up behind her and ran his crooked finger down her spine.

Tess gasped but did not move away.

"Now, that wasn't so bad, was it? To play the game a little?"

She pursed her lips.

"We're both adults here, Tess." He moved in front of her then pressed in on her. "Why keep on pretending that we don't both feel this chemistry between us?"

"Chemistry can be very volatile." She shut her eyes. "Frankly, I can't afford the risk of having it blow up in my face right now."

"Just because something is volatile does not mean we have to let the situation get explosive." He murmured the words against her temple.

She swallowed hard but did not refute his opinion.

"We're not kids anymore, you know," he went on. "We can control this."

"Control?"

Her watchword. Her guiding principle. If he'd spoken of anything else, she might have given in.

"Control it?" Tess slipped away from him and stood firm in the hallway. "Says the man who once touched off a chemical fire in the science lab at high school. We had to have class in the Home Ec room for a week."

"It wasn't a fire, Tess."

"No?"

"It was a noxious odor."

"All the same, I think I'll pass."

"You sure about that?"

"Silence and denial are both vastly underrated as problem-solving techniques, in my opinion."

It was only a half jest and he knew it. "Is that right?"

"They have served me well—"

"Up until this ugly business with the notes."

"Most of my life," she finished.

"So you're ready to abandon those time-honored traditions yet? Not when you need their protection most?"

She set her jaw, her eyes sharper than thorns in a thicket. "Are we talking about just recognizing the tensions between us or acting on them?"

"Whatever you're most comfortable with."

"Comfortable?" She almost choked on the word. "Flynn Garvey when you are around, I am many things, but none of them comfortable."

"I like that."

"Well, I don't."

"I know."

"You just like having me off balance."

"I just like having you however I can, Tess. If you say it's got to be at arm's length, then I'll accept that. I won't like it, but I'll accept it."

"Good, because we still have a lot of work to do. How soon can you be ready to delve into Jerrianne's secret?"

"As soon as I get you out of that T-shirt . . ."

She scowled in warning.

"And into your street clothes."

"I have to shower." She jerked her head toward the end of the hallway. "Go watch cartoons with Max a while."

"I'd rather watch you."

"Go."

"Okay. I did promise to spend some time with Max after all."

"He's a great kid."

"Yeah, he is. Makes me think—"

"About having children."

Until the words came out of her mouth he'd never seriously considered having kids. Now, in a flash of emotion and insight, he realized that, if he had the right person to help him raise one, he would like a kid. Very much.

"I don't know." He lied because there was no point in doing otherwise with Tess on this subject that would never be of any significance between them. "I have so many issues with my own upbring-ing."

"Well, I know how that feels. Still . . ." Her gaze trailed off to the darkened hallway and the lighted rooms beyond. "When I spend any amount of time around Max, I do allow myself to dream a little. I wonder if maybe I couldn't resolve a lot of my own issues by having children and doing it right."

"You would, Tess."

"Hmm?"

"Do it right."

They looked into each other's eyes. The clock ticked.

Finally, Tess broke eye contact and cleared her throat. "I'd better go shower and get dressed."

"Yeah, I'd better go check in on Max."

"Help yourself to whatever breakfast food you can scrounge up in there." She hurried off, calling behind her, "Half my pantry is cold cereal."

Flynn chuckled to himself. The Martha Stewart of the South, and half her pantry was cold cereal. The Tess who ran that damned sham magazine and the woman wearing his favorite T-shirt seemed more and more to have less and less in common. Nothing but the loyalty of friends, the gratitude of the whole town, and the admiration of one foolish, horny, and helpless-to-do-anything-about-it man.

* * *

"Productive morning?" Brother J stacked tattered hymnals on top of a black upright piano.

"Yes, it was." Flynn picked up a couple of the red-covered books and handed them to the preacher as Max's footsteps faded into the kitchen of the storefront church. While Tess waited in the car, making supersecret arrangements via her cellular phone, he had brought the boy in and planned to stay no longer than the minimum acceptable small-talk-time—which, southern manners dictated, could be "quite a spell." "Didn't catch any fish but it was time well spent just the same."

"Somehow I thought it might be. Good for both of you, I suspect." He slid the last hymnal on the stack, then motioned for Flynn to grab a chair as he took a seat on the piano bench. "There's a kind of healing takes place when you stop stewing over your own troubles and reach out to someone who really needs a friend."

"Healing, huh?" He ignored the cold metal chair in favor of perching on the edge of a large table.

"You think of a better word for what happens when we share ourselves with others?"

Healing. That was it. Flynn had thought that what he had come back to Mount Circe to find was hope, peace, acknowledgment, maybe even some atonement on his father's part. But what was the sum of that if not healing? All these years he had carried the *wound we don't flush clean, the piece of glass under the skin, the sliver we can't find,* as Brother J had once described it to him. It had festered for a long time. Flynn had thought only one thing could resolve that, but as he stopped and considered his time with Max today, he realized that the man standing before him in faded jeans and a scraggly ponytail was right. He felt better. Could he have begun to heal without so much as setting foot in P. Pearcy McLaughlin's presence?

The older man stretched his long legs out, crossed at the ankles. "I put a lot of stock in the importance of healing. Don't you?"

Flynn looked at his hands, and shook his head. "Tell me something, Brother J."

"Surely."

"How'd a ornery old street preacher like you get so wise?"

"Careful, not you're tempting me to quote chapter and verse at ya." His eyes twinkled.

Flynn held up his hand. "Don't bother, I just . . . well, I guess I just . . . that was my awkward way of trying to say thank you."

"Thank me? I should thank you. You've done right fine ever since you got back. Won over quite a few folks around town, judging from the gossip that wafts this way out of the barber shop."

"You're a big part of that, I'm sure. And, though I know you never set out to do it, you've been a big part of my life." Flynn stood and held out his hand. It did not seem a large enough gesture to offer someone who had set him on the right path with only a few kind words and a belief that the boy he was could become the man standing here today.

"Well, thank you, then." Brother J got to his feet and clasped Flynn's hand with a firm shake, then placed his other hand on Flynn's right arm, holding him there a minute longer. "When you do the kind of work I do, people come and go. Not many think to come back and let you know you made a difference."

"You did, Brother J." He patted the sleeve of the preacher's rumpled work shirt, gave another shake, then released his hand. "You made a difference."

"Mind if I ask how?"

"You told me fourteen years ago that I had the seeds in me to be a man others could look up to and admire. No one—no *man*—ever told me that before. Funny how that small piece of encouragement could change the way I thought about myself."

"Changed it some, I surely do see that. But no *so* very much. You still think of yourself as that boy who wanted nothing so desperately as the love of the father who had forsaken him."

Flynn had been in bar fights. He'd been in street fights. He'd even gotten gouged and mauled trying to intervene in a cat fight. But he had never taken a blow that knocked the wind out of his sails like Brother J's solemn observation.

"I know how you can change that, Flynn."

"I already have a plan, thanks."

"Oh?"

"I plan to meet him, face to face, man to man . . ."

"You'll come up one man short, then, because whoever fathered you, whoever would father any child and then just walk away, is not a man in my book."

Flynn chuckled by way of offering his agreement. "Still, I want to look the old guy in the eye, just once. Is that too much to ask?"

"No, not to ask. But after what? Nearly forty years? If he hasn't wanted to meet you in all that time, it probably is too much to *expect* that he'll come 'round now."

"I have to try."

"You'd do better to expend your energy on others and on one single act that will, indeed, change who you are forever."

"Look, Reverend, I—"

"You can forgive the man."

"Forgive?" He said it like he was spitting rocks.

"You think you're a tough man, a hard man in many aspects, and you count yourself successful."

"Yeah, but . . ."

"*But* until you can set your bitterness aside and forgive the one who dealt you this disappointment you will always remain that injured little boy. You will never find what you want."

"Healing." He spoke it aloud though he had not intended to.

The older man put his arm around Flynn's shoulders. "The devotion of a parent for a child is the closest thing to divine love most of us get the chance to practice here on Earth. If it's not there you cannot force it or fabricate it."

Flynn nodded. He could not have spoken then if his life depended on it.

"Things gone another way, you might have been the best friend your father ever had. Somedays I don't know how I would have gotten along without my Jerrianne and Max. I often wish I'd done better by them and pray that I will do better in the future. But I wouldn't have given up one moment of sharing their joys and sorrows for anything. That your father didn't have that from you is his . . ."

"Yeah, his loss." Flynn stepped away. "Now you're in my territory, preacher. That's a text where I can quote the clichés chapter and verse."

"Doesn't make it any less true."

The ache in Flynn's heart confirmed that sentiment. "I gotta go. Tess is waiting in the car."

"If you ever want to talk about how you can get beyond the hurt and anger at your biological father, whoever he might be . . ."

"You honestly have no idea who it is, do you?"

"Won't pretend I haven't heard the gossip. Everyone from old Mr. James—"

"Jobie?"

"His daddy."

"Oh."

"To some traveling salesman who never left a calling card, I've heard the speculations. But no, I have no idea who your earthly father is."

"Earthly father?" Flynn folded his arms. "You implying some folks think I was left here by aliens?"

"Could be some folks do." Brother J gave him a one-eyed once-over worthy of a vintage *X Files* character. "But I was making reference to your Heavenly Father."

"Okay. Time for me to leave before you haul out the bullhorn and brimstone. I didn't come here for preaching."

"Grandpa! Grandpa, come look'n see what I found," Max called from the back room.

"Coming right along," J called out to his grand-child. Then he turned to Flynn, his life-lit eyes warmed by a kind of mercy and understanding not often seen in this cold world. "When you're ready, I'll be here, son."

Son. It still cut through him. It still carried so much power and pain. He held his hand up, then turned to go. The uneven floorboards creaked with every step toward the open door, where fresh air and Tess waited beyond. Every step took him away from the only man who had ever tried to guide and encourage him.

Sunlight slanted across the toe of his shoe when he pulled up short and twisted just his head to ask over his shoulder, "Do you really think I have it in me to do it? To forgive the bastard who abandoned my mother and me and never looked back?"

"Yes. I do."

Flynn nodded slowly, then picked up his pace and strode over the nearby threshold. He did not share the depths of Brother J's faith on this issue, but he could not discount the idea completely. He'd give it some thought. Later.

Right now he had to take Tess through the motions of pawing through Jerrianne's most private past, even though he could probably tell her exactly what they would find and where they would have to go to deal with it.

13

Silence and denial are both vastly underrated as problem-solving techniques, in my opinion.

Even as she cringed at her words, Tess could not dispel her relief at having dodged the bullet. But for how long? Sooner or later Tess knew she and Flynn would have to talk about the past, about that night.

"No time like the present." Flynn climbed behind the wheel of his convertible.

"What?"

"Brother J has taken charge of Max, or maybe it's the other way around." He slammed the door hard enough to gently rock the car. "You've set aside the morning, the tank is full of gas, and I'm full of—"

"Baloney? Piss and vinegar?"

"I was going to say optimism about the day's project."

"Oh, that's much better then."

"So, we agree, there's no time like the present to plunge into secret issue number two."

"Right. Yes." She took a deep breath. The aroma of chicken and dumplings filled her senses, and she could almost taste the hot lunch Brother J would be serving to the poor and elderly today. She shut her eyes but she could still see the storefront with SALVATION BRETHREN FELLOWSHIP painted in huge black letters on the window and the SALVATION DELIVERANCE van parked right out in front. "But I have to warn you of something before we start."

"That sounds ominous."

"To eliminate Jerrianne as the target of the blackmail we may have to go to someplace . . . unsavory."

He feigned a high-pitched gasp.

"Be serious," she snapped. "I just don't want you to go assuming anything or reading too much into that. I know what I have to do, where I have to go. I'll direct you there and then I'll give you your instructions."

"Now it's my turn to say 'be serious.' "

"I am serious."

"Yeah, a serious pain in the butt." He turned the key and the engine purred to life. "Barking out orders, '*I* know what I have to do.' Like you're the only one involved. Not to mention trying to pull that that lame BS about wanting my help but not telling me why or what we're going to do."

"Did it ever occur to you that Wy and Jerrianne and even Reni have kept these things to themselves for a reason?"

"I'd say 'duh,' but you'd probably slap me, toss me out of my own car, and drive off to save the world on your own."

She'd have denied it but the idea held a certain appeal to her. Save the world. It had been her duty, at least to save her own personal world and to keep her friends and family and their secrets safe from outsiders, for all her life. Letting someone else in on her life's mission, especially the only man who had ever posed a threat to her maintaining her strict vigilance over that goal, was the hardest thing she'd ever done.

"Flynn, I know I seem overprotective, but these are not things my friends want anyone to know."

"I'm not just anyone."

No, he wasn't. This was someone her friends trusted despite Tess's inner struggles over him. "Still, I certainly don't feel that it's my place to go blabbing to you about Jerrianne's painfully private former life."

"Fine, then how about I tell *you*?" He gunned the motor. The convertible zipped back out of the parking space. Then Flynn made an illegal U-turn and headed straight for the Plantation Pines section of town.

"Just where do you think you're headed?"

"To the Lure."

She gasped. "You know?"

"That our sweet, innocent-looking Jerriane worked as a stripper her senior year in college?"

"Only the last semester of her senior year, to make enough money to graduate."

"I don't know how long she worked there or her motivation, Tess."

"But you saw her, didn't you?"

"I saw her." Town—what everyone called the downtown district—faded behind them as he wound down familiar, then less-familiar streets. "But I never caught her act, if that's what you mean."

"You saw the picture?"

"Picture? What picture?"

"I'll explain that later. First you tell me how you saw her but you didn't see her working at the Lure."

"It happened the night of graduation." The car tires thumped over four sets of railroad tracks.

Tess tensed up like a treed raccoon. She grappled with different ways of avoiding the topic of that certain night but like that animal up high in a Georgia pine, she knew her only option. She had to go out on a limb. "Keep talking."

"It just so happened I encountered her sitting in her car in the parking lot of the Lure, crying. I asked her what was wrong and she told me."

"I remember you said that night that you were

going to go there to squander your fortune on naked women."

"Well, I didn't."

"You just said you did go to the Lure."

"I went past the Lure. There's a difference."

"It's not exactly on the main thoroughfares, Flynn. Why would you go past it if you weren't determined to go to the place?"

"After I . . . left your room, I went driving. Drove all night, all around town."

"You promised me you wouldn't drive. You'd been drinking."

"One drink," he said. "Over an hour of hanging out in the Rebel Tavern, just to get my nerve up and to add a certain aura to my act."

"Act?"

"Tess, I . . . I don't know what to say about it now. It was so long ago and so much has happened since."

"You put on an act to get rid of me?" She put her hand to her forehead and rubbed her fingers over the dull ache building there.

Digging deep, she dredged up the memories of that night. If she had a truly twisted sense of humor, she'd have appreciated the irony of forcing herself to recall what she had spent so much time and heartache trying to purge from her mind.

"Tess? Are you all right?"

"Why, Flynn? Why would you put on an act? By

not contacting me that whole school year, by not calling me when you moved home, you'd already made it pretty clear that you didn't want me."

"But I did want you, Tess. I wanted you and far more frightening to me at that time, I cared about you."

She curled her fingers against her temple, half tempted to cover her ears, to silence the confession she could not bear to hear.

"That's why I had to do it," he said softly. "Why I had to make sure."

"Make sure of what?"

"That you hated me."

She managed a brittle laugh. "What's the saying? Be careful what you wish for—you might get it?"

"At the time I thought it was for your own good."

"You never were much good at thinking."

He chuckled. "Back then I wasn't much good at anything but making trouble. I didn't want to bring that on you, Tess. For once in my life, I found a person I didn't want to destroy with my bitterness and anger. And that's what would have happened if we'd have stayed together then, I know it."

They stopped at a red light and sat in silence.

When the signal turned green and the car rolled slowly forward, Tess had to ask, softly, "Then it wasn't because of the professor's wife?"

"What professor's wife?"

"Reni said you got kicked out of school because

of some incident concerning a professor's wife and two one-way tickets to South America."

"When did she say that?"

"That night, not long after you and I parted company."

"And you remembered it all these years later?"

"Trying to come to terms with what went wrong between us had a profound effect on the choices I made, choices that haunt me to this day, Flynn."

Even watching him in profile, she could see his jaw tighten. He kept his gaze fixed on the road.

"Between that 'act' that you put on to sour me on seeing you and that rumor, well, let's just say it didn't leave me in the most logical frame of mind."

"So, that was why—"

"I know how many people around here thought of the SuiteHearts as hell's belles and bitches to boot but we were not heartless and self-absorbed."

"I know that."

"The things we did, at least the three I know about, the things we have tried to live down and keep quiet about all this time, they were not whims or treachery. They came from somewhere, they had reasons behind them."

"I know that, Tess. I don't suppose I let myself believe that back then. I'd just done what I saw as my first and only noble act and all I could see was how my gallantry had turned on me. Guess I was pretty self-involved back then."

"Back then? You mean back when you still thought of my actions that night as the ultimate betrayal to you? Like, oh, way back as long ago as when we got the first note?"

The first orange and black sign pointing the way to The Lure loomed on their right, proclaiming "fun times ahead."

"Okay, you got me. But in my defense, I have to say, I have grown a lot since then."

"You've grown?"

"Yup."

"In the last couple weeks?"

"Uh-huh."

"From what?" She batted her eyes for heightened effect as she poured on her deep-fried, honey-dipped accent. "Just being around li'l ol' me?"

He gave her a glance, then gave her another that bordered on a leer that somehow managed to be too sexy and yet self-effacing. "It's true. You have helped me grow."

"Oh?"

"Oh, yeah. Being around you has inspired numerous personal growth spurts."

"That's it. We've crossed the line. This conversation is officially over."

"What? Why?"

"Call me old-fashioned, but it just sort of ruins the mood of a sincere heart-to-heart once veiled comic references to erections start popping up."

He laughed—a good, solid, wonderful laugh.

Tess joined him, amazed that sharing something so seemingly insignificant as laughing together could go so far toward repairing the hurt between them.

The wind ruffled through her hair as they sped on. Up ahead the Twilight Lanes came into sight. Later tonight she'd meet her dear friends there for a league game. She hoped she'd have some good news for Jerrianne by then and perhaps be able to move on to learn what Wy had concealed for so long. Her stomach knotted just wondering what that might prove to be.

She looked at Flynn. "So, you seem to know all these secrets—you don't happen to have some clue as to what Wylene might think she could be black-mailed for?"

"Not a clue."

"Damn. I'd hoped you could tell me it was something just as inane as Reni's and Jerri's. That would at least confirm my worst fears—that it's all my fault."

"Don't be so hard on yourself. I still believe you're reading too much into this whole note business. It's a prank or someone who has issues with you or your magazine trying to rattle your cage."

"Who? Who would want to do that and have access to any information regarding me and something as personal as the SuiteHearts?"

He shook his head.

They came up on another black and orange arrow-shaped sign announcing, THIS IS IT!

Tess shifted in her seat. "Of course, *you'd* heard the truth about Jerrianne, *you* had pretty substantial suspicions about Reni, and *you* knew beyond the shadow of a doubt what I would never want revealed from my college days."

"You intimating that I might have sent those notes?"

"I'm not *intimating* a damn thing. If I truly thought that, I'd come right out and say it to your face."

"I see." He pulled the car into the gravel parking lot and cut the engine.

"But don't think the possibility never crossed my mind."

His eyes fixed on hers with his lids lowered but that did not lessen the intensity of his searching gaze.

"You had the information, the access to the Suite-Hearts—our whereabouts and all—and the notes arrived not long after you came back to town."

"All true."

She let her lips curve into a telltale smile with delicious slowness. "However you are sorely lacking in the most essential area."

"Ouch, Tess! No man likes to hear that from a former girlfriend."

"Motive."

"Oh, right. Motive."

"You don't need the money." She held up her finger.

"True."

"You've already kept everything you know about us quiet for all these years."

"My lips were sealed."

"You don't have any reason to want to hurt anyone in the group—but me, of course."

"Tess . . ."

"You were even content to stay clear of me completely rather than make an issue of the past."

"For all the good that plan did us once the notes showed up."

"Uh-huh. Unless of course you've set up this phony situation to get on my good side, to play hero, and have me beholden to you." She laughed.

He didn't.

She gripped the door handle and told herself what she had told him when they'd first gotten in the car—don't read anything into this. Their lives had already been damaged enough with assumptions and misinformation, among their other problems. She refused to see his nonreaction to her joke as a threat. And whether she liked it or not, that in itself was another big step.

LIVE GIRLS! LIVE BAIT! Flynn eyed-up the boast painted two feet high on the cinderblock building. It had all been fun and games, but now the idea of Tess going into this place did not sit well with him. "Now what exactly are we planning to do here?"

"There's a picture."

"Ah, the picture." He remained unconvinced about the wisdom of her going in. "You really think that a fourteen-year old photo is big enough to blackmail someone for?"

"No, I don't. But Jerrianne does. It would kill her father to have this come out."

"He survived her having a baby out of wedlock, how much worse could this be?"

She bestowed the granddaddy of all steely-eyed looks on him.

"What?" he asked. "You implying he didn't?"

"Why do you think she still lives at home with a child of her own at age thirty-six? He keeps an eye on what she does and never lets her get too confident about her own judgment."

"I know he can be a little over the top."

"What'd you call him once? 'A few loaves and fishes shy of feeding the multitude?' "

"More like one ham and a blue-haired church lady short of a Sunday social." He put his hand on her shoulder. "He can let his enthusiasm rule over his common sense but he's a good man."

"Yes, he is."

"His problems with Jerrianne—is that a religious thing?"

"It's a daddy thing." Her face lit with a tender wistfulness Flynn had never seen in her before. "You know how southern fathers are about their little girls."

"I don't know how southern fathers are about anything, Tess."

Without saying a word about his fatherless upbringing, she expressed the most eloquent empathy simply by laying her hand on his cheek. After a moment, she sighed and shook her hair back. "Well, they usually don't think highly of men ogling their precious princess baby girls *au natural*, if you know what I mean."

"So Jerrianne's brief dancing career would crush Brother J on more than just the preacher level."

"Yes, and add to it that one of the reasons Jer did it was because her father couldn't afford to pay for her college education, and you see why she does not want this to get out."

He tried to imagine giving a rat's ass what your father might think, but he couldn't muster so much as a rat's eyelash. "I still don't think it's what's behind the notes."

"Neither do I."

"Even if it was, it'd be her word against a blackmailer's."

"You're forgetting the picture. When she worked here, Jerrianne earned an extra chunk of change to pose for a photo for them to put on the wall."

"Like a promotional poster?"

"No, more like those delicatessens you see in movies and TV that have celebrity photographs up." The fact that he did not know this about the place registered somewhere in the back of her mind. "They only did that with the really pretty girls who worked here. They call it the Prize Catch Showcase."

"Classy." He shook his head. "And she thinks it could still be there after fourteen years?"

"I have no doubt Jerrianne was one of the prettiest girls who ever worked at this place, Flynn. Don't be fooled by all the glamour of the live bait counter and fancy aquamarine cement façade. This place does not attract the supermodel set."

"You know me. I'm a sucker for a gilded lily." He winked. "But I'm still not convinced that picture would still be up here."

"Look at it this way: Do you recall back when I was in junior high, you were probably in high school already, two cast members from *Hee-Haw* got lost passing through town? They stopped into the Chat 'n' Chew Café?"

"Vaguely."

"Well, long story short, the menu they autographed that afternoon still hangs in a two-dollar frame behind the cash register. 'Nuff said?"

"Good old Mount Circe." He should have felt annoyed, irked, or at least a little smug that he was above such small-town triteness. Instead he felt . . .

contented. He turned toward the building before them, realizing that as sleazy as it got, Tess would be fine going in the place. This was Mount Circe, after all. "So how we going to get in there?"

"Hmm, this is just a wild concept but I thought maybe we'd use the door?"

"*Tess Redding* is going to waltz into Georgia's finest nude dancing club and bass fishing outlet? Under what pretext? Asking for a job?"

Her eyes flashed with mischief. She shimmied her shoulders. "You don't think they'd hire me?"

"Yeah, like I'm going to answer that question. You'd kick my ass to Atlanta and back no matter what I said."

"Well, a girl does need her exercise."

"Maybe you should get in there and shake your groove thing."

"You never quit, do you?"

He leaned across the car seat and touched under her chin. "You used to like that about me, Tess."

"Yeah, well, we're both a lot older now."

"But with age comes patience, experience, the ability to delay gratification—"

"Translations? The need to stop and nap halfway through?"

He traced his finger down her neck. "If you really want to find out . . ."

She jerked away. "What I really want is to get this over with."

"We still haven't come up with a cover story."

"How about this one—it's a summer morning in Georgia."

"Yeah."

"You and I have sought out this one place that we feel can fulfill our special but burning needs of the moment."

"I'm following you."

"Because we simply cannot wait. We have to have—"

"Go on."

"Bait."

"Huh?"

"Bait, you idiot. I know it probably isn't the kind of thing you have ever paid the least bit of attention to, but one of the few unique aspects about this nasty, rotting hole in the wall is that is does offer a full-line, always stocked bait shop."

He groaned. "The bait shop. And here I'd gotten my tub of worms for fishing with Max from Brother J."

"Well, you can make up for your lack of vision right now. You are going to go in there and cause just enough of a distraction for me to scan the wall of photos and grab Jerrianne's—she told me exactly where it should be if it's still up."

"And you really think it still might be."

"Someone came into the Fellowship for a hot meal a little over a year ago and recognized her from the photo he'd seen the night before. So yes, I still think it could be here. But not for long."

"Let's do it then—for Jerrianne."

"For the SuiteHearts."

"For Brother J and southern daddies everywhere."

"For crying out loud, let's go!"

The place smelled worse than she'd even imagined. Worse than a stagnant pond on a hot day. Worse than the back alley of the old Rebel Tavern on margarita night after the college kids had heaved up their weight in tequila and onion rings. Worse than the perfume counter at the Dreamland Discount Mart after the parochial schoolgirls stopped in to douse their uniforms and dab on as much sample makeup as they dared before heading to the public library. She pressed the back of her hand over her nose and mouth. The place smelled, she decided, like a horrific collision of all three.

She stood just inside the door, taking shallow breaths while her eyes adjusted to the serious lack of light. Flynn seemed oblivious to the stench and the darkness. He sauntered off into the big open room on their left. She squinted after him, amazed by the reddish-orange shag carpet, black stage, and light-lined catwalk jutting into clusters of plastic tables and chairs. He did not seem to notice those either, but fixed on the task of finding someone to distract.

Busy work, she told herself. She had not really needed his help to accomplish this minor act of petty thievery. But at least she could keep an eye on him this way—or an ear, she thought, listening to him banging into the chairs in the main room.

"Hey! Anyone here?" Flynn called.

"Be-yout theyur in a minute," a man's ragged voice replied. "Dancers don't start uhp fer 'nother 'our yet, though."

Tess shook her head. She had no idea such things went on virtually round the clock, and here in tiny Mount Circe, too. *That* certainly never made the pages of her magazine.

She started down the hallway to her right. Jerri-anne's direction would take her straight to the show-case wall not too far off the main room.

"That's okay." Flynn kept it just below a holler, obviously trying to keep her apprised of his—and more importantly the other man's—whereabouts.

Primed to act, she turned the corner again and there it was. The Prize Catch Showcase. Tess had never seen so many naked women in one place and one time in her life. From the chair rail to the ceiling the entire length of the hallway was lined with their photographs, their bare breasts proudly thrust almost menacingly outward. She took a step and swore that like eyes in certain paintings, the things seemed to follow her no matter which way she moved.

"Bait 'n' stuff like 'at's in the back." The man running the place sounded like he had a throat full of sandpaper and a mouth full of marbles. "If you want a drank you'll have to hang onna bit, I'm fixin' to set up them heating lamps for the buffet."

"Buffet?" Tess found herself mouthing it the exact time Flynn said it out loud.

"Yessir, we got us a happy 'our buffet. Noon to four."

"You mean nekkid women aren't enough to bring the guys in? You got to serve food too?"

Tess didn't know whether to smile or be worried that she and Flynn had such similar sentiments about the matter. Trying not to gawk too much at the often Dolly Partonesque proportions in the pictures, she began to count just as Jerrianne had instructed her—third row up, ten or twelve over from the left.

"Well, them fellas gotta eat, too," the man said above a clatter of metal that Tess recognized from her own line of work as the trays in a buffet table. "It ain't no big deal er fancy fixin's anyway. Fried cheese, 'tata skins, chicken wings, that kind of a thing. All you can eat with the cover fee and purchase of a lap dance."

"And no one complains?"

"Complains? 'Bout what?"

"You mean to tell me no one has ever come in here for the buffet and ended up saying to one of the dancers, 'Hey, don't be shaking that over my hot wings'?"

Tess bit her lip to keep a sudden outburst of laughter from giving away her presence.

"No one ever said nuthin' to me, that's all I know."

"What about health regulations? You know, no shoes, no shirts, no service. Come to think of it, it doesn't say a word about no *pants*, no service, does it?"

"Reckon not."

"But, jeez, man, even a lunch lady has to wear a hair net."

That did it. Maybe it was the image of naked lunch ladies in hairnets or the way Flynn was taking this fellow for a ride, but she just couldn't help it. She let out a short, sharp laugh that she simply could not contain.

"What wuz 'at?"

"Maybe one of your dancers came in early?"

Tess held her breath and bit her lip. Time had just run out. She had to get what she came for and get out. She scanned the area she was supposed to search a second time and then a third. She wondered if it was possible to get breast blindness, inhibiting her ability to single out the one photo she needed.

"Who's out theyur? Who's in that hall?"

The gravelly voice was headed toward her. She glanced over her shoulder at the door and thought of giving up and running. She gave one more furtive sweep of the wall—and there it was. *Geralyn Monroe*, the signature read. The brilliantly clever Suite-Heart/Sweethearts switcheroo should have clued Tess in that Jerrianne Munroe would have selected for herself such an impenetrable alias.

"Hey, where are you going, man?" Flynn sounded closer too, and she envisioned him putting his very body between her and the kind of man who ran a place like the Lure. "You never even found out what I wanted here."

She grabbed the photo off the wall.

"Okay. Fine," the stranger grumbled, no longer seeming to be walking in her direction. "What d'you want?"

"I was going to get some bait, but man, hearing about that buffet thing—now I've lost my appetite."

"Huh?"

If Flynn yanked the poor man's chain again, she did not stick around to hear. In a flash she had the photo tucked up under her shirt and had hit the door. The summer air hit her like the first blast of heat from an open oven. She plowed on.

She had just hunkered down on the floorboard of Flynn's car, staying out of sight if the man came to check things out, when the driver's side door opened.

"Let's get out of here." Flynn slid behind the wheel.

"Drive, man!" She gave him the thumbs-up.

He tore out of the lot in a cloud of gravel dust and a gale of her exhilarated laughter.

She didn't get a chance to climb back into the seat proper and fasten her safety belt until they rolled to the stoplight by the Twilight Lanes. Exhaling slowly, she settled back and shut her eyes.

"You did it, Tess."

She looked at him through her lowered lashes.

He beamed at her like he sincerely took pride in her reckless, ridiculous achievement.

No one had given her that kind of encouragement and approval since long before her mother got sick. No one had offered to help her without expectation of personal gain in almost as long. "Flynn?"

"Yeah?"

"Thank you."

"For what? You did the work."

"But I couldn't have done it without you."

"Honestly?"

"Well, maybe I *could* have." She reached out and gave his arm a squeeze. "But I am more grateful than you will ever know that I didn't have to."

14

Two things stayed with Flynn: Tess's gratitude for his help and her joke suggesting he had taken advantage of the situation so that she would be beholden to him. One humbled and thrilled him, the other made him want to slink off like the mangy, odious dog he was.

Not that he could slink anywhere carrying this flimsy cardboard tray filled with four sodas, a soft pretzel, and two orders of nachos. Melted orange cheese glistening with oil globbed over the thick yellow chips. It oozed toward the edges of the tray.

"Hey, Flynn, whatcha eatin'?"

"It's not for me, Jobie. I'm playing flunky to the terrors of lane eight tonight." He clunked the food and drinks down on the table on the landing nearest the Sweethearts ' seats. "They asked me to fill their order and get a table so they can run up and sneak a few bites between frames."

"So you're working tonight." His odd, eternally young expression lit with what Flynn could only describe as shared pride.

"Yeah, I guess you could say that. The ladies keep me hopping, that's for sure." He wiped a blob of cheese from between his thumb and forefingers with an almost translucently thin paper napkin.

"They paying you?"

Flynn reigned in a warm-hearted chuckle and narrowed his eyes over the group of women who had come to mean so much to him these past weeks. Well, three of the women. For the second time in the short history of their minileague participation, Wy had begged off coming. Now Flynn understood and even shared Tess's concerns over that situation. Maybe he ought to go over and have a talk with Joe Brent. See what he could find out about it. But tonight, he had the remaining Sweethearts, as their retro-style bowling shirts dubbed them, to cater to.

Reni, who had just picked up a tricky spare, pumped her fist in the air, bellowed like a drunken redneck, and yet still managed to undulate her hips provocatively. Jerrianne dropped a kiss on her son's head while they both laughed at the antics. On her feet in a New York minute, Tess embraced her oldest friend, then spun easily on the slick floor to pick Flynn out of the clutter of noise and color behind her. She gave him a genuine, spontaneous smile that would stay with him long after this misadventure had faded from their collective memories.

"Don't you worry about me, Jobie." He gave Tess a double thumbs-up, a grin, and a wink. "I'm getting rewarded ten times over for my efforts."

"Folks always pay me when I work for them. They pay me good. Real good, most of 'em." The sweet old guy nodded his head as he spoke. Up and down over and over. "Thems that don't, well, Mama says what goes around comes around."

"That right?" Flynn found his own head bobbing as he spoke.

"So I figures sometime somebody gonna do them wrong too." Jobie's head went still for a moment. His watery eyes grew somber. He stuffed one hand inside the front of his filthy old jeans.

Flynn wondered if the poor fellow might be fixing to start up his own version of the pledge of allegiance.

Instead he looked Flynn square in the eyes and said, "I don't take no pride in saying that, though."

"I know you don't, Jobie." He slapped the older man on the back, lightly but with his hand cupped to give it a good resounding *whomp*. "You're a good man."

"You are too." Jobie walloped him on the back

hard enough to nearly knock the wind out of his sails, then grinned big as a Cheshire cat with brown, crooked teeth.

Flynn sputtered out a cough. "So what brings you here tonight? You bowling?"

"Naw, I don't bowl. The fella who used to own this place, he used to let me put up the bumpers when they needed them for bumper bowling." He made a strange jerking gesture that Flynn could only assume mimicked the movement of putting up the bumpers.

"That right?" Flynn pulled out a chair and settled in.

"For a fact." Jobie leaned down close, his eyes bulging. "I was hoping if I hung around here sometimes they'd let me do it again."

"They might just do that."

"They used to pay me a dollar plus a foot-long wiener with cheese and a large soda from the fountain." Jobie pulled up straight and turned toward the snack bar like a needle finding true north.

Flynn contemplated the glistening hot dogs rotating on a metal rack behind dingy glass. "Oh, yeah. Well, hard to resist that, huh?"

"I didn't do it for the money and food, though."

A one lane over, the Sweethearts had just entered the eighth frame and still held the lead.

"I did it 'cause my mama says a man got to work to feel good about himself."

Flynn shook his head and uttered words he never

imagined he'd speak. "Pretty smart observation on your mother's part."

"You didn't used to work. Just lived off your folks' money, and you was an awful mess."

"I was indeed." He patted the small, grubby elf of a man on the back, gently this time, very gently. "Would you like me to have a word with the manager here about your doing the bumper work sometimes?"

Jobie patted Flynn's back in return. "I can polish the bowling balls, too."

"I won't neglect to mention that." He smiled.

Jobie glanced around like a stray dog looking for his next scrap. He seemed especially keen on the activity at the main desk.

If Flynn hoped to ask him anything he had to do it fast. "Say, Jobie, have you heard or seen anything more of the fellow who had you bring those envelopes out to Miss Tess and Miss Reni and all?"

"No sir."

"I don't suppose you could tell me something about that person, something you remember? Anything at all might provide a great help to me."

"Is there trouble? Mama warned me never to be a party to no trouble."

"Of course not. No, I understand." He understood he wouldn't get any information tonight. The distractions of the place weren't exactly conducive to probing questions anyway. "But can you do me one small favor?"

"I always like to do a favor, all right. I'm good at doing favors. And running errands. I'm the best at running errands in the whole town. Did you want me to run ya an errand?"

"Maybe later," Flynn said, making a mental note to look for opportunities for Jobie to work that would be positive and not demeaning. "Right now all I want is to ask you, if you should run into, see around, or even just hear about whoever had you take those envelopes to the ladies, would you let me know?"

"That sounds more like a job than a favor." The man's bristly white eyebrows came down over his cloudy eyes. He looked around.

"Yes, you're right." He stood and pulled his wallet from his pocket.

Rifling through the bills, he knocked loose the business card he'd taken from Tess's office with the information about her meeting with his father on it. Flynn's stomach clenched. The last thing he wanted was for Tess to see that and start asking questions— or worse, jumping to conclusions—before he talked things out with her.

With astounding spryness, Jobie bent down and scooped up the incriminating slip of evidence and gave it back to Flynn.

"You're a shrewd businessman, Jobie. A job it is." He shoved the card back in quickly, thinking he'd move it from in front of his driver's license later. Then he placed a stack of one-dollar bills in the old, gnarled hand. Jobie James didn't know squat about twenties or tens or even fives, but ones were his area of expertise. "Here's advance pay for keeping your ears and eyes open, and give this"—he handed the man a five—"to the man behind the counter and he'll fix you up with a great big soda and a foot-long."

"With cheese?"

"With cheese."

"Hey, what's the holdup?" Tess pulled at the bowling glove on her right hand as she walked up. "We're dying for some relief out there. Kicking bowling butt is thirsty business."

"You'll be kicked out of the alley on your own butt if you try to take this stuff out there. Snack-bar food stays in the snack-bar area." He gestured like a flight attendant giving safety instructions.

"I gotta go now." Jobie had already stuffed the money someplace out of sight. "They got a new person working at the cash register. I gotta go see that he does things right."

"Okay, you do that. And don't forget your new job."

"I won't forget." He lumbered off.

"What job did you have for old Jobie?"

"I just paid him to . . ." He saw the energy and excitement in her face—why put a damper on this night by reminding her about the notes? "Hey, aren't you up?"

She twisted around to see the flashing pointer on the overhead score screen. "Oh, that *is* me. I'll be back as soon as I'm done. That should give you enough time to think up a darn fine answer to my question."

"I shall do my best." He gave her a salute, then added, "And send the girls over to grab a bite between frames."

She hurried off, stopping to say something to Jerrianne, who in turn spoke to Reni before Tess took up her ball and started her concentration ritual.

Flynn was aware of the blonde and brunette ambling up to him but his real attention stayed on Tess. He couldn't help it. He liked watching her move, watching her take so seriously a game he doubted she'd ever played until her pals roped her into it. He liked that in this place, as in many places where her friends gathered and where he had been alone with her, she was not the phony woman of *Simply Southern* magazine. She was Tess. *His* Tess.

He'd have thought more about that possessive turn in his attitude but Jerrianne plunked down in the chair across from his and Reni right beside him. He didn't pay them much heed, either. His eyes stayed on Tess, waiting . . . watching.

Then she did it. She did that totally unnecessary step in her approach where she stopped, bent at the waist just enough to stick out her great, grabbable ass, then lifted the ball. She rubbed it slowly with her free hand, poked her tongue out—just the tip—then gave her hips a shake. If the routine had another step as she moved to release the ball, Flynn could honestly say he'd never seen it. By that stage he no longer had enough blood circulating in his brain for higher functions like visual input or even blinking.

"I don't think I ever got the chance to thank you proper for all you did in getting that awful photo of me back."

"And in getting me squared away with the college."

"I was happy to do whatever I could."

"I can imagine you were happy plum out of your gourd to spend some time in the Lure." Reni poured the southernism on thick making Flynn wonder if she did it to get in a jab at Jerrianne. "But to tote a statue head to the administration building in the middle of the night? That dog won't hunt, Garvey. You did that for some other reason."

If anyone could see through his self-serving motives, Reni could. And if anyone would understand them, and more to the point, tell him how to come clean with Tess about them, this was the very woman who could.

"I had my motives. But the longer I've been around Tess and the deeper I've gotten involved . . ."

"I thought so." She cut him off with a look that dripped self-satisfaction as she began fishing something out of her pocket.

Flynn narrowed his eyes. "You thought what?"

"That your reasons would have something to do with being around Tess *longer* and *deeper*." She pulled something blue and square from her pocket—though how she got anything in or back out of the tight-fitting pants again was beyond him. "That's why I went to the trouble of procuring these for you in the powder room."

"Good gosh-a-mighty, Margery Irene, have you taken leave of your senses?" He snagged the two packages of condoms she'd spilled out across the table and made quick work of putting them in his wallet. "Oh, look who I'm asking? Like you ever had a lick of sense to begin with."

"Better safe than sorry, that's what I always say." Reni snatched up her soda, grabbed a nacho chip, and, disregarding bowling alley rules, began to take her snack back to the bowler's area, where Tess had just left a five-nine spare. "Now if you'll excuse me, I have some balls to polish."

"Reni, you are awful." Jerrianne dropped a napkin to the floor and pressed on it with the toe of her shoe. It didn't go far toward sopping up the telltale trail of liquid cheese her friend left in her wake. "Don't listen to her, Flynn. No one really thinks you are helping us as a means of getting through to Tess."

He rolled a paper-covered straw between his fingers. "Yeah, well . . ."

"If I ever doubted your motives were anything

put pure and sincere, all I'd have to do is look at what you've done with Max."

Max. Just hearing the kid's name made his heart heavy. "Wish I could tell you I'd made big progress in granting his wish, Jerrianne."

"If you can't do it, I'm sure he'll understand." Her face practically glowed with love for her child. "We both know you're trying, and if there is anything I can do to—"

He put his hand on her arm. He hadn't intended to get into this now with Jerrianne, but she'd brought it up and it needed to be addressed. "There is."

"What?" She blinked in confusion.

"There is something you can do. It won't be easy, or pleasant, but if you do it, I swear you will be taking the first step toward making Max's wish come true."

"It's really important, then?"

"Jerrianne, if you don't do this, I am convinced that absolutely nothing I accomplish will help Max realize the one thing he wants most in his young life."

He had her attention now. She took in a deep breath.

Out of the corner of his eye he saw Tess approach. The last thing he wanted, with Jerrianne on the very brink of listening, of doing the right thing for herself and her child, was Queen Tessa barging in to start her rescue routine. If Jer didn't do this now, she might remain under Brother J's roof and subject to his benevolent authority for the rest of her life.

He stuck his hand out under the table to stop Tess from barging in and leaned forward, commanding Jerrianne to keep her eyes only on him.

"What do I have to do, Flynn?"

"You have got to tell your father about your past, all of it."

"No I don't. We got the picture so he never has to know."

"Screw the picture. This isn't about the picture. This is about you finding the strength to stand up for yourself and to take responsibility for life, even the mistakes."

He heard Tess murmur but did not acknowledge her.

"You have got to stand up to Brother J like the mother of a terrific child and a woman who is ready, willing, and able to chart her own course in life."

"I can't." Her hand went to her throat. She scooted her chair back until it banged into the empty seat behind her. "I could never let my father know what I've done. He'd never forgive me."

"I believe he would. But as long as you feel that way, you're depriving him of the chance to prove to you what a really good man, what a *damned good father,* he can be. And you're holding yourself hostage to the past, and to anyone who might want to use it against you."

Her cheeks flushed. She pressed her lips together and shook her head.

"Jerrianne, the only power anyone ever has over you is the power you give them. Take back your power. Don't surrender the rest of your life to trying to make your father love you. He either does or he doesn't."

He could not believe he had spoken those words, or what's more, that finally he had begun to truly understand them. He hung his head and pinched the bridge of his nose between his thumb and forefinger. But hiding his face did not disguise the anguish he felt as he finished in a raw whisper, "And your father loves you. If you give him the chance, I know he will show you how much."

Tess walked up quiet as a cat and put her hand on her friend's back.

He braced himself for a scolding over the harshness of his words or for Tess to rush in to volunteer to fix this mess on Jer's behalf.

"Listen to Flynn, sugar." Tess crouched down and looked Jerrianne in the eyes. "He's right."

"He is?"

"I am?" he asked as softly as Jer had. Then he cleared his throat and crossed his arms. "That is, I know I'm right, but I didn't think you'd see that, Tess."

"Actually, I've thought it for a long time." She gave him a fleeting smile. "You have to stand up to your daddy, Jerrianne. It might get ugly and awkward, but he'll get past it, and you'll all be better off afterward."

"It's the wound we don't flush clean, the piece of glass under the skin, the sliver we can't find that festers. It stays tender and makes us weak. Left untended long enough, it can eat us alive."

Tess studied his face, her eyes wide. "Speaking from personal experience?"

"I'm quoting a pretty decent guy." How often had he thought of that night and those words, but they had never held as much meaning as they did now. His eyes met Tess's as he reached out to lay his hand on Jerrianne's. "Brother J told me that the night y'all graduated from Lassiter."

Tess put her hand to her throat and closed her fingers as if fondling an unseen necklace.

Flynn remembered that necklace and his voice went gruff with emotion as he added, "It's taken me a long time to see the truth in those words myself."

"That's so . . ." Tears welled up in Jerrianne's huge eyes. She curled one finger in her pale ponytail and bit her lip.

"You're up, Jerrianne." Reni waved to them with all the subtlety of . . . well, of Reni. "Tess! Flynn! Drag your lazy butts back over here—we're winning!"

"Promise me you'll consider what I've told you." Flynn stood.

"I will."

"You bet she will." Tess gave her pal a hug, then a delicate shove in the right direction. "Now go bowl a strike so we can wrap this baby up with a win, okay?"

"Okay."

Flynn took Tess's arm so they could hang back a few steps as he whispered to her, "You've come a long way from 'silence and denial are the best problem-solving tools.' "

"Hey, I'm one of those 'do as I say, not as I do' teachers."

"Last week I would have had a smart-ass comeback about you being a phony, but now . . . I know you're anything but a phony."

"Thanks, Flynn. That means a lot, coming from you." She punched him lightly in the arm but before she could pull her fist away, his hand enveloped it and he pulled her to his chest.

When their bodies collided, what had started as playfulness took on new significance. Her breasts swayed against him. Their legs slid into a perfect fit, her thigh between both of his. She lifted her chin, her lips parted. That moment made a mockery of what he'd just said about no one having power over you unless you gave it to them. Tess had power over him and he had to set things right with her.

"I liked what you said about not letting a small thing fester until it becomes unmanageable."

"I only repeated some good advice."

"It's some advice I wish I had a long time ago."

"I did have it a long time ago, but it didn't do me much good until I was ready to take it to heart."

"Have you done that now?"

He nodded. "Can you forgive me for the way I hurt you?"

"Yes, if you can forgive me for—"

"Shh." He touched his finger to her lips. "I don't have a damn thing to forgive you for, Tess. I see that now."

"I hurt you, Flynn."

"I brought that hurt on myself, and on you."

She started to say something but he cut her off.

"You don't have to come to my rescue on this, Tess." He pulled her closer to him and laid his open hand along her face, his thumb stroking her full, sensuous lips. "For once, let someone else take the sole responsibility for something, okay?"

Her bright eyes shimmered with tears. She put her hands on his chest and let out a long shuddering breath. "Okay."

"I know that wasn't an easy thing for you to do."

"To forgive you?"

"To surrender being Queen Tessa, even just a little bit." He kissed her temple. "*And* to forgive me. I was a pretty big jerk for an awfully long time."

"You are not that same man, Flynn. I know that. I know you'd never do anything to hurt me, to make me feel used or keep anything from me."

Flynn's conscience grabbed him by the throat. He

glanced away to get a quick fix on things, to make sure he kept things clear and straightforward. But when he looked in her eyes again that all dissolved. He put his forehead to hers. "Tess, I—"

"Hey, Flynn! Miss Tess! Why ain't you eatin'?"

They jumped apart so fast that Flynn knocked over the chair beside them. "Did you need something, Jobie?"

Tess smoothed back her hair and acted absorbed in the activity on the lanes before them.

"You know how you said to tell you if I heard about them what asked me to take them notes to the ladies?"

"What? What are you talking about?"

Flynn gripped Tess's arm but stayed focused on Jobie. "Did you see them? Did they ask you to deliver another message?"

"No, but I heard them. That's still good if I tell you that I heard them, ain't it?"

"Yes, that's still very good. Where did you hear them? What did they say?"

"While I was helping out at that new cashier, he took a phone call. He asked me if I knew who was Miss Tess and her Sweethearts and I said yes, I did."

"Someone asked about me, about the Sweethearts, by name?"

"Sure enough, Miss Tess. Then he said did I know when you'd be done bowling and would I tell the person on the phone."

Flynn moved close to the excited old fellow, hoping to pick up every nuance and bit of information. "And what did you tell them?"

"That they was about done bowling."

"And?"

"And then he asked me, did I know if Miss Tess went straight home after?"

Fear sparked in Tess's beautiful eyes for only a moment before it transformed to gritty determination. She jerked her chin up. "What did you tell them, Jobie?"

"I told them I didn't know."

"Good," Flynn muttered.

"But then I said she gotta go home sometime, though—it's her house. And they said 'good point' and thanked me. I did good, huh?"

Flynn shut his eyes. "You did fine, Jobie. Thanks."

"I'm gonna get me that footlong now."

"Go on, you've earned it. We're going to watch Miss Jerrianne bring home the win for her team." He put his hand on Tess's back to direct her toward the lane where her friends waited.

Her spine went rigid as steel under his hand. She did not move.

"Don't let this worry you, Tess."

"Worry? Why should I worry? Jobie's going to get a hot dog, Jerri's going to win the game, and I'm going to have to watch my every step when I go home tonight because I have no idea what's waiting out there for me."

"No reason to get worked up."

"Weren't you listening? The person who sent those notes is trying to track down my whereabouts and you say there's no reason to get worked up?"

"It's not going to solve anything." He turned to take her face in his hands. "We can call the police but they aren't going to be able to do anything just because someone asked about you at a bowling alley."

"I know. You're right. Truth is, I strongly suspect whoever this is is just trying to figure out where to send the note making the money demands. I'm sure they checked around last time before they sent notes, too."

"Makes sense."

"In some ways, I feel relieved to think we may have one more piece of the puzzle soon."

"And once each of you has cleared up her youthful indiscretions *and* we get a note with actual extortion demands in it, we *can* go to the police. I know I'll feel a lot better then."

"I wish I could say the same." She placed her thumbnail between her teeth and stared off into space.

"Don't worry, Tess. It's going to be all right."

"You can't promise that."

"No, but I can promise that no harm will come to you tonight."

"How could you possibly make a reckless guarantee like that? I live pretty far out in the country. It's isolated and I'm alone."

"Not tonight."

"Oh, don't you even think about coming out to spend the night at my house, Flynn Garvey." She said it like a shotgun-totin' mama protecting her young virgin girl child.

He laughed. "I have no intention of going out there."

"You don't?" In the blink of an eye her expression became all petulant-belle pout.

"Like you said, it's too far out, too isolated. And it's exactly where Jobie told the person on the phone he would find you."

"Well, Jerrianne and Brother J don't really have the room, but I guess I could stay with Reni . . ."

"If that's what you honestly think this is going to go down, then you've got another think coming, girl."

"Oh no, Flynn." She stepped backward, with her hand outstretched. "I am not going through all this mess to head off any potential scandal while I'm working on this potentially huge business deal just to have it all blown out of the water when some gossip learns I spent the night at your house."

"No one will find out. And if they do, what of it? It's hardly the kind of thing people think twice about, much less something that would interfere with your business deal."

Beyond them, Jerrianne bowled a strike in her third and final time up in the tenth frame.

"All the same. With emotions running so high between us tonight, I don't think—"

Flynn caught Tess by the wrist and pulled her to him again.

The Sweethearts and Max leapt up and cheered.

"That's the right idea, Tess, don't think. It's already been decided for you anyway." Their gazes locked and their bodies nearly entwined. "You're spending the night at my house tonight."

Tess opened her mouth.

"And I won't hear any argument about it," he said just seconds before he kissed her, sweetly enough to keep from seeming a total jerk, but hard enough to back up his declaration.

15

Flynn took the long way home. The winding back roads took them up into the mountains just enough so they could see the small town of Mount Circe spilled out below them. Yet it gave them the sense of being alone in the world with no one but God and each other. Why he did that, he did not care to speculate. He was a man prone to act first and reflect on things after. Sometimes that proved the most interesting way to go through life.

"Mind if I pull to the side and look over the old town for a minute or two?"

"I suppose it's safe enough."

"You admitting you feel safe with me?"

"Nope. Just thinking that even if someone would come barreling around that curve yonder, they couldn't miss seeing this magnificent . . ." She opened the car door and ran her hand with tantalizing slowness along the edge of the window. "Throbbing, red . . ."

"Tess, are you flirting with me?"

"Adolescent symbol for surging manhood." She shut the door with a solid *clunk*.

If she thought she'd delivered the same kind of slam to his ego, she really had not been paying attention these last few weeks. "Awww, and I didn't think you'd noticed."

"What?" She looked at him over his shoulder.

"That I had the kind of . . . surging manhood that could stop traffic."

"I wouldn't be so all-fired proud of that in a place where more than one car sports an I BRAKE FOR ROADKILL bumper sticker."

Somewhere there was a smart-ass reply about comparing his goods with a stiffened-up wild animal, but before he could form one she shrugged her shoulders and continued.

"Actually, it was just my way of saying how interesting I find it, you having the same kind of car you had when you lived here before."

"Nothing funny about it." Obviously, she wanted small talk. He could deal with that. After that kiss and the implied threat of the phone call, he understood the need to put some normalcy in her evening and some distance between the two of them. "When I made up my mind to come back here, I traded in my boring old black sedan for this flashy number."

"Why?"

He came up beside where she stood and leaned against the car fender. Looking out at what he could see of the town, he folded his arms and smiled. "Guess I just couldn't see myself tooling around Mount Circe in anything but a red convertible."

"Like the old days."

"Yeah. Like the good old days."

She nailed him with quick but sure look. "I didn't say 'good.'"

He had to touch her but did not dare risk scaring her off. He shoved his hands in his pants pockets instead. "Were they really all that bad, Tess?"

She did not answer for a long time. They stood there, both under the same sky, looking down over the same scene, but he had to wonder if she saw something he did not.

Most of the town lay in darkness except the cluster of lights out at the dairy and through Plantation Pines, where the Lure and the Twilight Lanes and a couple of all-night gas-and-go places kept things brightened up. The old-fashioned streetlights staggered down along Main Street glowed dim compared to the rectangle of brightness around Lassiter College. It all looked so right to him, so peaceful. The nearest thing to home he'd ever known.

She sighed. "No, not that bad at all."

"But you still cannot fathom why I would want to come back to a town named after the Greek goddess who turned men into pigs?" He took her hand. "Like that was a very big leap, huh?"

She gave him a sly sidelong look. "She wasn't a goddess, she was an enchantress."

"Ah." He curled her hand against his chest.

"And she changed men into swine until she found one that her magic had no power over."

"And he changed her."

"She fell in love with him, and turned the beasts back to men again."

"And women have been trying to perform the same trick every since."

"You said it, not me."

"Still, the idea of a town that had the power to change people—how can you not be charmed by that?"

She stared out over the lights and pressed her lips closed.

"You want to escape this place that much?"

"I want to escape, that's true enough." She did not smile, or frown. She neither seemed saddened nor elated at the prospect of making her getaway.

Still, Flynn felt the depth of emotion stirring beneath that calm surface. "From what, Tess? What do you want to escape from?"

"I would tell you, Flynn." She faced him. "But I don't think you could understand unless you knew more about my family, how I grew up, what was expected of me, what I expect from myself—"

"And what you're afraid of."

It was one of those surreal moments when, if this had been a movie, they'd have heard crickets chirping to show the vastness of the silence between them. And crickets were chirping.

Tess twisted her hands together. She crossed and uncrossed her arms, then finally stepped away from him, her head down and her voice barely audible. "You have no idea what I'm afraid of, Flynn."

"Oh, I think I do—"

"Just because we've reached a kind of understanding about our past, don't make the mistake of thinking you know me."

"But I do know you, Tess." He took her by the shoulders. "I know the woman who has worked her tail off to accomplish her goals and in doing so never stepped on anyone to do it. The woman who struggled instead to lift everyone else up the ladder with her as she climbed."

She turned her face toward the town. "With all its flaws, this has been my home for a long time. I feel responsible for leaving it a better place."

"It is a better place. Not that place you sell in your magazine, the fantasy you want to take to the national market, but a better place for you having given so much to the town you love."

"I never said I loved this town."

"But you do. I can see it in the way you deal with people, give back to people, in the way you care about what happens here."

"Those are observations. They still don't mean you know me."

"I know the woman who is smart and funny and honest and has more balls than most of the men I've ever met, more balls than they even have in the whole of the Twilight Lanes."

That got a laugh. A small one—but sincere—so he appreciated it all the more.

"I know the woman who is scared to death she's going to end up like her mother, alone, dependent, and pitied by the whole town, if they knew the truth of her existence."

Tess gasped. "How did . . ."

"Look, growing up, I heard the gossip about your mother being . . . disabled."

"That's the kind version."

"Yeah, well, let's not get into a tug of war over the cruelty of small town gossip, between the two of us, we'd be here until long past daybreak and never solve a damn thing."

She looked away. "I can't believe I'm this transparent."

He rubbed his hand up her arm and went on. "If it makes you feel any better, human nature is my business. Trying to think how someone else thinks, to see what choices they might make so I can get one step ahead of them, that's a part of what I do."

"I never considered that."

"Yeah, well, it's no big stretch to understand the choices you're making. You have to make everything seem outwardly perfect no matter how big a mess it is underneath."

"So I like things pleasant and tidy."

"You have to maintain total control over everything within your grasp and a few things that exceed it."

"I'm task-oriented, so shoot me."

"And someone so much as cracks an innocent joke about going crazy and you throw up a barricade that could keep out an army and ten tanks."

"You can see that?" She put her hand to her mouth. "You can see how much I'm afraid of ending up like her?"

"It's not a crime not to want to repeat a loved one's mistakes."

"Mistakes?" She dropped her hand and pulled her shoulders up. "She was *ill*. That wasn't her choice. She couldn't help it—"

"No, she couldn't, but she could have sought help for it. And your father certainly did not have to manipulate your entire family into covering up what was happening. I understand she suffered greatly, and I won't downplay her pain and your family's, but there might have been better ways to deal with it."

"What are you saying?"

"I think you know."

"I think we'd better go now."

"Are you mad at me?"

"For speaking your mind? Gosh-a-mighty, if I was to get ticked off every time you did that—"

"We'd pretty much have the exact same level of give and take we have now." He gave her a kiss on the cheek, purely preemptive against her slapping him silly for virtually calling her a liar. Then, as he hurried off to his side of the car, he called, "I just want you to think about what I said, okay?"

"And I just want to go home and go to bed."

"Gotta love a woman who knows what she wants."

"Alone," she must have felt compelled to add.

"Ah, Tess, hon." He revved up the engine of his symbolic surging manhood and laughed. "I don't think you really know what you want yet. But when you do decide, I know everybody better get out of your way."

All Tess wanted ever since she could remember was to feel safe, that she alone wasn't responsible for the fate and happiness of the world, and that she had control of her life and choices. She had wanted to please her daddy, meet the expectations of all the right people, raise her sister free of the obligations that burdened Tess, and make her mama well. Those objectives weren't compatible.

She could not have them all, and so much had suffered that she never fully realized any of her goals. She had never fully felt the things she dreamt of and she had let her family down. Anita Lynn's purely selfish actions had proven that time and time again. Daddy had died a young man and Mama had never, ever gotten the help she so desperately needed.

She huddled alone in an enormous canopied bed. The closed-up old house smelled of dust. The T-shirt Flynn had picked out for her skimmed her bare breasts and fell to her thighs. The air conditioner, a window unit that roared and sputtered like a vintage crop duster's airplane engine, whooshed frigid air into the high-ceilinged room. Now, somewhere out there someone might just want to hurt her. Tonight she had none of the things she had always craved and she was helpless to do anything about it.

She hugged her knees to her chest beneath the soft, pale sheet and eyed the locked door. Flynn had insisted she lock it. It had not been her idea. He wanted to protect her from potential intruders. He did not tell her how to protect herself from the intrusive thoughts that had her wide awake an hour after they'd said their good nights.

He had asked for her forgiveness and refused to allow her to take the blame for what had happened between them. That they had come to this momentous conclusion in a bowling alley did not lessen its significance. They had made a breakthrough tonight and now . . .

Now she was in Flynn's bed. She had on Flynn's

T-shirt. She could smell his hair on the pillow and feel his presence in every object on the chest of drawers and nightstand. She touched his alarm clock, the black gooseneck lamp, and his leather wallet. Though he was asleep on the couch in his office downstairs, he was also here with her, all around.

She took a deep breath, slowly dragged her fingertips over the smooth surface of the wallet he carried every day in his pocket. It would be wrong to take a peek inside. Very wrong.

A flutter worked its way from the pit of her stomach to high in the back of her throat. No matter how much she yearned to know more about him, to know *everything* about him, she couldn't stoop to becoming a snoop. Could she?

"Tess?" A gentle tap came at the door. "You asleep?"

"No." She pulled the hand that had touched the wallet under the sheets. "I was just . . . um . . . did you need something?"

"I couldn't sleep so I thought I'd come up and get a book to read."

"Oh." She reached out to flick on the bedside lamp.

"If you don't mind letting me in for a minute . . ." His voice trailed off.

Letting him in? She shivered to imagine the possibilities. Of course, for those she'd need more than a minute, much, much more. If she had had a robe she would have slipped one on, but she didn't, or rather Flynn didn't, so she had to go unlock the door as she was. She padded over the expensive hand-loomed rug and called out, "Sure. No problem. Come on in."

The brass lock resisted.

"Get a good grip then give it a little jiggle to get it going."

"Hey, I am not going to let you in here if you're going to talk dirty like that," she teased. Instantly, she felt torn between wishing she'd kept her mouth shut and telling herself that the best defense against her anxieties about letting Flynn in the room was humor, as usual.

The bolt went gliding back with a solid click.

The old hinges creaked out a wary welcome as the door swung inward.

Flynn stood in the opening, one arm braced straight against the frame at shoulder level as if he thought she might suddenly dart out and he'd have to contain her. She guessed he had no idea that he could stop her in her tracks with just a look. If he said the right words, she'd fall into his arms and never let go. Well, *never* being a relative term for not turning him loose until they were both so spent from satisfying their lust that the Mount Circe fire department would have to be called in with the jaws of life to pry them apart. That kind of never.

The yellowed glow from the lamp brought out the golden highlights in his brown hair. It looked thicker, somehow, or if not thicker, spikier. As if he'd done that running-his-hand-through-it thing over and over again while hot and sweaty.

Tess toyed with the neckline of her borrowed shirt. "Don't you want to come in and get your book?"

"Sure, I . . . uh . . . just let me . . . just let me savor this for a minute."

"Savor?" She dipped her chin and let her hair fall over one eye and shifted her weight to one hip, then the other. Lands, if she had been any more coquettish she'd have made herself sick. Still, she wet her lips and cooed, "Savor what?"

"The cool air. The AC isn't working downstairs and I'm suffering with it." He stepped across the threshold. His white T-shirt clung to every muscle on his back and upper arms. "It's hotter than blazes tonight."

"Yeah, I know what you mean." She fanned her face and exhaled in a long stream through pursed lips. "So you say you have no air conditioning at all downstairs?"

"Yeah, and opening up the windows doesn't do much good, nor do I think it's particularly wise given I'm trying to protect you from a potential stalker."

"That's ridiculous. You can't put up with that. You have to sleep up here." She thought it. She said it. She wished she had thought about it a second time before she'd said it but there it was, out there.

She wasn't going to be ungracious enough to take it back.

"Thanks but no thanks. I'll be fine. I wouldn't have even come up here except—"

"Except you wanted to get a book." She folded her arms. Apparently she wasn't the only one who spoke without wasting a lot of valuable brain cells double-checking what was about to come out of her mouth. "What an extremely plausible excuse—if you disregard the fact that there are no books in this room."

"There aren't?" He whipped his head around but he didn't fool her. He knew he would find nary a tattered paperback in here.

"Not a one that I can see. Meanwhile, back where you had bunked down . . ."

"In the library," he filled in, his smile growing.

"Ah, I see you're following my line of reasoning."

"You're the one who told me once that nothing between us involved reason."

"Truer words . . ." She let her voice trail off, sighed, then set her shoulders rigid. "Nonetheless, it is reasonable that you stay here tonight. With this house all closed up and no air, you'll burn alive down there."

"I am far more worried about the kind of burning I'd do up here, Tess." He swept the back of his hand along the sleeve of her shirt, his fingers grazing the edge of her breast.

She gasped in nothing but sheer delight at his touch.

"No, it's one thing to acknowledge the sexual tension between us, but my staying up here tonight is like standing a little too close to the fire."

She pinched the fabric over his taut abdomen and peeled it away from the damp skin there. "You'd do better to stand too close to the shower."

He shut his eyes. "That sounds like a slice of heaven about now."

"Then do it," she whispered.

"The only clean bathroom with a shower stall is right through there." He pointed to the door at the end of the room.

"Go." She gave him a little push. "Take a shower. You'll feel much better."

"You sure?"

"What? You afraid I might go wild, crawl in there with you, jump your bones?"

"Wouldn't lower my temperature, but it would go a long way toward eliminating the insomnia I seem to have developed since our paths crossed again."

"You too, huh?"

He tipped his head and gave a half-smile.

"It's a totally impossible situation, of course," she whispered.

"Of course."

"We both have these feelings, these longings, we've admitted that much. But as two mature, right-thinking adults, we know nothing will be gained by giving into them."

"Absolutely nothing."

She had never noticed before, but the way his lips moved when he said that looked like a kiss waiting to happen. She mouthed the words herself.

He traced his fingertip along her temple, her jaw, then downward, to her neck.

She could not keep her eyes open. It had been a long time since she'd been with any man and it had been too long, far too long, since she had been with Flynn. Every fiber of her being vibrated in sync with his touch.

"Absolutely nothing gained," she murmured again.

The old needs still lingered, but her new realities must prevail. She was still going to try to take her business to Atlanta. She had to. The business was her security, and as precious as the moment of forgiveness had been between herself and Flynn, it promised nothing for the future.

"You'd better go take that shower." She put her hand up. "Make it a cool one."

He stepped backward and chuckled. "Don't worry about that."

The bathroom light came on and almost immediately the door shut to blot it out. What a perfect metaphor for their nonexistent sexual relationship.

The water came on. Shower curtain rings scraped over the metal bar twice.

Having Flynn so close soothed her in ways she had not anticipated and unnerved her in the familiar ways she had come to expect. Now, in his bedroom, in his clothes with him only a few feet away, hot and wet and naked . . .

She flattened her palm against the bathroom door. She shut her eyes. The scent of soap and shampoo filled her nostrils. She held her breath.

It was one thing to acknowledge their desire for one another, but to act on it?

The water splashed in the next room. Flynn mumbled something. It didn't matter what. His deep voice resonated in the tiled walls and penetrated Tess's being. Then she asked herself another question. Perhaps they stood to gain nothing if they gave into their desire, but what did they stand to lose?

Tess was no longer some silly schoolgirl with notions of forever loves and passionate romances that culminated in something borrowed and something blue. She was a grown woman with real needs and the means to have those needs met with no strings, no expectations. And after they parted ways—no regrets.

They say it's not the things you do but the things you left undone that you regret. Her own words, spoken to Flynn himself, came back to her. She bit her lip.

All her life she had wanted to feel safe, like she alone wasn't responsible for the fate and happiness of the world and in control of her life and choices. Flynn's nearness definitely made her feel safe. From the first time he had spoken to her, even before she knew who he was, until tonight, when he had taken the responsibility for the pain between them, he had showed his willingness to shoulder some of her burden. If she wanted the last thing, to be in control of her life and choices, that too was within her grasp. She had only to take it. She had to seize control of this situation. Now or never.

The water cut off.

She took a step backward.

She could hear the shower curtain whisk open and the ruffling of a towel over Flynn's naked body.

She swallowed hard, steeled her resolve, then hurried back to the bed, stripping off her T-shirt as she went.

The door opened.

If she didn't act fast, she'd lose her nerve.

Flynn, dressed only in sweatpants that hung low on his hips, stepped barefoot into the room. He rubbed a big white towel briskly over his head as he said, "I, uh, hung my shirt up in there to dry out. I don't think I'll need it downstairs tonight."

"I don't think you'll need it upstairs tonight, either."

"Tess, I've thought it over, and it's really not a good . . . Oh . . ." He let the towel drape over his neck. Even in the dim light she could see the hint of his sinful smile. "I know the perfect hostess does whatever is necessary to put her guests at ease, sugar, but if you're going topless just so I won't feel self-conscious . . ."

"Come here."

He walked toward her, slowly, not tentatively but with an air of restraint and caution. "Tess, do you really think this is a good idea?"

She threw the sheets back to reveal her naked body.

"I'll take that as a yes."

It had been so many years since he'd seen her this way. Then she had been young and perfect and untouched by time or cynicism . . . or by any other man. It took every ounce of courage and determination to let him look at her like this. Yet, she could think of no other man she could be so open with, so vulnerable. She trusted Flynn.

He rewarded her trust with a look so endearing yet so intense, so reverent, and so hungry that her heart soared.

He moved to the edge of the bed. "Tess, you know that if we do this, things won't ever be the same between us . . ."

"Shut up and take off your pants."

He lowered his head.

She saw his chest move or she would not have known he was laughing.

"You really are a control queen, girl, you know

that?" His hand went to the cord in the waistband of his sweatpants.

"You got a problem with that?" She put her hand over his, ready to finish the job for him if he hesitated.

"Not tonight I don't." He held his hands up.

"Good." She gave the cord a yank.

That the baggy pants did not fall smoothly down gave testament to the effect she'd had on him.

She ran her fingers along the inside of his waistband.

He must have liked the contact, as his skin drew into gooseflesh and he sucked in his breath.

She smiled, placed a kiss on the bare skin just above the bulge in the clinging fabric, then pulled his pants free to reveal the man in all his glory. "Oh, Flynn . . ."

"If you're having second thoughts, speak now or forever hold your peace, because darlin', once I climb between those sheets I don't know how I'll hold myself back."

"Don't hold back, Flynn. Don't hold anything back." She lay on the pillows before him, offering herself like the very first time.

He moved over her, and bracing his arms to keep his weight off her, kissed her on the neck, on the jaw, then on the lips.

She felt aware of every inch of him. Of the hair on his body chafing against her smooth skin, of his muscles tensed and hard-pressed to her soft flesh.

He took her breast in his hand then pulled his mouth off hers and trailed his kisses downward.

When his tongue played havoc with her straining nipple, she cried out.

"You like that?" He kissed the valley between her breasts.

"I do, but Flynn?" She took his face in her hands. "Maybe . . . maybe when we've done this a couple dozen times and I've worked out fifteen years' worth of missing having you inside me, then we can concentrate on the foreplay. Right now I need you in me . . . now!"

"A couple dozen times? Hon, I only have two condoms."

She writhed beneath him. "Now!"

"Yes, ma'am." He reached out for the wallet on the nightstand and deftly pulled out one packet.

She tried to help him.

"I can be responsible for this part." He pushed her hands away.

"But I can do it."

"Yeah, I know you can do it all, but not this time. I'm afraid if you touch me now, if you unroll this baby over me, I'll go off like a rocket and we won't need it anymore."

She smiled to think she still could do it to him.

And when he did it to her, her smile grew tenfold.

Tess had never gone hungry, or been parched by real thirst. She had never wanted desperately for any physical necessity. Yet the moment Flynn eased his

body over hers and moved inside her, she knew
what it must be to feel those things and finally find
satisfaction.

She could never have known that if they had not
first found forgiveness and now . . .

Now. Now. Now. It echoed in her mind, resounding through her body, building, harder, faster, harder
still. Now was all that mattered.

Flynn was with her now.

He groaned and called out her name. Then again
and again.

"Yes," she hissed, through teeth clenched tight as
her entire body. She peaked in tune with only Flynn
and the present, with what they were sharing now. If
it was all they had, it would still be so much more
than she had hoped for . . . though, for the first time
in nearly forever, making love with the man whom
she had loved a lifetime gave her cause to hope for
more.

16

"Well, you were right about one thing."

Flynn rolled over to the sound of Tess's voice and winced as sunlight came streaming into his eyes. He moaned. "What's that?"

"We did sleep well last night." She placed a kiss high on his cheek.

"Yeah." He chuckled and pulled her nude body close to his, murmuring against her neck, "So well we didn't even get a chance to use that second condom."

"Oooh, second condom!" She practically squealed like a kid in a candy store, then lunged across him to reach for his wallet.

"I just want you to know I don't usually carry those things around at the ready." Flynn scrubbed both hands over his face, trying to wake up enough to enjoy what was about to happen. "Reni foisted them off on me last night. Of course I'm glad she did it now, but—"

"What is *this*?" Her soft voice wavered.

Flynn froze. He lowered his hands but he did not have to do that to know what she had discovered in his wallet. A cold heaviness filled the pit of his stomach. He should have told her before they'd made love. "Tess—"

"Why do you have this?" She flipped the card over once, then again.

"That's *my* sliver left to fester," he said quietly. "My piece of glass buried under the skin."

"I don't understand." Her lips were pale and her eyes troubled. She thrust the card out toward him. "Why have you written down the date and time of my appointment with P. Pearcy McLaughlin?"

"I wanted to come clean with you about that earlier tonight. I tried to in the bowling alley, but I kept getting interrupted."

"Come clean?" She dropped the business card on top of the covers. Clutching the sheet to her chest, she sat up. "I don't like the sound of that."

"It's nothing awful, at least not in the big picture. But I do feel like I owe it to you to let you know that your scheduled appointment with McLaughlin is the real reason I first insinuated myself into this business with the notes."

She pushed her fingers back through her hair.

"This sounds like the kind of conversation best carried out fully clothed, over coffee in the kitchen."

"No!" He reached for her. "I've been a long time coming to this. I'm ready to talk about it now and I'll be damned if I'll give myself time to backtrack."

She brushed her fingers over the new growth of whiskers along his clenched jaw.

He kicked at the covers with one foot to get them from between their bodies then stretched his legs out alongside hers. He drew her close until she filled the circle of his arms.

"So?" She flicked her nails through the hair on his chest. "What's this about my business deal being why you horned in on the blackmail mess?"

He caught her wrist to stop her. He needed all his faculties to do this story justice and he found her touch far too much of a distraction. "Maybe you don't realize this, but when you first got those notes—up until last night and that phone call, really—I didn't take this extortion and fear of scandal business very seriously."

"No newsflash there."

"At first I only wormed my way in on your problem so I could stay close to you and get on your good side."

"If last night is any indication," she said quietly, "it worked."

He lifted his head trying to get a read on her expression, but he couldn't pinpoint what he saw there. Disappointment? Resignation? Peace? He folded her into a deeper embrace and sighed. "The important thing, Tess, the thing that I want to make sure you understand beyond all reasonable doubt is that all that has changed now. I've changed in these last weeks."

"I know, Flynn." She pushed up onto her elbow and looked into his eyes and smiled. "I would not be in bed with you now if I didn't know that."

"Really?"

She rolled over, sprawling half over him, with her hair an enticing tangle of gold falling over her eyes and down her graceful neck. "Well, I am thirty-six and single and obviously in desperate need of a great big dose of hot monkey love, but even I have some standards."

He ran his thumb along the shell of her ear. "Do tell."

"I could never be with a man I don't respect or who I don't think respects me."

"I do respect you. My respect for you keeps growing all the time." He sounded like a lovesick pup but he didn't care. It came straight from his heart and she deserved to hear it. "I respect you as a friend, as a smart businesswoman, and as a truly decent human being."

"A decent human being," she echoed softly.

"Coming from a man who does not think there is an overabundance of those in the world, that's a real compliment."

"I believe you."

Tess Redding believed him. He tried to comprehend the implications of it but couldn't.

"What's more, I believe *in* you, Flynn." She spread her open hand over his chest, above his heart. "I believe in the man you've become and the man I think you will always be. You've turned your life around. You've done so much good for kids like Max."

"Before I accept any medals for that, Tess, you ought to know that McLaughlin is the driving force behind all those good and charitable acts on behalf of those kids."

"McLaughlin?"

"In fact, he's the reason behind most of my decisions, including trying to piss off everyone in town, getting thrown out of colleges, trying to live fast and die before I was twenty-five. He's the reason I have used my trust fund to pursue men who turn their back on their parental responsibilities."

"What are you saying?"

"What I did for those kids, by and large, I did to get back at the man who had rejected and ignored me all my life—my father."

"Flynn . . ."

"The space on my birth certificate may say 'father unknown,' but my mother was pressured to write that in order to secure my future financial security." He held no bitterness toward his mother. He hoped that came across in the gentle tone of his voice. "The one concession allowed in that agreement was that, as long as I did not go by it, I could have the legal name Phillip McLaughlin Garvey."

She mouthed the name silently.

"Phillip Pearcy McLaughlin is my father."

She sat up. "He's your . . . ?"

"Father." The term felt hard and odd on his lips. Saying it evoked in him a cascade of emotions like no other single word could.

Father. All his life it had been synonymous with distance, selfishness, cruelty, and even hatred. But today, having felt the approval of Brother J and the empathy for little Max, today the word *father* no longer held only bitterness for Flynn.

"I had no idea," Tess whispered.

"No one does. Can you imagine that? *I'm* really the one with Mount Circe's best-kept secret?"

"I'm stunned." She pulled the sheet over to cover her body and the business card he'd cast aside slid onto her legs. She reached out and plucked it up. "But what effect does that have on my appointment with him?"

"None, really. I just . . ." He clenched one hand into a fist. He hated to confess his plan to her and hated more that he wasn't sure why. Was he more ashamed of his early willingness to manipulate and use her or more afraid that once she knew what he wanted she would have the power to take it away from him?

He forced his hand to relax, took the card from

her, then looked her straight in the eye. "I had hoped you would let me go to that meeting with you."

"Why would *you* want to go to my business meeting?" The bedsprings groaned as she moved away from him. "It has nothing to do with you. It's about my magazine, my hopes and dreams for it and about my future."

"Yes, I know. But I had my own agenda then. I wanted to see my father and he refused to see me."

"Refused?"

"Would not talk to me on the phone, had the sheriff escort me off the grounds the day I showed up at his office and decided to wait for him to come out. He will not see or speak to me. He has closed and locked all doors between us. Your meeting with him was my way in."

"No." Her head barely shook, her mouth hardly moved. "My meeting with him was *my way out*. If you hadn't told me about this relationship . . ."

"But I have told you."

"That was not your original plan."

"No."

"You would have weaseled your way into that meeting at my side." She began to inch backward, to the side of the bed, the sheet clasped in both her hands. "And in doing so, knowingly dashed my chances of achieving everything I've been working so hard to accomplish."

"Yeah, when this all started out I would have, yes. But now . . ." He didn't finish because he didn't

know what to say. He wasn't the same man that had
first hatched this scheme. Just moments ago she'd
said she understood how much he'd changed. And
yet, seeing her reaction, exposing his innermost lifelong pain to her only to have her worry how it might
affect her precious sham rag of a magazine, well, it
made him wonder if the Tess he had grown to
admire wasn't just as big a phony.

"Now what?" she demanded.

"Tess, my whole life has led me toward that
point. Finally, to look that bastard in the eyes and
say . . ." Both of his hands curled into fists. He bat-
tled back the stinging threat of tears. He turned his
back on her and buried his head in his hands. "Well,
I don't know what I'd say, but is it so hard to understand that a man might want, just once in his life, to
look into the face of his own father?"

"At what cost to me, Flynn?"

"*What* cost to you?" He raised his head but did
not look at her. He could not. "You aren't in danger
of losing the magazine, are you?"

"No. But without McLaughlin's backing I won't
be able to take it to national distribution, perhaps
even to a monthly format."

"Oh, I see." He turned his neck to peer at her over
his shoulder, his hands folded over the sheet pooled
in his lap. "My getting a once-in-a-lifetime shot at
confronting my father might just throw a little saw-
dust in that well-oiled fantasy machine of yours, is
that it?"

"Don't try to paint me as the villain in this, Flynn. You are the one willing to risk everything I've worked for all my life for a few seconds of revenge before we both got our butts hauled off by the cops."

"*Was* willing," he corrected.

"You would have *used* me. Just like everybody else in my life, you didn't do anything for me or with me that was just because I mattered to you." Her voice cracked. When she went on it came out as a hushed accusation. "It was all for yourself and what I could get you or do for you."

"The instant I told you all this, Tess, that no longer became an option, though, did it? It no longer became a secret agenda. It became—" He cut himself off. His chest rose and fell in heavy, labored breathing. He glared at her across the bed they had shared in passion and in absolute trusting sleep last night.

"Say it," she said, her mouth tight and her eyes narrowed.

"It became your choice, Tess." He put his back to her. "I never expected you to invite me to that meeting knowing what you now know. And understanding how it would have hurt you, I never would have gone, even at your insistence."

Her silence cut him to the core.

"But that you never gave my feelings in this the least consideration, that first and foremost you thought about that damned magazine . . ." He raked his curved finger slowly over his scalp. "Well, I guess that says it all, doesn't it?"

The bedsprings creaked. The mattress shifted as her weight moved off of it. The covers rustled. Then in one fluid jerk, the corner of fabric was whisked from his lap.

He sat there naked and alone as Tess stormed into the bathroom cloaked in her shabby pride and the rumpled bedsheet.

The second time in his life he'd done the right thing for the right reason. He'd been honest and set his own motives and desires aside for another's sake, and what did he get? The same thing it had before and from the same woman—a kick in the gut and a mind-numbing dose of reality. If this was the reward for caring about someone, Flynn figured he'd take a pass on the whole experience.

Idiot! Idiot! Idiot! If she could have pounded her head against the bathroom door without Flynn thinking she'd gone stark raving mad, she'd have done that very thing. Tess stumbled to the old claw-foot bathtub and perched on the edge.

The one man alive whose very existence posed a threat to everything she had worked and sacrificed and built toward for so many years. The only man who had already taken advantage of her love once, who had used her before and who she had let into her heart and bed for the chance to do it again.

How could she have been that naïve, that trusting . . . that out of control? Okay, they had reached a kind of understanding about the past. He had shown her she could count on him. And it had been a long, long time since she had been with any man. But none of those were acceptable excuses for rushing into that level of intimacy that quickly.

It was the kind of thing Reni would do, for Pete's sake, or Jerrianne. Or maybe even . . . *Wylene*. The very name pulled Tess's proud tirade up short.

Tess *had* acted this rashly before. And she'd been burned by that experience as well.

"Stupid, stupid . . ." How could she think he wanted her without any strings attached? When had anyone ever wanted her for anything but what they could get from her?

Flynn was no different. He said he only started out using her to get to his father but . . .

His father.

Shit. How could she have it within her reach to give the only man she'd ever truly loved the thing he had wanted all his life? The thing that nearly drove him to destruction in his youth and motivated his every action even now—to see his father? How could she deny him that?

By the simple act of telling her, of baring his soul to her, he had made it almost impossible for her to say no, no matter what he claimed was his intent. This was one secret he should have kept to himself.

She hung her head and rocked her upper body. "Stupid, stupid."

She clenched her teeth until her jaw ached and thought of every name in the book to call herself, to call Flynn. But mostly herself. She was the one who was supposed to have been in control. This was, as everything she felt pressing down on her so hard she could scarcely breathe, her own fault.

She wanted to cry. She wanted to scream. She wanted . . .

The *wham* of the outer bedroom door slamming resonated through her bones and flesh and into the small, dark center of her lonely being.

She just wanted someone to hold her.

17

"Tess?" Jerrianne's voice rang hollow in the long hallway leading to Flynn's master bedroom.

As soon as she'd pulled herself together, she'd called her assistant to come pick her up at Flynn's. Then she'd promptly gone off on another crying jag.

Tess scurried back to the bathroom, tucking her bowling shirt into her pants as she went. She'd thought of borrowing another of Flynn's shirts, or even wearing the one she'd had on before bed, but under the circumstances it did not sit well with her. She'd have to settle for trying to cover up the effects of last night's high and this morning's all-time low with a splash of cold water and a quick comb through her hair.

Make herself presentable. That was the goal. She

turned on the water. Then she'd get her ducks in a row. She cupped both hands under the cold stream gushing from the faucet. She had a plan. She inhaled sharply as the water hit her skin. She would get into her office, make some calls, and get everyone working, and then . . .

She raised her face to check the result in the mirror. "No."

"Tess? You in the bathroom? I'll just wait out here."

"No. No." She put her hand to her cheek and gazed in disbelief at the woman she saw in the mirror. Dark circles under pain-dulled eyes. Features pinched with determination and anxiety. The face of a woman pursuing a goal she did not really want and was not in the best interests of anyone she cared about. A woman making her most important life choices based on fear.

"Mama," she whispered.

She could have sought help for it. And your father certainly did not have to manipulate your entire family into covering up what was happening. I understand she suffered greatly, and I won't downplay her pain and your family's, but there might have been better ways to deal with it.

By refusing to ask for help, whether with the blackmail or the business, Tess had become the one thing she had fought all her life to avoid: her mother.

Like her mother. Not crazy, not depressed, not sick, not weak, not confused or any of the things people had said about Mama but like her mother just the same. A wave of anger welled up in her chest.

"How could you let this happen?" she murmured, then raised her eyes. "Daddy, how could you have sacrificed me and Mama and even Anita for the sake of keeping up appearances in *Mount Circe, Georgia*? How?"

She seized the bar of Ivory by the sink and pressed it to the cold, smooth surface. She slashed the soap across the mirror leaving pale streaks that blurred her reflection, but did not obscure her image or the truth she knew she could no longer avoid.

In driving ahead to make the deal with McLaughlin she was not moving forward, but backward, with her life. Back to the time when she did what was expected no matter how much it took from her or hurt others.

How often had Flynn spoken of washing clean the wounds so they could heal? That was his lesson to learn in life, she had thought. But seeing her mother's eyes in her own weary expressionless face, Tess knew different.

She saw in that moment the likeness of the walking wounded that she had become. Falling in step behind every woman who had ever sacrificed her worth, her dignity, her very life to be a "good girl," to put on a brave face, to get over it and get on with things, to hide the truth and never let her real emotions show.

She was still doing what Daddy had trained her well to do. She was not her own woman, she was the

young girl who wanted to win Flynn Garvey's heart
so desperately that she never gave him the chance to
really know her, to really love her. She was the sister
so determined to make a life for Anita Lynn that she
took away the young girl's chance to make a life for
herself. She was the friend who so deeply feared
being discovered for a fraud that she turned a blind
eye to Wylene's needs in the guise of protecting her.
She was Daddy's little girl, Mama's little helper.
She was the picture on a magazine cover, the business woman who understood that perception is
everything . . . and the tiny child who knew it was
nothing at all.

As Flynn's secret longing to face his father had
been his hidden hurt, this was hers. Until she got it
out of her system, she could never be whole, much
less move on. But how could she do that? Unlike
Flynn, she could not even hope to look her father in
the eye in this lifetime and ask him why, tell him
how unfair he'd been, and find a way to repair the
damage done between them. She had to work with
what she had here and now. She had to find a way in
her own heart to resolve her anger and begin again
as the woman she knew she truly could be.

Outside the door she could hear Jerrianne stirring
around in Flynn's bedroom.

What Flynn said was true. There was another
way to get what she wanted with the magazine,
from her life. There was a way to deal with the
threat of blackmail against her without endangering

Wylene's privacy and perhaps the very quality of her life. There had to be. If there wasn't she might as well send a big fat check to her greedy sister, hand the running of the magazine over to that piss-poor excuse for a human being who had let his own son down for so long, and lock herself away in her secluded farmhouse.

That was never going to happen. She was Queen Tess, damn it. She would not *let* that happen. She would find another way to do it all.

The possibilities filled her with a sense of power and energy she had not known in years. She dried her face on the towel as she walked to the bedroom.

"Reni and I looked over the whole of the Heritage House first thing this morning." Jerrianne had tossed her purse on the bed and stood with a pad and pencil, waiting for Tess to begin barking out orders, no doubt. "We didn't find a note or any evidence of anyone lurking around."

"You didn't have to do that." Tess grabbed her hairbrush from inside her bowling bag and began going after the tangles in her hair. The bristles snagged just once and she stopped to think of Flynn's fingers catching in her hair as they made love, of his body over hers.

They had gone so far last night toward mending the rift between them, toward maybe building something together. And now . . .

"Flynn came by to pick up Max to see if they could get any use out of the metal detector he bought for him. He said he'd gone out to your house and didn't find a note or anything there, either."

"He did?" And now, maybe they actually stood a chance of doing just that, if she could resolve the last lingering issues of her past and find a new way to approach the future. "Did he say anything else?"

"No. But I wasn't in a listening mood. We got a request from McLaughlin—another set of documents he wants you to bring when you come for the presentation. I was up to my neck in those. In fact, we should go back and dive back into that right away."

McLaughlin. She rubbed her fingertips over her forehead and squeezed her eyes shut. "Never mind that, Jerrianne. In fact, let's stop all work on the deal with McLaughlin right now. Oh, but don't tell him we've done it and don't cancel the appointment."

"What? Tess, are you—"

"Crazy?" She looked up and grinned. She felt so light she thought she could fly. Really, she had no reason on earth for this surge of optimism, but she couldn't help it. "If anything was crazy it was the idea of going into a partnership with that ruthless loser. There has got to be a better way to take the magazine to the next level, Jer."

"Are you kidding? There are probably a dozen ways, but they might mean you giving up some . . . you know . . . control."

"All the better, then." She went to her old friend and put her arm around her shoulders. "You have been so much help to me, Jerrianne. You've gone over and above the call of duty, supported me, and worked like a dog even when *I* was the one being a bitch."

"Don't be so hard on yourself, hon."

"No, I was. I admit it. One hundred–proof, aged-in-the-barrel, southern-stubborn bitch."

"No, you were only eighty-proof stubborn bitch." Jer slid her hand around Tess's waist. "The rest was a mix of sweet tea—"

"Aw."

"And the devil's own rotgut corn-liquor orneri-ness."

"You have been spending way too much time around Reni, girl." She pinched her friend's arm. "Unfortunately, that can't be helped right away because we need to call her and Wy and have a little reunion over by the old dorm."

"What are we going to do?"

"Remember that box we buried in the southwest corner?"

"It was in the northeast corner, but yes, I know what you mean."

"We are going to go dig it up."

"We're not supposed to do that for another six years."

"I have a feeling we might not all still be friends in six years. We need to do it now." She couldn't undo what had happened so long ago, but she could go back and face it, if for no one but herself.

"Tess, this doesn't sound like you."

"Actually, for the first time in a long time, it does sound like me." She pushed the hairbrush into the bag, zipped it up, then seized the handle.

"How will we find the box?" Jerrianne grabbed up her purse and tucked the pen and pad inside. "You think it's one place, I think it's another."

"Don't worry." Tess headed out the bedroom door without looking back. Her looking-back days were officially over and she had never felt so strong or sure in her entire life. "We'll find the box, even if we have to get a little help from our friends to do it."

"Try over there, Max." Jerrianne directed her son, with his brand-spanking-new metal detector compliments of "Uncle" Flynn, toward an empty flowerbed. The low electronic hum of the gadget faded into the background but never quite disappeared.

Flynn pitched the bent spoon from Max's first sweep around the lawn, into a nearby trashcan.

Wylene shaded her eyes with her hand and shifted her weight like a person who wanted to be ready to get out of there fast if the need arose. "Tell me again why we're doing this now instead of when we had agreed we would?"

Slapping his hands together to get some of the dirt off them, Flynn walked back to where Wy, Reni and Tess stood. "Hey, had I known y'all had a box with information about your college days buried in your old dorm lawn, we'd have been out here with shovels a hell of a lot sooner than this."

"Like that li'l bit of junk has anything to do with those 'I know what you did in college' notes." Reni rolled her eyes and somehow managed to make even that simple gesture a big production and occasion to shake her ass.

Flynn clenched his teeth. Like it wasn't bad enough, him being here at all, he had to put up with that attitude.

"You are getting on my very *last* nerve, Reni, so kindly knock it off before I knock you out." Tess jerked her thumb over her shoulder like an umpire threatening to toss a player off the field.

Leave it to Tess to take charge and take no prisoners. Intellectually, he figured he ought to resent her pulling her Queen Tessa act, but in his heart he just couldn't hold it against her. It didn't help matters any that she had come to him not less than an hour ago and asked him for the one thing he thought she never would—his help.

And he, fool that he was, could not tell her no. She'd probably counted on that fact when she showed up, so he tried not to put too much stock in her *asking* him to come here instead of telling him.

"Besides, being here isn't about the blackmail notes. I don't give a hoot about the blackmail notes anymore anyway."

"You don't?" Wy twisted a strand of her dried-out hair around one finger.

She doesn't? Flynn thought. That was news.

"Y'all were probably totally right in thinking they were nothing, someone yanking my chain. And it worked. But I hope they got their jollies, because I'm past that now."

Flynn studied her. From the relaxed confidence of her stance to the clarity in her eyes, she seemed to mean every word of it. He wanted to ask how she had reached this point, wanted to hope . . . but he was still a bit too tender from this morning's let-down to risk it. This gathering, this moment, was about this mysterious box, not about the ways they had failed each other.

Max's metal detector blipped once, weakly.

All their heads turned in the boy's direction. Silence.

"You know it is possible that someone found your box in the last fourteen years." Flynn had to say what he knew the women each thought but would not voice themselves. "It's possible it's not here at all."

"It's here," Tess said, her eyes narrowed as she scanned the grounds. "If not physically, then here." She tapped one finger over her heart. "And here." She extended her hand into the circle of her friends. "I don't have to unearth some object to accomplish what I came for today. I just have to go inside myself and hope my dearest friends in all the world can do the same, and after it's all done . . ."

"We'll still be friends." Reni grasped Tess's outstretched hand. "I believe that with all my heart. That's the prediction I made on my scroll."

Tess curled her fingers around Reni's hand.

"That's why I came home to you all when my world crumbled. I came home to the people I knew would love me without conditions, without questions, and without taking any of my bullshit." Dark eyes gentled by a wash of tears, Reni looked one by one to the other women. "The thing I put in our memory box was a small, framed photo of the four of us."

"Oh, Reni." Jerrianne put her pale blond head next to Reni's dark hair in a sideways sort of hug. Then she placed her hand on those of her two friends. "My prediction was that we would each be good, strong, self-sufficient women. And I believe that has come true."

They murmured their agreement.

"I told my daddy about working one semester as a . . ." Jerrianne glanced to make sure Max could not hear, then lowered her head and whispered, "stripper at the Lure."

"Shit." Wylene clapped her hand over her mouth, her eyes shifted. When she lowered her hand, a mask of composure as old as belles themselves graced her face. "That is, oh, my! I never imagined that you'd ever ... that you had pursued ... that you ..."

Flynn could hardly stand to watch her wallow like that. But what else could he do?

Wy waved one hand in the air in the universal sign of someone choking—on her own politeness— exhaled in a sputter, the clamped her hands on her hips. "No, no. I can't do it. I was right the first time—shit, girl, what were you thinking?"

Jerrianne was the first to laugh. That was as it should be, but the moment she let loose, they all joined in.

Damn, but Flynn did like these women. And he was proud of them. He would not have brought that up right now. They'd have turned on him and reminded him, rightly so, that they did not need his approval or pride. This was a closed circle, and the half of the human race that peed standing up need not apply for entrance.

"So how'd your daddy take the news?" Tess asked, the laughter still lingering in the curve of her lips, the light in her beautiful eyes.

"He was not happy, but he's working on getting past it." Jer raised her head and her gaze met Flynn's. "I never would have done it without Flynn's urging. And the next thing I'm going to do is find a way to move into my own home."

A house of my own for my mom and me. Flynn smiled to himself. He'd done it. Not the way he'd quite expected, not by using the tools of anger and revenge against his indifferent father, but by encouraging someone to trust the deep, abiding love of a good, decent daddy. He'd helped to make Max's wish come true.

He looked out at the boy who was moving with precision in small increments toward the southeast corner of the old dorm. He couldn't help but feel a little pride in what he'd done and in the kid who had helped him look at fathers and sons in a whole new light.

"The thing I put in the box was one of my dad's fishing lures." Jerrianne shook her head. "At the time I thought it represented independent choices. Now I think I was really just trying to bury my guilt instead of dealing with the real source of it."

"I know how that is," Tess whispered. She raised her somber eyes to Flynn's.

"I put my room key in." Wylene looked left, then right, then at the ground. When she looked up again, she moved in to complete the knot of hands at the center of the circle of friends. "Promise you won't laugh, now."

"No."

"We won't."

"Never," they each assured her.

They drew her in close and put their heads together. The summer sun glanced off their hair. For an instant, they seemed to have stepped back to a time when anything was still possible. Somehow, Flynn thought, anything *was* still possible for them, with their friendship intact and their willingness to help one another.

They raised their heads. Someone sniffled. Another woman laughed. Seeing them like this, Flynn felt at once excluded and yet privy to something almost sacred.

"Go on, Wy," Jerrianne urged. "Tell us what you put in the memory box."

"I put in my room key as a symbol of closing the door to the past and entering a new phase of my life." Wylene bit her lip, clearly trying not to cry at the bitter irony of how her life had not lived up to that expectation.

But Flynn's mind focused on something else altogether.

"Your room key?" Tess asked. "The one to the outer door of our suite?"

Flynn cocked his head, focusing in on Wy's answer.

Wylene laughed. "Of course. It's the only door we kept locked."

Somewhere behind his back, Flynn registered the *blip-hum-blip* of Max's metal detector.

"So *you're* the reason we didn't get our deposit back." Reni elbowed the redhead in the ribs.

"Shut up, Reni." Tess bumped shoulders with the brunette. "We all know about the scuff marks you left on the ceiling."

The blips grew longer and faster. *Blip-blip-blip-blip.*

"We just don't know how you got them there." Jerrianne grinned.

"And we don't want to know." It only took a flash appearance of Queen Tessa to set that straight. "But, Wylene, I remember clearly gathering up everyone's keys—each with the proper name taped to it—on the morning after graduation."

Flynn rubbed his thumb and forefinger together, trying to recall those keys, how one had looked and felt in his hand.

"The morning after graduation was when I told you Joe Brent and I were engaged, Tess, and you made some excuse and hurried away. You never even asked for my key."

Tess went pale. "Oh . . . I guess . . . that could be right."

"It's right. I'm telling you that key is in the box."

"What was on your scroll, Wy?"

"I don't . . ." She looked away. Her shoulders lifted slightly, then slumped. "I wrote that I . . . I wanted us all to be happy."

Flynn gritted his teeth. Joe Brent Spivey had been his best friend—a lousy best friend, but maybe no better than Flynn had deserved back then. No matter how rotten that sniveling jerk behaved, Flynn had only wanted to deck him once. He had not done it then, but right now he wished he had. He wasn't certain, if Joe Brent were here, that he wouldn't take that long-delayed punch on the spot.

"Uncle Flynn! Mom!" The metal detector's blips

grew faster and faster until the machine let out one long *bleeeep*.

"I found something, Mom! I think I found it!"

The women rushed toward the place where the boy now knelt.

Jerrianne put a hand on his shoulder.

Tess dropped to her knees and began gouging away at the rich soil with the garden trowel they'd brought for this purpose.

Flynn hung back, wondering if he should go to them at all. Much as he admired these women, this was none of his affair. Much as he had come to care for Tess—care for? He folded his arms and took a good long look. From her grab-a-man-by-the-guts golden hair to her I'm-no-kid-anymore-and-aren't-you-glad curves, yes, and even the smudge on her face from the job of uncovering the box, she was amazing. Cared for her? Hell, he loved her.

At least he could be man enough to admit it to himself. No need to burden her with the unwelcome news of it, of course. She'd made her choice. She had her friends and her business and nothing else mattered.

And yet, she had not confessed what she had buried in the box, and something in him had to know.

"That's it! That's our box!" Jerrianne helped Max push away the dirt caked on the dented metal lid.

The smell of freshly tilled earth and sweet summer grass filled Tess's senses, and she drew the scent in deep. Without the burden of fear weighing down on her even the simplest things like this seemed more precious.

Max shouted in triumph as they worked the small treasure free.

Jerrianne hugged her boy like he had just pulled her to the shore from a storm-tossed sea.

Reni threw her arm around Wylene's neck, doing irrevocable damage to Wy's stiffly sprayed hairdo.

Wylene smiled—a real smile that came from inside not just a flutter of her lips.

The sights warmed Tess straight through to her weary soul, which suddenly did not seem so very weary at all.

Max held the box aloft over his dirt-speckled blond head.

"So much for that being the inspiration for those horrible notes." Wylene peered at the thing, her hands on her knees. "When they used the word *SuiteHearts* spelled the way we did when we lived here—"

"Wylene, I didn't think you got a note." Tess looked up and into her friend's wary green eyes.

"Actually, I did." She stood up and slid the strap of her little red purse off her shoulder. "I got one that first day, only I didn't know it."

"Joe Brent?" Flynn came close enough to spread his large hand over Wylene's back.

She nodded, her eyes downcast.

"Wylene," he said softly, "I'm not sure exactly what Tess wanted to accomplish by coming out here and unearthing this box."

She wanted to explain it to him but could see in his eyes, this was not the time to interrupt.

"But I am telling *you*, Wylene, don't let them open it unless you are ready to face the consequences."

"Flynn?" Tess's pulse picked up. Fear began to creep back over her. Something was up she had not counted on, something she could not have planned for. She could see it in Flynn's eyes.

She struggled not to launch into her lifelong control mode, to take over and start issuing demands and making disclaimers. Instead, she inched as close to the man as she dared and whispered, "What are you—"

He gripped Tess's upper arm with his free hand. Not hard, not a warning to back off, but more a reassurance that he knew what he was doing.

"Wylene, I know this is a friendship thing here, but I'm telling you, I know a few things about the night this box was buried. Don't open the box if you don't want to know the truth."

Wylene ran her thumbnail along her purse strap and blinked. "Gosh, the way I've lived my life, I'm not sure I'd recognize the truth if it bit me on my"— she conjured up a weak laugh—"nose."

The others exchanged glances.

"I had big plans and dreams when we buried that box." Wy's gaze never seemed to land on any one thing or person as she spoke. "I lost those a long time ago. I don't see how whatever 'truth' you think we'll find in a memory box can be worse than that."

Flynn put his hands in his pockets, those blue eyes trained on Wy alone.

She fixed her gaze in his, trusting him so openly that Tess felt a pang of shame over her foolish misgivings about the man. Wy squared her shoulders. "Let's open it."

Max held the box out to his mother.

Jerrianne pointed him toward Tess.

If ever in her life she wanted to call out for help, this was it. But she took the box from the little boy.

"You know what, Max?" Flynn fished around in his jeans pocket and pulled out a handful of change. "If you go inside those big doors over there, you'll find a lobby with public restrooms where you can wash your hands. Then right next to that is a vending room. Get yourself a soda and a snack, how 'bout it?"

Max looked to his mom, who gave her nod of approval, then he took off running, calling back, "Thanks, Uncle Flynn!"

"Thank you, Max. You did a good job." Then Flynn turned to the group, pointed toward the stone steps at the side of the building, and said, "Maybe we should take this over there."

"We?" Reni pushed back her hair, her gold and diamond jewelry glinting in the afternoon sun. "When did *you* become a SuiteHeart, sweetheart?"

"Reni," Tess growled, holding the box in her white knuckled grasp.

"I know." Reni rolled her eyes and started toward the steps. "Shut up."

"Let's get this done before Max comes back." Jerrianne gave Tess a nudge.

"And before Joe Brent wakes up and gets hungry enough to come looking for me and realizes I'm not working in the studio," Wylene whispered.

"Oh, Wylene." Tess couldn't say any more than that. But she didn't have to.

Her friend wiped a knuckle along her lower lashes. The smudges of mascara left by her tears in the soft layer of concealer did not detract from the redhead's still fragile beauty.

Reni opened her mouth, but for once had the tact to keep her opinion to herself.

Jerrianne looped her arm through Wylene's.

Wy stared at the eyeliner and makeup on her fingers. She sniffled. "So much for finding happiness, huh?"

"It's not too late for that," Tess whispered.

Wy laughed, rubbed her hands together, then raised her chin and looked at Flynn. "I'm ready. I think it's time I found some truth in my life, don't you?"

18

"You need a little help, Tess?" Jerrianne's knee banged against Tess's shoulder as they huddled on the cool stone steps of their old dorm.

Tess looked at the red stains on her fingertips from trying to pry open the rusty box in her lap. "No thanks, hon, I can get it. Just needs a little more elbow grease but it's nothing I can't handle on my own."

From where he stood just outside the cluster of women friends, Flynn leaned his hip against the stair rail and chuckled.

"You know, Jerrianne." Tess stood. "On second thought, that's not a bad idea. I do need some help getting into this thing."

"Can't you just cajole it open with your"—Flynn stopped to give her a smile but she saw the bristle beneath the thick, lazy accent and expression—"southern charm?"

"No, I can't." Any more than she could help letting Queen Tessa show through in moments of personal challenge. "But I could just bust it open by cracking it over something hard and unyielding. Say, you don't seem to be using your head right now. Why don't we try that?"

"Why not? You've already had your way with my . . ." He stopped himself.

The way the other girls cleared their throats and stifled giggles, she knew they thought this was some kind of sexual gambit. But looking into those deep, soul-baring eyes, Tess knew otherwise. Tess knew the word left unsaid. You've already had your way with my *heart*, it echoed through her mind as clearly as if he'd actually spoken it to her.

"Good gosh-a-mighty, Flynn," she heard herself whisper without having meant to make a sound.

She wanted to tell him she felt the same way. She wanted to apologize for the way she had acted. She wanted to fall into his arms and never let him go again. But they had something to accomplish before she could even try to do any of that.

She held the old box out to him. "Give it a . . . Would you help me get this open, please?"

He put both hands on the container. His fingers brushed, then caressed, then closed over hers. His touch and the box slipped away seconds later. "I'll give it a shot."

Only fragments of the metal object showed under his large grasp, a rusted corner, a grimy seam. Metal groaned over metal. A shower of dirt and pebbles rained down on Flynn's shoes. "There!"

"Oh my gosh." Jerrianne turned her head.

Wy pinched her nose shut. "Gross."

Flynn held the mold-filled box at arm's length. "When y'all put this together, I'm assuming the word *waterproofing* never came up?"

"We were idealistic," Jerrianne argued.

"We were idiots," Tess countered, daring to look inside at the dank-smelling mess. "The scrolls are history. Looks like the wooden part of your fishing lure is cracked, Jer. The framed photo looks warped. But the key to our suite *is* there."

"Look again," Flynn said. Then before she could do as he directed, he reached in and plucked out the silver key.

"I'm looking," Tess said. "Aside from some brackish gunk growing along the edge, it looks like your plain old average dorm key."

"Except there's no tape on it with Wylene's name."

"Of course not, it rotted off."

"It never was there."

"How could you know?"

"Because I know this key. It's to the back door of my mother's house."

"How on earth would your mother's backdoor key get in our box?"

"Obviously someone stole it from my key chain and swapped it out with Wylene's key."

"Who would do that?"

"Someone who knew she'd be out at parties all night and if her key didn't work she'd blame the celebrations, someone would let her in, and she'd turn the key in the next day and never be the wiser."

"Joe Brent." Wylene sighed.

"I think he wanted to be waiting in your room for you when you got back home that night," Flynn said.

"He wasn't in his right mind. He took our breakup hard. Harder than anyone suspects. In fact, that's my secret. That's what I didn't want anyone to ever know."

"What?"

"Y'all think Joe Brent ruined my life. You think his selfish ways are all within his control and I should make him shape up or give him the boot. But I know the sensitive side of the young man he once was. I know what I drove him to do that night."

"You *know*?" Tess's hand trembled as she raised it to cover her mouth.

Flynn moved swiftly to her side. He slid his arm around her waist, as if he thought she might just fall apart on that very spot and he'd have to pick up the pieces.

"I know and I want you to understand, I don't hold it against you . . ."

Tess held her breath.

"Flynn," Wy finished.

"Flynn?" Tess blinked.

"Me?" He jabbed his thumb to his breastbone. "What the hell are you talking about?"

"I know, Flynn. I know about the accident. I know that he was so distraught the night I told him we'd never get back together that he threw himself in front of your car. That's how he hurt his back and why he has never been able to keep a job for long."

"Accident?" Tess shook her head.

Flynn's whole body tensed beside her. "Hurt his back my . . ."

"Joe Brent didn't ruin my life, y'all." Wylene held both her hands up to command everyone's full attention, waited to make sure she had it, then concluded, "I ruined his."

Flynn swore under his breath.

Tess clenched her teeth. She had come here to find personal closure. She had come to prove to these old friends that it wasn't Queen Tessa holding them together, but their special bond and love for one another. A bond that would withstand no matter what later was revealed about her, at least for the others and especially for Wy, so she would never be left alone at Joe Brent's mercy.

She had *not* come here to make her own confession, and she was not convinced it was the right thing to do. But how could she let Wylene go on blaming herself for something she had no part in? Her stomach twisted into hard knots.

"I've taken credit for a lot of crap in my life, but

doing a hit-and-run number on someone who was, at that time, my best friend is not an accusation I can let roll off my back."

"You mean he didn't throw himself in front of your car because he was suicidal over my breaking up with him?"

Flynn held the key from the box up and said nothing.

"He had *your* keys, your *car* key, too." She didn't ask it, she said it. "It never did make sense that he'd be hit by a car and not have a scratch, just neck and back injuries. Sometimes I'd ask him about it but . . ."

Jerrianne scooted over on the step and put her arm around Wylene.

Reni laid a hand on their friend's leg.

"People saw you driving all around campus that night," Wy said. "And tearing out of our dorm parking lot about the same time he said it happened."

Flynn moved close to Tess, angling his body slightly in front of her.

Tess appreciated the protective stance. She sank her fingers into the tense muscles of Flynn's shoulder to let him know it.

"I saw your car that next day, it did have a huge dent in it." Reni threw her ever-helpful two cents' worth in.

"After . . ." Flynn moved over again, all but shielding Tess entirely from their sight. "After something set him off, he ran out and stole my car. He didn't get out of the parking lot before he drove it into a lamppost. I came out, hauled his sorry butt out of the seat, and left. Didn't hear till the next day that he'd taken himself to the hospital."

"And that the two of you were suddenly engaged," Jerriane added softly.

"He lied." No anguish or anger colored Wylene's almost inaudible realization.

"Are you okay, sugar?" Reni touched their friend's cheek.

"I'm fine. I just . . ." She looked up, her features unreadable. "You know, I think I've known this for a long time. That he had manipulated me into marrying him, that he kept on manipulating me with guilt to stay."

"And when guilt didn't work?" Flynn asked outright what they had all wanted to know and feared finding out for too long.

Wylene bowed her head. She pulled her purse in her lap and kneaded the leather with her fingers. "He made me feel like I was the lowest creature on earth."

"Did he hit you?" Flynn pressed on.

She shook her head too quickly to be convincing, but she did raise her chin, her gaze fixed on something low in the distance. "He never had to hit me, not really. Between the guilt and humiliation I pretty much did whatever he expected of me."

"Wylene, if you want out . . ." Reni was the one to broach the subject first.

"We will help you," Tess moved from behind Flynn and reached out to take Wylene's hand. "Whatever you decide, these friendships will survive."

Wylene gave Tess's fingers a squeeze. "I can say the same to you, you know. Now that I have made myself down this one last bitter taste of truth, now that Joe Brent can't pressure me into caving in to him, *our* friendship will survive anything . . . Tess."

It felt like the life had drained right out of her. She put her hand to her throat. "You know?"

"No, nothing concrete. But over the years I've had my suspicions. Now that you know it wasn't all-consuming passionate love that motivated me to marry my husband, maybe you can fill in the missing pieces. That was your secret, wasn't it?"

Tess drew in her breath. She had not come here today to confess her sins to anyone. Now it looked like she was going to have to do it in front of everyone she held dear. She wondered if she was strong enough.

She looked over her shoulder to Flynn.

He nodded.

She was asking for his help yet again. She did not have to give it words; her eyes said it all. He could not refuse that plea. No matter what happened after this, he would be here for her now. He placed his hand on her slender shoulder and urged her to go on.

She shut her eyes. When she opened them, her eyes fell on the box.

"The thing I put in the box was the gold heart necklace that Flynn gave me the summer we were together. My scroll was an empty page—I couldn't see any future for myself that night."

A twinge of sadness sweetened with sentimentality took Flynn by surprise at her sudden revelation. He had braced himself to hear something else altogether.

Tess brushed her fingers over the place where the small heart had dangled on that night fourteen years ago. "I did that that night because I was hurt and angry. The guilt came later, though, and made me glad I'd done it. I was glad not to have that necklace as a reminder of what I'd done."

She took a deep breath then let it out slowly. When she lifted her chin, she did not take on the air of regal command but appeared simply like a person looking into the heart of a good friend. "Wy, on the night we buried this box and said we'd always care about each other, I betrayed our friendship by sleeping with Joe Brent."

"Tess!" Jerrianne's expression looked as dazed as a drunk winding her way off a Tilt-O-Whirl.

"And you never told me!" Reni landed a light backhand across Tess's upper arm.

"I walked in and found them together." Flynn thought nothing short of the devil with a cattle prod could have dragged that information out of him and yet it spilled out freely, and it freed him in a way he had not expected. "Joe Brent let out like a scalded pup. I was blind with rage at Tess, though I had no right. I had no right at all, after the way I'd behaved that night. And . . ."

"And now here we are, all these years later," Tess said. "Older and hopefully a little wiser."

"Speak for yourself," Reni sniffed.

"Okay, I'm a little wiser. Reni here is still a moron."

She scowled.

"A beautiful, youthful moron," Flynn corrected.

"Thank you."

The exchange broke enough of the tension for Tess to regroup. "Wylene, sugar, you understand, I didn't set out to do it. I just felt so bad about what happened between me and Flynn, and Joe Brent felt so bad about what happened between the two of you, and . . . well . . ."

"She was young." Flynn doubted his less than brilliant insight helped much, but in for a penny, in for a pound. He put his arm around Wylene's slender shoulders. "They were both young and not thinking right and besides that, Joe Brent was an asshole."

"Flynn!" Tess stepped forward.

He held his hand up for her to back off. "I

thought you weren't going to hide behind pretty lies anymore, Tess."

"It's an awful big leap from a pretty lie to an asshole." She blinked then cleared her throat. "Well, you know what I mean."

"I know you wasted all these years not telling Wylene about that night because Joe Brent held both of you and your friendship hostage."

Wy's brow furrowed. She seemed untouched emotionally by Tess's confession and Flynn's harsh words for her husband. Had her friends let her slip too far away so that none of this even mattered anymore? He knew that kind of numbness to life and knew it was not life at all.

"Wylene," he said, "it doesn't take a brain trust to see that Tess kept quiet because she knew Joe Brent would make you choose between the SuiteHearts' love and support of one another and him."

"And he would have won," Tess said with genuine grief in her tone.

"Tess is a good friend, Wylene."

"I . . ." Wylene stood.

She looked smaller than she had earlier. In fact, in a summer outfit of bright pink pants and sleeveless checkered top, she looked almost childlike. Beneath that face full of makeup, the redness that started in her cheeks began to spread over her pale skin. She twisted the tiny handbag hanging at her side in both hands, then looked down at it. "Y'all understand I can't leave him. I don't have two pennies to rub together and my only means of making a living is in a house where his name is on the mortgage."

"I can't tell you to break up a fourteen-year marriage, especially with two children involved." Tess put her hand on Wylene's. "But if the issue is money . . ."

"Hell, I have money." Reni snapped her fingers and took the step above where Jerri and Wylene stood. "Money cannot be an issue here any more than it was when we got those lousy notes. What we are talking about here is taking care of ourselves."

"That's what we did when we decided not to deal with the blackmailers." Jerrianne held her head high, her blonde ponytail swinging. "When we decided to deal with the pain of our past instead. Those petty blackmailers don't have any power over us. Except to embarrass us."

"Oh, hell, Reni does that to us all the time." Tess laughed. "If we can survive her we can survive anything."

"Excuse me?" Reni cocked an eyebrow and planted one fist on her hip. "Have you forgotten I just recently made space in my bowling bag for somebody's head? Don't make me go looking for my hacksaw again."

Tess gave her that dead-eyed look.

Reni gave it right back.

Jerrianne laughed, just a little.

Tess joined in, then pulled Wylene into a hug. "See, now, Reni has money *and* a hacksaw. Flynn and I have experience sneaking all around town in the dead of night. Jerrianne and Max know the single-parent routine forward and backward. So, if you need financial aid, advice, or somebody's body parts spirited away in a bowling bag by night, *we have got you covered.*"

"What's that?" Flynn leaned in to put his lips near Tess's delicate, enticing ear. "You're not offering to do it all yourself?"

She lowered her chin and raised her gaze to his. "Much as the idea of being alone in a room for a few minutes with Joe Brent Spivey and a hacksaw appeals to me, I'll have to pass."

"I hear you." He chuckled. He'd take a few minutes alone with the jerk himself, but he wouldn't need the saw. Just one good punch, flesh hitting flesh, and a satisfying *oomph* followed by a thud would do the trick.

"And while I'm happy to spare you anything I can moneywise, sugar"—Tess tapped Wy's purse with one finger—"I have to be very prudent in that area right now."

Oomph. Thud. The blow hurt just as much coming on an emotional level, Flynn discovered. Actually, it hurt more, he amended as the feeling from this morning rushed back. "Yeah, she has a big business deal pending. Gotta make sure everything looks financially flush, gotta buy a bunch of doilies to hang all over the place."

"Reni, where did you say that hacksaw was?" Tess folded her arms and aimed that look his way.

He reflected it right back at her.

"Now, y'all, don't get ugly." Jerrianne pushed her way between the two of them. "Here comes Max. Besides, we need to cover up the hole we made, decide what we're going to do with this box, then go home and get cleaned up—we've got bowling tonight."

Each of the SuiteHearts turned to look at the blonde barking orders.

"Who died and made you queen?" Reni asked.

"Well, somebody has to keep this crew in line." Jerrianne stepped from the shade of the building into the bright light, called out to her son to fill in the hole, then turned back to the group. "Wylene, honey, do you need someone to go home with you? I'll do it or Flynn will or we can even go get my daddy. He's a little on the older side now, and sometimes his enthusiasm gets the better of him, but he can handle just about anything you throw at him."

"I can't believe you're not busting in and taking command," Flynn grumbled as Tess sashayed past him.

"Why should I? Jerrianne is doing fine."

He watched her as she headed over to lend a hand to Max. He wanted to read more into this new attitude, but how could he when she had made no overture to show she understood his feelings regarding the meeting and his father?

"I can handle Joe Brent," Wylene said with a

quiet confidence she had not shown since Flynn had come back to Mount Circe.

"Then you go on." Jerriane leaned in and kissed the redhead on the cheek. "Will you make it to bowling tonight, please?"

"If I don't show up, call the police, because something awful must have happened." Wylene returned the peck on the cheek and started off toward her car, her head high.

"Are you serious?" Reni called after her.

Wy kept on walking, but there was a definite spring in her step that had not been there before.

"Is she serious?" Reni turned to Flynn and Jerrianne.

Jerrianne shook her head. "I just hope she shows up so we don't have to worry about it."

19

"Tess, I am going to say something to you now that I never dreamt I would ever say to any-one—ever." Reni took her by the shoulders and locked gazes, with just centimeters between them. "I want to win that bowling trophy."

"You do?"

"More than I thought humanly possible." She gave Tess a shake. "So get your act together and concentrate on the game."

Tess shuffled backward on the highly polished surface by the ball return. "Look, I'm sorry, Reni, but I just keep wondering if Wylene is going to show up."

"We're all concerned about Wylene here."

"I had Daddy go pay a call on her, Tess. If he encounters any problems, he'll let us know."

"Oh, great." Tess feigned a laugh. "Glad to know Brother J is on the job. He didn't take that bullhorn he uses for street preaching, did he?"

"You know, I tried to get him to leave it at home, but he says you never know when you might need that extra surge of power to get your point across."

"I could have used one of those in my marriage." Reni squinted one eye and held up an invisible bullhorn to her mouth. "Hey, butthead, behave or be prepared to pull to the side of the rocky road of love and surrender half your worldly assets."

"Throw your practice ball, Reni." Jerrianne pointed to the lane. "We're only given so long to warm up."

To Tess's surprise Reni obeyed, though she took her sweet, sweet time about the process.

"You!" Jerrianne crooked her finger at Tess. "Get your mind on the game. Focus."

"Jer, I—"

"We'll do some Zen thing, you know, 'Ommm, I am at one with the tenpin.' "

"This isn't—"

"C'mon, say it with me. 'I feel the power of the curve ball, hallelujah.' "

"I know what you're trying to do." Tess folded her arms. "And it's not going to work."

Reni and Jerrianne understood how difficult it was for her to wait this out on the sidelines. In fact, keeping her from rushing out to Wy's rescue was probably the real impetus behind Reni's all-consuming passion to possess a cheap wood-and-gold-toned plastic trophy with a little bowling man perched on top and Salvation Brethren Jerrianne's Zen bowling conversion act.

"Okay, let me try this." Tess assumed a serene pose, but kept one eye open. "Ommm...I am going to worry about Wylene until she walks through that door and tells me there is nothing to worry about."

"Funny." Jerrianne flicked the sleeve of Tess's pink bowling shirt. "So what about Flynn?"

A few feet away Reni released her ball and it went thundering down the lane.

"Flynn doesn't strike me as the worrying type."

Jerrianne clucked her tongue. "What about Flynn walking through that door?"

"Ain't going to happen, friend." Tess spun the words out with an extra dash of sass to make it seem like she really believed them and couldn't care less if he showed his handsome face or not. "Not gonna happen."

"I know."

Reni's ball slammed into the pins and the sound echoed through the lane. "Strike!"

"You know?" Tess blinked.

"He called me just before I left to wish us luck and say he didn't see the point in his coming down tonight."

"And why would he?" She tried to inject a light

laugh after the question but it faltered. She exhaled slowly and sank her hand in her pocket to touch the card she had tucked away to give him.

Her mind had been on Wylene most of the afternoon but her heart had never strayed very far from Flynn. From the way they had made love last night, as if it were the beginning and end of everything all at once. From the way he had looked at her as they stood on the dorm lawn and the way he stood up for her when she made her confession. Tess had convinced herself that it all meant something—that Flynn Garvey . . . cared for her.

"Why would he?" she repeated as soft as a final echo.

She'd acted like nothing but a thorn in his side for far too long. She'd been impossible, preposterous, and rude. She'd been bossy. Heavens, she'd been the queen of bossy. Yet he hung in there with her. And when he finally shared his deepest sorrow with her, she latched on to her fear like a kid with a tattered blankie and ran away.

"Can you believe that, Tess?" Reni swung her hip into Tess's and almost knocked her down. "A strike and it doesn't count. Jerrianne's warming up, aren't you going to watch?"

"I'm watching," Tess mumbled, but her gaze had wandered to the front door, then to the door of the lounge. He wasn't coming and now she knew it.

"Hey, Miss Tess!"

"Jobie James, you startled the pee-waddin' out of me!" She put her hand to her chest.

"Sorry, Miss Tess, but I want to tell you, someone was looking for you."

"They were?"

"Tess, look, look." Reni tapped her furiously on the shoulder. "Jer's going to get a spare."

"Shhh! Would you just go away?"

"All right." Jobie hung his head. His shoulders slumped and began to shuffle off. "But they paid me some dollars and let me get a footlong to tell you."

"No, Jobie, not you." She took a few steps to catch up with him. "You said something about getting paid?"

He pulled up short and nodded vigorously. "Some dollars and a footlong."

Flynn. Giddy warmth rushed through her. He did come after all. She pulled the business card out of her pocket and held it in both hands over her chest like a child with shiny new coin. "Where is he?"

"Ain't just a 'he.' It's that fat'ead who give me the notes an' he got a lady with him."

"The notes?" She whipped her body around to stare down the length of the alley. "Where, Jobie? Which *fathead* do you mean?"

She had not intended for the word *fathead* to come out so much louder than the rest of her question, or to imply that she needed help pinpointing a single fathead in a virtual sea of them. But that was exactly how it sounded. Everyone within shouting distance of her turned in her direction.

She thought of issuing a blanket apology, but knowing that one of these faces might be that of her friendly local extortionist made her grab Jobie by the arm and whisper. "Who paid you? Who was looking for me? What fathead are you talking about?"

"Not fathead." Jobie looked at her like she'd lost her mind. And when a man who has been on the receiving end of countless such looks himself decides to bless you with one—it's a beauty. "Fat'ead."

"Fathead?"

"Fat'ead," he corrected nice and loud.

"Fat . . . fat . . . head?" Oh, how the mighty had fallen. Last month the Martha Stewart of the South was headed for national acclaim, and today stood in the Twilight Lanes bowling alley yelling fat head over and over at a sweet, grubby, disabled man. She gritted her teeth and tried it one more time, exactly as he had said it. "Fat'ead."

"Yeah. Fat'ead!" He raised his hands like they'd crossed the finish line together in record time.

She clutched her card, blinked, and looked around, casting smiles about her like a beauty queen on a parade float. All the time her mind whirred. *Fat'ead. Fat . . . 'ead. Fat . . .* "Oh, my word, fat Ed? Is that who you mean? Ed? Ed Hacker?"

At the mention of the name, Jerrianne's head went up.

"Tess, what is it?" Reni rushed up, barely stopping just inches away from them.

Jerrianne came within a hair of rear-ending her. "Did you just mention Ed?"

"Jobie, was the lady with him my little sister, by any chance?" Tess put her hands on her hips.

"Wull, does your li'l sister look just like you . . . only little and not so much like you?"

"She kind of looks . . ." Tess threw her hands up. "Jobie you know my little sister. Is that who was with him?"

"Yup."

"Where the hell are they?"

"You shouldn't say 'hell.' "

"Jobie!"

"In there." He pointed toward the lounge.

"Ed's here? He's in town and he didn't even try to contact Max?" Jerrianne kept at Tess's heels.

With every stride Tess picked up speed. Dodging kids and winding past onlookers, her eyes stayed on one thing, the door of the Twilight Lounge.

Reni hurried along as fast as her skintight capri pants and half-size-too-small bowling shoes would allow. "Where are you going ten minutes before our final game and what is so all-fired urgent?"

"That's a damn good question." Flynn caught her arm just a few feet from the shoe rental counter, but it was not his grip that held her in place. Around them the discord of bowlers and video games, light and dark, the stale air of the building and the gushes of fresh air from the doors opening and closing all faded into background haze. For one second it was just Flynn and her.

"You came after all," she whispered.

"Like I could ever stay away from you." He grinned. Those blue eyes all but danced with mischief and emotions that only a damned fool would trust.

Her heart did a number to rival the pounding rhythm of the band in the lounge.

"I brought you something." He reached into his shirt pocket.

"It's going to have to wait a minute." She slid the business card in the same pocket with his fingers still stuffed inside. "This is for you. Hang on to it and I'll be right back."

"Where are you going?"

Tess patted his solid chest and resumed her stride. Knowing Flynn had come had doubled her resolve to handle this swiftly. "I am going to hand out a little *Simply Southern* whoop ass to the person who has turned our lives upside down for the last few weeks."

"Her sister, Anita Lynn," Reni said none too quietly as she fell back in line behind Tess.

"And Ed." Jerrianne was not a half step behind.

"Your Ed?" Flynn called out. "Max's Ed? The man I've been searching all over creation to find?"

Flynn's footsteps hammered quick and hard but he had not caught up with Tess when she hit the swinging doors with a wallop and burst into the lounge.

She heard Anita yelp before she actually found her in the dark, smoky room.

"Tess, be reasonable, now," Flynn cautioned.

She ignored him. When she picked out her little sister, sitting at the bar next to the man who had betrayed Jerrianne and ignored sweet, innocent Max, she made a lunge.

Flynn's arm wrapped around her waist so fast that, combined with her forward momentum, it lifted her feet right off the ground. "Let me go 'cause I'm going to have to kill that little rat, and I don't care who I have to go through or take down with her to get the job done."

"Sisters," Flynn said calmly to the bartender, who nodded and started passing the word along.

Anita Lynn jumped up. She would have toppled her barstool if not for the actions of an entirely unruffled patron who caught the seat by the rim without so much as a glance to see the source of the hullabaloo. Anita backed away. "Now, Theresa Jo, I would not have done this if you hadn't . . ."

"Oh, don't you lay this flaming bag of donkey crap on my doorstep, you little . . . blackmailer!"

Now that did cause a few heads to turn, more so than the fact that Flynn still had her snagged up against his body, her arms and feet flailing.

"If you had just given me the money—"

"Given you the money? Come over here, girl, and I'll give you . . ."

The band stopped playing.

In the lull everyone looked Tess's way, as if they expected her to provide the entertainment.

She smiled most graciously. Or as graciously as one could dangling above a barroom floor in the grasp of the man whose hold had her pink bowling shirt gaping and was giving her breasts a push-up effect that Victoria would spill her very last secret to duplicate. "Nothing to see here," she managed to say like a Sunday-school teacher cooing to her class. "Just a family spat."

The crowd moved listlessly, and began to talk again.

She fixed her eyes on Anita and jerked her head. "Outside."

The summer air hit them like a wall as they trooped out the side door of the lounge. Flynn kept a loose hold on both Tess and her sister. Reni flanked Jerri-anne, who kept her cold, hard glare on chubby, bumbling Ed Hacker.

"What were you thinking?" Tess demanded of the young woman who shared her parentage and the same glowing complexion but little else.

"It's your fault," Anita shot back.

"My fault? I didn't send any threatening notes! I didn't . . ."

"Like fire you didn't! Who was it sicced the detectives on Ed, trying to get back child support and who knows what all?"

"How did you know about that?" Flynn was renowned for his discretion and skill. Had his personal involvement with Max made him sloppy in this case?

"He has a kid. He's never paid child support. The first person who called was a friend who just had to check where the call came from. Mount Circe?" Her narrow-eyed gaze shot daggers at Tess. "We knew."

"So since I'd already said no more money, you hatched a scheme to get me, Jerrianne, and our friends to pay your debts for you? To make Jerrianne pay her own back child support in essence, is that it?"

"You can afford it. Ed can't."

"Ed made a baby and walked out. I didn't," Tess shot back.

"Mercy me, what a total mess." Jerrianne threw up her hands.

"What I want to know is how you knew what any of us back did in college, you little brat?" Reni, who had forever treated Anita like a best friend's annoying baby sister—an intrusion on and competition for Tess's attention—shoved her way between the two sisters.

"I didn't." Anita practically spit her answer in Reni's face. "But I didn't have to know Jack about you all because I know Tess."

"And?" Flynn glared at the girl.

"And I knew the only way to get to her would be to go after the people she cared about."

"Man, that is so true," Flynn muttered under his breath, but when Tess turned troubled eyes to him, he sighed. "That's exactly what I did when I tried to weasel my way into your good graces. I did it by ganging up with your friends, offering to help them instead of being direct with you about what I really wanted."

"Yes, you did." She spoke softly, then wet her lips like she was about to say more.

"That's why I came to see you tonight. That and the thing Brother J told me on your graduation night, about taking care of hurts when they are fresh, before they begin to eat away at you."

"I'm glad you did." She touched his cheek. "And I suspect Anita is, too, because if you hadn't been here I'd have skinned her alive."

"But now you're not so mad anymore, right?" Anita Lynn twisted her fingers together. "I was just . . . well, you always took care of things."

Tess turned to her sister.

"You always had it all under control. You never needed me for friendship, to talk to, or help out around the house or at your work . . ." Anita looked down. ". . . or to take care of Mama."

"If I told you that was about to change, would you be willing to try again?"

"Try what again?"

Tess raised her shoulders then let then fall. "Being my little sister . . . being my friend?"

Anita smiled, then her eyes shifted. "What about Ed?"

"I am not done dealing with Ed." Jerrianne stepped forward.

"That's not for me to handle." Tess held up her hands.

Ed, Anita, and Jerrianne all began to talk at once, a heated discussion confined to the three of them.

Flynn looked at Tess and made a show of wiggling one finger in his ear. "Um, did I hear that right? You're not going to tell them how to deal with this?"

"Jerrianne is a smart, capable woman." Tess turned and placed her hands flat on his chest. "She can handle this just fine on her own."

"On her own, my aunt's fat fanny. She's got me on her side now. So look out, because heads could roll." Reni jumped in, adding her emphatic opinions to the already animated fray.

Tess laughed and never looked back.

Flynn laced his arms around her. "I have something for you."

"Oh, and I have something for *you*."

The both plunged their fingers into his shirt pocket at the same time. He pulled her hand away and she did not protest. "Allow me."

He pulled out the piece of paper she had put in there a few minutes earlier. "I don't get it. The business card I wrote your appointment with McLaughlin on?"

"Not my appointment." She pushed his own hand, still holding the card toward him. "Yours. I've decided not to go to McLaughlin for the money. It may take longer, but I think there are other ways to make this dream happen, if I'm just willing to accept a little help."

"That's . . ." His heart filled with awe and joy. He recognized the emotions at once, because although he'd never felt the potent mix, he'd often imagined it. And after all his years of waiting, Tess had made it happen by giving him the two things he'd always longed for—real love and a means to meet his father. "Here . . . I brought this for you."

He reached into his pocket again.

"My necklace. I mean, *your* necklace."

"No, it's yours, Tess. I want you to wear it." He held up the glittering gold and diamond ornament that he'd spent all afternoon cleaning. "I want to see you in it like you were that night before all the garbage happened, and . . ."

"If I put this necklace on, what does it mean?"

"You're going to make me say it, aren't you?"

"I don't have the power to make anybody say or do anything."

"The hell you don't."

He grabbed her up and kissed her, deep and hard and long.

"What is wrong with y'all? Have you lost your ever-loving minds?" From somewhere beyond their kiss, Wylene Spivey's voice called out. "They are looking all over for the Sweethearts in there and if you don't haul your behinds back inside in the next two minutes you are going to forfeit the game."

Reni and Jerrianne scrambled toward the door back into the bowling alley, ordering Anita and Ed to come along.

Tess ended the kiss and moved away just a bit, but her gaze stayed lost in his.

"Good gosh-a-mighty, Miss Theresa Jo Redding," he murmured. "You do know that I love you, don't you?"

"And I love you."

"Hey, Tess," Jerrianne called out from the threshold of the open door. "Wy says things are strained over at her house and can she and the girls stay with you tonight?"

"Sure, they can stay at my house," Tess called out, her eyes fixed on Flynn.

He tensed.

She smiled and cocked her head in perfect kissing position again, then added for only his ears, "They can stay at my house . . . but I won't be there."

He wrapped her in his arms again and they kissed each other senseless.

20

"So?"

"So." Flynn flipped through the contractor's estimates for modifying his mother's home so he could do his part for the Anna May Garvey Foundation from there. He raised those be-mine baby-blue eyes to hers, then grinned the most obviously obtuse grin possible and said, "So, I think that the girls have gotten in deeper than they've bargained for. A fall bowling league is going to provide much more competition than that mini-fun league they won."

"Yeah, well, what can I say? Once Reni got her hands on that trophy it was all she wrote. And if that's how they want to spend their free time, who am I to interfere?"

"You still committed as their permanent substitute?"

"Stop avoiding my question."

"And your question was again?"

"So?" She pushed aside his stack of paperwork and plunked herself down on the desk right in front of him.

He planted both hands on her thighs and kneaded the muscles. "So *what*?"

As much as Tess enjoyed his touch they had a very serious issue to clear up. She pushed his hands away and leaned forward. "So what about the appointment tomorrow? Have you decided if you're going to go or not?"

He sat back in the chair and ran one hand back through his hair. "Would you think I was a jerk if I didn't go?"

She kicked off her pump and put her toes on the arm of his leather office chair, giving it a little rock. "Would you think I was trying to take control if I asked you why not?"

"I'd think . . ." He met her gaze. His face went somber. He blinked, then sighed, then took her foot in his big strong hands and began to massage it. "I think I owe you an explanation."

"You don't owe me one, but I surely would appreciate hearing one."

"Truth is, so much has happened since I first thought ambush was the best way to make the man acknowledge me. Now . . . now I see things differently. I understand that if a man wants to be a father and loves his child, nothing can break that bond."

"It's been pretty amazing seeing how well Brother J has adapted to Jerrianne's old secret and her new independence, hasn't it?"

He nodded. "At the same time I see that no matter how terrific a kid is—"

"Like Max."

"Yeah, no matter how good or smart, or cute or even how much a kid needs his father, if a man rejects his responsibilities, that's his shortcoming, not the kid's. That man—and I use the term lightly—is the one missing out."

She sighed. "At least Ed has chipped in with some money and has promised to send checks regularly."

"I can't force myself on McLaughlin, Tess. It wouldn't change anything." He put her foot on his lap and gave it a pat. She brought her other foot up and as he rubbed it, he looked out the window and said, "The only thing I can do is forgive him."

"Forgive him? Where the hell did that idea come from?"

"From about as far from hell as you can get."

"Been talking to Brother J, I see."

"And he didn't even need a bullhorn to get through this thick skull of mine."

"Forgive him." Awe infused her tone. "And you honestly think you can do that?"

"I don't see how I can do anything else. I don't think I have to lecture you on how heavy a burden a grudge becomes when you carry it with you 'round the clock, year after year."

"Heavy enough to bury everything good and hopeful inside you. I have felt that weight myself, for sure."

"Have you forgiven Anita Lynn?"

"I think it was easier for me to forgive her than it was for her to forgive me. I thought I was doing right by her and I just made bad things worse and worse."

"Maybe the question I should have asked is, have you forgiven yourself yet?"

"For . . ."

"For not being perfect."

"I never thought I was always perfect," she said softly.

"Oh?"

"I thought I was always *right*!"

He chuckled. "Then have you forgiven yourself for being wrong?"

"Most days, yes. Though sometimes I still think . . . hey, stop that!"

He let go of her foot.

"No, not that. Stop leading the conversation away from the real topic."

"Real topic?"

"Your relationship, or lack of one with your father?"

"I'm working on it, Tess. I'm learning to forgive him and I won't give up. I'll keep trying to get through to him, trying to make contact. Who knows, maybe someday I'll call for an appointment and he'll say yes."

She slid her foot from his hands, then moved to

sit in the man's waiting lap. She looped her arms around his neck and gave him a kiss on the cheek. "We'll send him an invitation to the wedding."

"Okay." He laughed and kissed her on the neck. "And a copy of the first issue of *Simply Southern* to go national."

"The Christmas issue?" She gave him a newly modified look, one she'd honed to affect his particular sensibilities. "The one with your picture on the cover dressed as Santa reading my magazine?"

"A little poetic justice, don't you think?"

"In more ways than one."

"I can't believe we got the money together so quickly, and right here in Mount Circe."

"Well, you knew Reni would kick in, and she'd shame her folks into an investment," he said.

"And your check was one of the first to clear the bank, thank you very much." She touched his nose. "Of course the real shocker was Miz James."

"Who knew?" He laughed. "Imagine, money that came into Brother J's church because of your magazine going to fix up the house of the woman who had enough socked away to become one of our primary investors."

"And had an authentic autograph book with all the celebrities from the Atlanta premier of *Gone With the Wind*, to boot."

"You know when she made that dummy book for the museum, you'd have thought she'd at least have looked at the real names to copy."

"You'd have thought she'd have done a lot of things, like found a better way than hoarding stocks, cash, and valuables to provide for poor Jobie after she's gone."

"Yeah, well, I've got that under control now."

She kissed his temple. "Isn't it lovely?"

"Me being Jobie James's guardian?"

"No, silly, that everything is under control now. Everyone we care about is safe, if not deliriously happy. Queen Tessa only rarely has to make an appearance to keep things in line and even then, I don't have to shoulder the weight of it all by myself."

"Yeah, that's very lovely, indeed." He pulled her into a deep, sweet kiss.

She gave herself over completely to him, surrendering to his love and to the moment entirely.

The phone nearly jarred them apart like a jolt of electricity.

"Garvey here." Flynn picked it up before the third ring. "Yeah? Yeah? Uh-huh. Okay, we'll be right over."

He hung up and nudged her gently off his lap. "C'mon, girl, time to take Queen Tessa out of mothballs."

"What now?" She leaned on him as she slipped back into her low-heeled pumps.

"Big doings over at Granny Pistol's." He walked briskly ahead of her, stopping to hold the door open. "Seems the neighbors are taking exception to the idea of turning a section of the old place into Wylene Spivey's House of Charm and Cheerleading."

"Somehow I knew that Jerrianne, Wylene, their kids, and Reni sharing that house was going to be trouble." She hurried along and out onto his porch.

"That's why after we get married we're moving into your house, where we'll be safe from the inter-ference of neighbors, townfolks, and the assorted meddling of the Sweethearts of the Twilight Lanes."

"Uh-huh." Tess smiled behind his back at his naïve assumption and did not bother to try to correct him. She knew what any southern belle worth her smelling salts knows: When dealing with a head-strong man, it was best to save some surprises for after the wedding.